Ivy's Ever After

Dawn Lairamore

Holiday House / New York

Library of Congress Cataloging-in-Publication Data

Lairamore, Dawn.
Ivy's ever after / by Dawn Lairamore.—1st ed.
p. cm.
Summary: Fourteen-year-old Ivy, a most unroyal princess, befriends Elridge, the
dragon sent to keep her in a tower, and together they set out on a perilous quest to find
Ivy's fairy godmother, who may be able to save both from their dire fates.
ISBN 978-0-8234-2261-6 (hardcover)
[1. Fairy tales. 2. Princesses—Fiction. 3. Dragons—Fiction. 4. Fairy
godmothers—Fiction. 5. Conformity—Fiction.] I. Title.
PZ8.L1363Ivy 2010
[Fic]—dc22
2009043288

For Dad and Mom

CALLING ALL PRINCES!

HIS ROYAL MAJESTY THE KING OF ARDENDALE

announces

A COMPETITION

to win the hand of

HER ROYAL HIGHNESS

PRINCESS IVORY ISADORA IMPERIA IRENE.

Who, in accordance with The Dragon Treaty,
is to be imprisoned in The White Stone Tower, guarded by

A DRAGON

of enormous strength, cunning, and ferocity.

The noble Prince who slays the dragon will be crowned

THE NEXT KING OF ARDENDALE,

winning in the process

THE HAND OF THE PRINCESS,

GLORY AND HONOR, and

THE DRAGON TREASURE.

Applications can be made directly to

HIS ROYAL HIGHNESS THE KING OF ARDENDALE

at his royal seat.

PART ONE

The Princess

1

Ivy

I vy might have been a proper princess if her mother had lived, or her fairy godmother had seen to her upbringing instead of vanishing without a trace one winter's night, or her father hadn't lost his mind. But as it happened, her mother did die, her fairy godmother did vanish, and her father did lose his mind, so Ivy never really had much of a chance one way or the other.

Her real name was Princess Ivory Isadora Imperia Irene, but she hated it and insisted that everyone simply call her "Ivy." This was the first impropriety. Many others followed. For instance, the princess spent an unnatural amount of time in the castle's musty old library. She was often to be found curled up most unladylike in a frayed armchair by the window, engrossed in some unsavory story about pirates or goblins or children who didn't do as they were told. And rather than play with the dolls in her tower bedchamber, Ivy made friends with the children of the kitchen staff, even the filthy stable boy, and joined in their loud games of Capture the Flag in the courtyard or jacks under the stairs in the entry hall. Worst of all, she sometimes spent entire days out of doors without a veil or parasol, flitting about under the sun until her face became as brown as bread crust and as freckled as a swallow's egg.

Ivy's nursemaid, Tildy, had a very good sense of what was proper, having raised Ivy's mother to be the perfect princess. But these days Ivy's father was very careless about things, as anyone could see from the rather tumbledown state of the castle. He was inclined to let his darling Ivy do whatever she pleased, and who was old Tildy to argue with the king? Not that she didn't try to persuade him, mind you, but their conversations always went something like this:

Tildy: "Your Majesty, I think it high time that Princess Ivory take up music. The harp is quite a lovely instrument, most suitable for a young lady of her station. It will teach her poise and discipline."

The king: "Ivy insists the harp is of no practical value whatsoever. She believes her time would be better spent learning a more sensible skill, like archery."

Tildy: "Archery? Are you sure that's an appropriate pastime for a princess?"

The king: "Archery is quite a worthwhile pursuit for any person. Why, many a grave battle owes its victory to archers, and archery has its everyday uses as well. Arrows are excellent for peeling parsnips, provided one remembers to use the pointy end. Indeed, I have discussed the matter with Frederick, and we agree that harp lessons are entirely unnecessary." (The king was very fond of his horse Frederick and never made any important decision without consulting him.)

Tildy: "Yes, of course, Your Majesty." (This was usually said with a slight droop of Tildy's shoulders and a well-hidden sigh.)

So Ivy escaped most of the lessons one would expect a princess to have: embroidery ("Stitches should be small, neat, and evenly spaced"), elocution ("Three-gray-geese-in-the-green-grass-gra-zing"), and etiquette ("A princess must never put the entire soup spoon in her mouth; rather she must sip daintily from the side of the spoon, taking care to make as little noise as possible"). After a while, even the king's counselors gave up trying to convince him that the royal princess should be taught to behave more—well, royally. After all, things weren't as they were before, back when the queen was alive, when the king still had the sense to care about what was proper. Why, the king hadn't thrown a single ball or hosted a foreign dignitary since his wife had died that sad night Ivy was born, so it wasn't as if anyone important ever saw the princess, anyway. And as for attracting a suitable husband, well, that was taken care of.

The king ruled a small kingdom called Ardendale, a patchwork valley of fragrant meadows, rich farmland, and wandering streams so full of silver-brown trout that even the worst fishermen went home with a heavy basket. For all its beauty, Ardendale was an isolated place, difficult to reach from even the closest neighboring kingdoms. South of the valley, past long stretches of pebbled beach, were the white-capped waters of the Speckled Sea. To the east were the Craggies, a collection of towering mountains, frozen in winter, barren in other seasons, and full of trolls no matter what the time of year. The highlands to the north were blanketed by the Fringed Forest, named for the hanging moss that had taken over the once-beautiful trees. It grew everywhere, draped from each branch like tangled gray-green hair, making the entire forest look ancient and weighed down. It was a favorite joke among travelers that if you stood still long enough, moss would grow on you, too.

To the west was a place not even the bravest of the King's Guard would dare to venture, the Smoke Sand Hills. Low and rocky, these sandstone rises were the color of rust and every morning turned a brilliant red in the rising sun. More often than not, curling tendrils of smoke could be seen drifting up from the hills, the steamy breath of dragons slumbering in the warm spaces beneath. Every once in a while, in one of the villages or farms closest to the Smoke Sands, some housewife walking home from the market or a shepherd grazing his sheep would spot a dragon itself, flying low over the hills, its wings spread the length of four wagons, blowing bursts of flames or clutching a wild goat in its enormous claws. It was a sight both majestic and terrifying, one that made many a staunch soul very grateful that the dragons never flew down into the valley kingdom itself.

Ivy grew up knowing there were dragons in the Smoke Sands, although she had never seen one herself. Since having dragons so close didn't seem to concern anyone else, Ivy had never worried about it, either. That is, until she was ten and learned, purely by accident, that she was going to have a lot to do with dragons—at least with one dragon in particular. It was a fine morning in early spring, and cottony clouds floated lazily in the sky. Ivy was gathering daffodils outside the castle gate with her friends Rose and Clarinda, the daughters of kitchen maids.

"Wouldn't it be wonderful if we could pick flowers every day for the rest of our lives?" Rose asked as she gazed happily at the profusion of blossoms, their sunny heads bobbing in the breeze like pecking hens. The lovely spring weather was making Rose, a fanciful girl to begin with, even more giddy than usual. "Maybe some kindly fairy will whisk us away to a magical forest where it's always spring, or turn us into flower maidens, or enchant the castle garden so the blooms never, ever fade."

"I don't think that's likely to happen," said Clarinda, who was soft-spoken and very practical. "One day we'll be grown, and I expect we'll have to work like everyone else. There won't be much time for gathering flowers."

"Yes, I suppose you're right," Rose said with a sigh. "I'll probably become just like my mother. She never seems to have time for fun. She's always in the castle kitchen, peeling potatoes or scrubbing pots or yelling at us to get out of her way.

"You're so lucky," she said to Ivy, twisting a curl the color of marsh marigolds around one finger. "You'll never have to scrub pots, and everything will always be puddings and pies. Well, except for maybe that tower business with the dragon.

But once that's over, you'll have a husband who will be king and not a single care for the rest of your life."

"The what business with the dragon?" Ivy had been busy tugging a caterpillar off one of her daffodils and thought maybe she hadn't heard right.

"You know, the *tower*, the *dragon slaying*." Clarinda's voice was even softer than usual. She was as quiet as Rose was bubbly, as delicate and dark as Rose was bright and golden. At the moment, her doe eyes were growing wide with alarm. "You do know about that, don't you? On your fourteenth birthday?"

"Of course she does, silly," Rose scolded. "She's the princess, after all."

"Of course," Ivy was quick to agree, but only because she was too embarrassed to admit she hadn't an inkling what her friends were talking about.

When they returned to the castle, Rose and Clarinda scampered off to the servants' wing, and Ivy headed straight for the library, where she usually found the answers to her questions. What could she *possibly* have to do with a dragon slaying, of all things? The thought filled her with unease.

But finding the answer proved more difficult than she expected. She was the only one who used the royal library these days, and it was something of a mess. It had been years since the castle had kept a proper librarian, and books were scattered untidily across the wooden tables that ran the length of the room and piled knee-high in crooked stacks on the floor. There were more books off the shelves than on, leaving the tall bookcases so full of gaps they reminded Ivy of the uneven smile of Boggs the gatekeeper, who was missing many teeth.

It took Ivy a while to comb through the piles, looking for anything she could find on dragons or towers or slayings. Finally, in a far corner of the library's history section, under a thin layer of cobwebs, Ivy located a crumbling old volume called *An Annotated History of Ardendale*. She flipped to the index, hoping to find something under *princesses, fourteenth birthdays*, or maybe *dragons, the slaying of.* Although she didn't have any luck with these, *dragons, agreements with* led her to a chapter called "The Dragon Treaty." When she finally found what she was looking for, it was far worse than anything she could have imagined. For there, within the book's worn bindings, as plain as the nose on her face, it decreed that she was to be locked away on her fourteenth birthday, imprisoned in a tower of white stone, guarded by none other than a dragon.

2

The Dragon Treaty

Ivy burst into Tildy's sitting room without so much as a knock, which was ill-mannered even by her standards. Tildy was by the window, darning a stocking the princess had torn while climbing pear trees in the overrun orchard next to the castle garden. She was so startled that she missed a stitch and nicked one of her thick fingers instead.

"Princess? What is it? What's the matter?" she asked at once, seeing the distraught look on Ivy's face.

"Is what this book says true?" Ivy thrust the opened copy of *An Annotated History of Ardendale* toward her nursemaid. "Am I going to be locked in some tower guarded by some horrid dragon?"

As soon as Tildy spotted "The Dragon Treaty" at the top of the page, her face drained of color, becoming almost as pale as the faded tapestries that draped the stone walls around her.

"Oh, Princess," she said, lowering her eyes to the flagstone floor to avoid Ivy's accusing stare. "Yes. Yes, I'm afraid so."

"But *whyyyy?*" Ivy wailed. She saw Tildy flinch at the shrillness of her voice—princesses were supposed to speak quietly and delicately, after all—but was too upset to care. "Why would anyone do that to me?"

"Princess," murmured the nursemaid, rising to take Ivy's hand and lead her to the cushioned bench by the window, "come here; come sit by me, and I'll tell you everything you need to know. Everything you should have been told a long time past."

Tildy was short, plump, and starting to wrinkle, but always made sure she looked as presentable as she had when the queen was alive, something most of the castle staff no longer bothered to do. Today she wore a wide-necked dress the same cornflower blue as her eyes, and her hair, which had been cinnamon-colored in Ivy's younger years but was now mostly gray, was pinned to the back of her head in a tidy coil. As always, she smelled of lavender water and clean, sun-dried cloth. Just the familiar scent of her was enough to make Ivy feel a little better.

"Ardendale was not always as peaceful or beautiful as it is now," Tildy began, speaking in the same soothing tone she had used to tell Ivy bedtime stories when the princess was small. "Hundreds of years ago, dragons from the Smoke Sand Hills terrorized our little valley. They carried off all the cattle and sheep, ate half the crops, and burned the rest with their fiery breath. The entire kingdom was a smoldering ruin. People were starving and afraid to set foot outside their doors, lest they be snatched up by some angry dragon.

"The king at the time was in a terrible bind, for Ardendale has always been too small to have an army of its own. There's just the King's Guard, and they're hardly enough to take on a whole slew of dragons." Tildy's voice had grown soft and low, as if in sympathy for the poor king's plight. "But this king was a clever man," she continued, brightening. "As you know, for as long as anyone can remember, no son has ever been born to the royal family of Ardendale, only daughters. This king had a particularly beautiful daughter, and knowing how much young princes like to prove their worth, he declared that the prince who could rid his kingdom of the most dragons by summer's end would have the princess's hand in marriage and be crowned the new king of Ardendale upon their wedding. (He was rather tired of ruling himself, anyway, dealing with the dragons having been so stressful and all.)"

Tildy explained that dragon slaying was a favorite sport among princes. They arrived in Ardendale with their swords and armor, their horses and flying banners, setting up camps the size of small villages on the valley floor, some with entire retinues of pages and squires and standard-bearers. "And you know how hard it is to get to our little valley, since you can only come by ship on the Speckled Sea or take that awful road through the Fringed Forest." Tildy took up her sewing so she could work and talk at the same time. "But you see, princes take their dragon slaying very seriously. There's a great deal of glory to be had, not to mention treasure.

You know about dragon treasure, don't you? Those horrible beasts are hoarders of the worst sort—their hidey-holes in the Smoke Sands are heaped with gold, gems, and coins from hundreds of years of raiding villages and caravans. And it's only fair that whoever slays a dragon gets to claim its treasure for his own."

Tildy deftly ran a stitch along the tear in the stocking, her silver needle flashing in the sunlight streaming through the window. "Nothing lights a fire under young princes like the promise of glory and riches. They scoured the valley looking for dragons. Some were even brave enough to venture into the Smoke Sands, right into the heart of dragon territory." Suddenly, Tildy's blue eyes clouded over. "Dragons are brutal creatures," she said, "and I'm sorry to say that more than a few of those princes never came back. When a prince did manage to slay a dragon, he'd have its treasure for a prize.

"In the end, a brave and mighty prince who had slayed eleven dragons ended up winning the princess's hand. He had built up quite a treasure trove by that point, finer than any dowry the king could have provided. On his wedding day, he was proclaimed the new king of Ardendale. You will be proud to know that this most valiant of men was a forefather of your very own royal family.

"Eleven dragons!" Tildy repeated, shaking her head in wonder. "Why, today you're lucky to find a prince who can manage to slay one. As for the contest to win the princess's hand, it was such a success that it was decided that all future kings of Ardendale would be chosen in the same manner—the prince who slayed the most dragons duly won himself a queen and kingdom, for the old king always steps down once his eldest daughter is married."

"That's a strange way to choose a new king," said Ivy.

"Well, it was useful all around," said Tildy sensibly. "So many princes were eager to win glory and fortune, and here was their chance. The dragons in the northern kingdoms had died out long ago, for they had princes and knights and armies aplenty to take care of such problems there. Arden-dale was one of the few places in the world where one could still find a dragon to slay. It was also very good for the king-dom because everyone figured that after enough princesses, there would be no more of those nasty beasts left."

"But there *are* dragons left," Ivy pointed out.

"Yes, well... it didn't quite work out the way everyone had hoped." Tildy's voice was heavy with regret. "The more dragons were slain, the angrier it made the ones who were left. They doubled their attacks on the kingdom, and even went so far as to stream dragon fire at the castle itself—at one point the entire southern tower had to be rebuilt. Their numbers were dwindling all the same, however, and it was enough to make the Dragon Queen nervous."

"I've read about her," said Ivy. "She's supposed to be the oldest, meanest dragon of them all."

Tildy nodded, then described how centuries passed in terrible discord, until one day the Dragon Queen made an offer to the then-king of Ardendale: if he would put an end to the dragon slaying once and for all, her dragons would never venture forth into the valley again. They would retreat into the Smoke Sands and live solely off the wild game in the mountainous wilderness on the other side of the desert hills. It would have been the perfect arrangement for everyone involved, except for one unfortunate detail.

"You see, before the dragon slaying, it had always been a bit difficult to marry off the princesses of Ardendale," Tildy said. "Not many princes were willing to journey all the way to our far-off kingdom just to find a wife, not when there were plenty of perfectly good candidates from much larger and fancier kingdoms nearby. But the chance to slay dragons and claim their treasure was an enticement only Ardendale could offer. The king knew that if there were no dragons to draw suitors, the royal family could very well die out."

"Couldn't the princesses just marry someone from Ardendale?" asked Ivy. "Or rule the kingdom themselves?"

Tildy looked aghast. "That would be highly improper. We've always been ruled by a king of noble blood. Anything else would be unacceptable.

"So the Dragon Queen agreed that for the firstborn daughter of every king, she would give one of her dragons to do battle. The first prince to slay the creature won the princess's hand and the dragon's treasure. This way, the Dragon Queen lost only one of her vastly depleted kindred, while the princess would still get a royal husband and the kingdom its new king.

"Both the king and the Dragon Queen swore on their honor that all future generations would follow the terms of their agreement, and it came to be known as the Dragon Treaty," said Tildy. "No one actually wanted a dragon to roam freely through the valley, so a tower of white stone was constructed at the foot of the Craggies. It was the perfect location, far from any village or farm, with plenty of rocky crevices nearby for the dragon to secure its treasure. The princess enters the tower on her fourteenth birthday, and there she remains under lock and key, guarded by the dragon until she is rescued by her future husband!"

Tildy said all of this as if it were some grand, wonderful thing, but Ivy felt only a hot rush of anger. Why hadn't she been told any of this before today? And did everyone in the kingdom honestly think she would have nothing to say about being tossed in a tower and left to rot like a sack of turnips until some sword-wielding prince saw fit to save her?

"I won't do it!" she declared.

Tildy's face was sad, but it remained set and unyielding. "I'm afraid you have no choice," she said wistfully, lowering her sewing to her lap. Then her eyes flared with sudden fire. "Oh, I knew something like this was going to happen. If only you had had a proper upbringing! Most princesses grow up knowing they're to be locked in the tower, so it doesn't come as such a shock. But no—your father didn't think it necessary to worry you while you were still so young." Her tone turned harsh and disapproving. "'Time enough for that later,' he said. 'Let the child have her fun. One must make hay while the sun shines, after all.' Bah! Foolish old man. Doesn't have the sense of a sand flea."

Even though she had to admit to herself that her father was pretty muddled most of the time, Ivy didn't like to hear anyone say it out loud.

"My father is not foolish!" she snapped. "And he's not going to lock me in a tower, even if there is some silly treaty." Her father, who loved her so dearly, would never let her be treated in such a manner. Ivy had to speak with him at once. Sparked by a fierce new determination, she dashed from the room and was halfway down the hall before poor Tildy could say another word.

3

The King's Final Say

When Ivy found her father, he was counting haystacks in one of the fields along the castle grounds. Frederick, who was a very old horse with a muzzle almost as gray as the king's own outpouring of hair, rambled along beside him.

"Ah, Ivy," the king exclaimed happily as she rushed up to meet him. "I'm so glad you're here. I have just discovered the most perfectly formed haystack you shall ever hope to see—"

"Father, I need to talk to you about this Dragon Treaty business," Ivy said in the most purposeful voice she could muster.

"Oh yes...the Dragon Treaty." The king suddenly looked very uncomfortable and started to fiddle with his long beard. The skin beneath his eyes sagged a bit the way the skin of a peach does if it's left sitting too long, but the blue eyes above were warm and kind, even if they did seem faraway most of the time. "I suppose you were bound to find out about that sooner or later. I didn't wish to trouble you unnecessarily. I know how much you love to play and run about under the sun and sky. But you needn't worry, dear; being shut in the tower won't be so bad as you think. Why, it actually has some very fine amenities—"

"What?" Ivy felt as if a large stone had been dropped into the pit of her stomach. "You're not actually going to make me do this, are you?"

"Well, of course you're going to do it," said the king matter-of-factly. "It's tradition. The princesses of Ardendale have been locked in the tower for generations."

"But that's not fair at all!" Ivy cried. "To lock me up and make me marry a stranger who could be someone completely awful, just because he can slay a dragon."

The king looked a bit guilty, and for a moment Ivy thought he would give in as he usually did, but then his face hardened and took on a gravity she had never seen before.

"You should not be so quick to scoff at dragon slaying," he said reproachfully, drawing himself to his full height beneath the worn sweep of his cloak. "It is not an easy undertaking. I should know—it is how I came to marry your mother."

Realization burst upon Ivy like tinder catching flame. Of course, since her father was king, it meant he had to have slain a dragon. She knew her father hadn't always been as simpleminded as he was now. Still, it was hard to believe that the old man before her, who had to be reminded not to use a fork to eat his afternoon bowl of pea soup, could have ever done something as daring as fight a dragon. Truth be told, she couldn't imagine anyone who looked less like a dragon slayer. At the moment, his hair was crinkly like a scarecrow's, sticking out in all directions from underneath his tarnished crown, and his eyes had grown soft and distant with memory.

"I often think of the first time I saw your mother," the king said, and his face was so thoughtful and composed, Ivy felt certain this was one of those rare moments he was thinking clearly. "It was right after I defeated the dragon. He had been a particularly nasty creature and had already sent several princes to a terrible end. I was no young buck, even back then. In fact, many people told me I had no business attempting to slay a dragon at my age—no business at all—yet I succeeded where all those younger princes failed." Ivy could hear a thread of pride running through his voice. "I was so exhausted, I could barely move, but somehow I managed to climb the steps of the tower, and there was your mother, standing at the top. She wore a golden gown and her hair was long and loose, flowing to her waist in waves as dark as a chestnut's shell. Sunlight was streaming through the window behind her, making her glow like an angel."

The king's expression was heavy and wistful, full of remembered longing. "But what I recall most was the look on her face. She gave me the most glorious smile. She didn't seem to care that I was battered and bruised, or so much older than she. She looked so happy, as if I was the one she had been waiting for all along. I have never seen a sight more beautiful in my entire life."

His words took Ivy by surprise, for her father rarely talked of her mother. Tildy said he had loved her so fiercely that her death had been almost more than he could bear. His mind had started to go soon after and grew worse with each year that passed.

The king tore himself from memories of his beloved queen. His gaze fell upon Ivy, heavy as a millstone.

"The Dragon Treaty is what saved Ardendale." His voice was somber. "Do you think our kingdom would be this pleasant and peaceful if there were still dragons despoiling our land and endangering our people?"

"Well, no... of course not," Ivy admitted in a feeble voice. Tears pricked her eyes, and there was a plunging sensation in her middle that made her feel as if she were sinking into a giant mud puddle. "But there has to be some other way to keep the kingdom safe. Maybe we could make some other arrangement, a new treaty—"

"And who would be our next king?" her father demanded. "What prince would come all the way to Ardendale just to marry you?"

His words stung sharply, and, seeing the stunned look on her face, the king was quick to soften the blow.

"Ivy, you know I think any man would be lucky to have you for a bride, but the matter is not so simple. There was a time when many a prince would have gladly ruled Ardendale, but that's no longer the case. The northern kingdoms have always been larger, and they've grown faster than we could ever hope to. We don't have their cities and palaces, their armies and knights, their sailing ships and merchants and wealth. Ardendale is a simple kingdom of farmers and peasants, pleasant enough for us, but most outsiders would consider it...well, backwater. And the castle and grounds have fallen into some disrepair these past years. I suppose I haven't been as good about the upkeep as I should have been," the king confessed, looking guilty. "Even the dragon treasure isn't what it used to be. Its enormity was always a bit exaggerated, I'm afraid, and now it's less than ever, seeing as the dragons haven't been able to raid anybody since the treaty was formed. When I slayed the dragon, I myself received but a small cache of coins, long since depleted, but we try not to make such things known outside the kingdom. Ivy, there is nothing to draw a new king to our shores except for the opportunity to slay a dragon and lay claim to its treasure. It's the only thing we have to offer."

The full weight of her father's words struck Ivy in that miserable moment, and she understood at last what he had been trying to tell her all along: the Dragon Treaty was far too important to be trifled with. It was the means by which their kingdom was preserved.

"Your mother was proud to do her duty and play her part in fulfilling the Dragon Treaty. It would be a disgrace to her memory if you didn't do the same," said the king. "Ivy, you will honor the terms of the treaty, and that's my final say in the matter."

It was the only command her father had ever given her. Ivy felt the last bit of hope drain from her like wine from a barrel, and when Frederick snorted and bobbed his head up and down as if to say he approved, she knew there was nothing in all the world that could change the king's mind.

4

The Ship of Bones

As sunny years drifted by, Ivy became quietly resigned to the fact that she was to be locked in a tower on her fourteenth birthday. Most of the time she managed not to think about it. It wasn't in Ivy's nature to dwell upon unpleasant things, not when there were so many curiosities and delights in the valley kingdom much more worthy of her attention: wild strawberries to be picked in the weed-dotted meadow near the miller's cottage, wiggling tadpoles to net in the reedy shallows of the stream that meandered past her father's favorite hayfield, and four entire dusty shelves in the back of the castle library dedicated to storybooks and tales of high adventure.

Ivy might have comfortably forgotten all about the tower for months on end if it weren't for Tildy. Unfortunately, the ever-sensible nursemaid thought it wise for the princess to know everything there was to know about the white tower at the foot of the Craggies, down to the last painfully uninteresting detail.

"The white stone is from a quarry in the kingdom of Marmor," Tildy explained one morning at breakfast, daintily stirring her tea, taking great care not to clink the spoon against the sides of the cup. "It cost a fortune to import enough to build a tower—why, we might be as grand as the northern kingdoms today, if the royal treasury hadn't been depleted to buy the stone."

"The chamber at the top of the tower is quite lovely," the nursemaid said another time, interrupting Ivy as she was trying to read one of her favorite books. "I'm sure you'll find lots of sensible ways to spend your time there. It was said one princess practiced posture so diligently that by the time she left the tower she could walk up and down stairs with two books, a teacup, and an egg balanced on the top of her head. And your own great-grandmother used her time in the tower to embroider an entire chest of handkerchiefs and linens for her bridal trousseau. They were the envy of every young lady in the kingdom, as you can well imagine."

Every once in a while, Tildy produced a piece of information that was actually worth knowing, for example, the bits about the wishing table, the golden goblet, and the magic mirror.

"Drusilla cast some spells when the tower was first built, all those hundreds of years ago," she said one afternoon as she tried to get the princess to stand still long enough to mend a fallen hem. "It's probably the only time in her everlasting life your godmother has done something truly useful." Her voice turned sour. She had never forgiven the princess's fairy godmother for running off after the queen died.

"There's an enchanted table that fills with food—whatever you wish, whenever you wish." Tildy's face shone at the thought of magically conjured meals.

"At least I won't starve," grumbled Ivy.

"There's also a golden goblet that fills with fairy nectar when you cup it in your hands," Tildy continued. "Fairy nectar isn't any old stuff, you know. Usually, it can only be harvested from the flowers of an enchanted fairy garden. I've never had any myself, of course, but I've been told that it's as golden as sunshine and tastes of honeysuckle, and those who drink it instantly feel strong and refreshed."

Ivy couldn't imagine why she would need to feel strong and refreshed while sitting around a tower all day but figured Tildy wouldn't appreciate her mentioning this.

"And the jeweled mirror that hangs upon the tower's wall is the most amazing of all," said Tildy. "It's no simple looking glass. You just have to ask, and it will show you whomever you wish to see—as long as they're human, mind you. It doesn't work on creatures like fairies or goblins or trolls, not that you'd want to see the likes of them. But you can see your father or me whenever you please, even if you can't speak to us. That should help some, if you get lonely."

Suddenly Ivy had a dreadful foreboding.

"What happens if no one saves me?" she asked. She didn't remember anyone saying how long she had to stay in the tower if no prince was successful at slaying the dragon. "When do I get to come home?"

The slightest flicker of a frown played upon Tildy's lips, a sure sign the princess wasn't going to like what she had to say. "Well, traditionally, the princess stays in the tower until she is rescued by her future husband or dies of old age."

"Old age!" cried Ivy, horrified.

"That's only happened twice," Tildy added quickly, but a flurry of nervous flutters had already started stirring Ivy's insides. "Luckily, both of those princesses had younger sisters to take their place. You see, some dragons are so fierce that no prince can slay them. The princess grows old and dies before anyone can win her hand."

"But wouldn't the dragon get old and weak, too?" Ivy asked desperately.

"Dragons live for hundreds and hundreds of years," Tildy said sadly. "Seventy or eighty years guarding a tower are nothing to a dragon. If the dragon can outlive the princess, it can return home to the Smoke Sands. And, unfortunately, the older the princess gets the less...eager some suitors become, although the opportunity to slay a dragon and claim its treasure is still enough to entice some third-rate princes, even if they have to marry a woman older than aged cheddar.

"But don't you worry." Tildy patted Ivy's hand reassuringly. "Your mother wasn't in the tower for more than two years before your father slew that dreadful beast—quite a feat at his age, I must say—and some brave prince will come and rescue you, too."

Ivy pressed her lips together and held her tongue, but inside her thoughts were reeling. Her mother had spent two years inside the tower—*two entire years*—without ever setting foot outside its high stone walls, without searching for long-legged crabs in the seawater that pooled between rocks on the beach at low tide or spending entire afternoons curled up with a cup of tea in the library or even being able to see a single person she cared about except as a reflection in a magic mirror. And some princesses had been in there much longer, some their entire lives, with nothing but a tower full of enchanted objects and an angry dragon for company.

Rose and Clarinda weren't much help, either. Rose found the whole being-rescued-by-a-prince scenario incredibly romantic and kept saying things like, "I imagine the prince will be very handsome," and "When he saves you, I bet he sweeps you up into his arms and whisks you down the spiral staircase to a white horse waiting at the foot of the tower." She thought lounging around a tower awaiting a princely rescue was a glorious way to spend your time.

Clarinda at least tried to be sympathetic.

"It could be worse," she said. "I heard in Anura, the princesses have to kiss a frog to get a husband."

Rose snickered at this, and Clarinda looked embarrassed.

"It's true," she insisted softly. "My sister says the royal family there slips potions into the wine glasses of princes to turn them into frogs. The only way they can change back is if a princess kisses them. The prince is usually so grateful, he marries her."

"That's ridiculous," Rose said, and Clarinda never brought up kissing frogs again.

Ivy had been born in autumn, after the air had grown chill and leaves had started to burst into their fiery displays of red and gold. It was a season she normally loved, but she spent her thirteenth summer dreading the coming of crisp and colorful days. Knowing the tower awaited her on her birthday, like a lurking monster eager to snatch her away from this world and swallow her whole, cast a shadow upon even the brightest of summer afternoons.

Just when she thought her trepidation couldn't possibly get any worse, old Boggs the gatekeeper rushed into the Great Hall one morning as summer was nearing its close, demanding to speak to the king.

The king sat swinging his legs under the long oak dining table, and they had knocked against the tabletop sending several boiled eggs rolling off his plate into his lap. Luckily, he was too busy to notice, so intent was he on wrapping apple slices in his napkin to take to Frederick.

"You are interrupting His Majesty's breakfast," Tildy told Boggs testily. She hated how the manners of the castle staff had gone to ruin since the queen had died—along with just about everything else.

"Begging your pardon, ma'am," Boggs said, bobbing his bald head in a clumsy bow. Boggs had once been a member of the King's Guard, but in his old age resigned himself to watching over the castle gate. He was missing his two front teeth, among many others, so his s's came out sounding like a muffled "th" instead. "A thip hath landed on our thore," he lisped, "and I thought the king should know. I've never theen the like of it before."

"We're not expecting any more merchant ships this summer," said one of the royal counselors from his high-backed chair at the king's elbow.

"Perhaps the King's Guard should be readied," suggested the other, looking nervous. "It could be a warship or an invasion of some sort."

"Nonsense," said the king, speaking around a large mouthful of porridge. "Who would invade us? We are a peaceful populace and have nothing that would be of value to another kingdom, although our haystacks are exceptionally fine, if I do say so myself."

"Nonetheless, I think we need to have a look at this ship to make sure it doesn't pose a threat," the first counselor insisted.

"Very well," said the king, rising from the table and sending an avalanche of eggs to the floor.

Although Tildy protested, Ivy left the Great Hall with the king and his counselors as they made their way to the beach with a small contingent of the King's Guard. It wasn't a far walk, as the castle perched upon a grassy rise a mere stone's throw from the pebbly beach that stretched down to the sea. Ships were uncommon in Ardendale, and Ivy wasn't about to miss a chance at such a rare sight. Maybe these were traders on a new route, bringing perfumes and cloth and curiosities from faraway lands.

As soon as they turned down the narrow path that led to the water's edge, Ivy could see Boggs had been telling the truth about the ship being strange. Although the beach here was lovely, the water was unusually deep and choppy. It was too dangerous for swimming, but the depth meant that vessels could pull in almost all the way to shore. The odd-looking ship that bobbed there now was smaller than the merchant vessels that brought wares to the kingdom two or three times a year. From the single mast hung an enormous sail that was dark gray and leathery-looking. Ivy wondered if it was made of some type of animal hide and, at the same time, wondered who would use hide to make a sail.

But the strangest thing about the ship was its color. It was white—a dazzling white so bright in the morning sun that Ivy almost had to squint to look at it. The color was so smooth and even, so much a part of the ship's timbers, it couldn't possibly have been paint or a wash. Ivy wondered what wood had such a color. The hull gleamed as if someone had polished it to the bone.

As they drew nearer, it struck Ivy with horror that the ship hadn't been *polished* to the bone, it *was* bone. Or, to be exact, lots of bones, enormous bones, polished smooth and carved and fitted into an entire sailing vessel. Even the bowsprit at the ship's prow was bone, a long tapered spiral that resembled a giant unicorn's horn, from which hung a massive, intricately carved bone lantern, used to light the ship's way after dark.

With its ominous trappings of bone and skin, of colorless white and gray, Ivy might have thought some phantom ghost ship had anchored on their shore, except that this ship looked crisp and clean and expertly made, and a crew that was very much alive was alighting from the two small boats they had rowed to the beach. There were well over a dozen of them, and all had very pale skin and hair so blond it was almost white. They were dressed in fine tunics and trousers made of the same leathery material as their sail and, despite the warm weather, boots of thick, spotted fur.

The most important member of the group seemed to be a handsome if somewhat somber-looking young man. There was white fur trimming his tunic, and about his neck hung a large bone pendant shaped like a bear raised on its hindquarters, claws exposed, with shiny black stones for eyes. His reed-thin lips and sharp cheekbones gave him a slightly chiseled look. He walked ahead of everyone else, flanked by a thin, distinguished older man with a neatly trimmed blond beard, long nose, and hawkish eyes. When they reached the party from the castle, the bearded man gave a curt bow and then turned to gesture formally at the young man with the pendant.

"Greetings," he said in a grand, sweeping voice, "from His Royal Highness Prince Romil of Glacia."

5

The Ice Prince

"This is most out of the ordinary," Tildy exclaimed for about the hundredth time since the king had returned to the castle with the pale-skinned prince and his men in tow. Each time she said it, her voice grew a little more frantic and high-pitched. "Most out of the ordinary."

It turned out that the kingdom of Glacia was far, far north in a very cold part of the world. Gar, the bearded adviser to Prince Romil, explained how the prince had had to set sail for Ardendale before summer was over, as it was the only time of year when the ocean passages were not completely frozen. And so the prince had arrived more than one month before Ivy was to enter the tower and the dragon was made available for slaying, and expected food and lodging not only for himself and the solemn Gar but for the sixteen members of his personal guard that he had seen fit to bring with him on his journey.

"It does seem a bit unusual," said the king. "When I came to Ardendale to slay the dragon, I pitched a tent in a grove of ash trees on the outskirts of the Craggies. I cooked gruel in a tin pot over the campfire and had no one but dear old Frederick for company. Yes, Frederick was in the prime of his life back in those days. What a fine specimen of strength and loyalty he was!" The king's eyes grew misty, and he seemed to drift off for a moment before pulling himself back to the matter at hand. "I suppose princes nowadays are not of such a rugged nature, what with all their servants and sailing ships and fancy clothing and such. Still, Prince Romil is our honored guest, and we must do our best to make him and his men feel at home in our humble castle."

"But where will we put them all?" cried Tildy, wringing her hands fretfully. "It's not like we have eighteen spare rooms, let alone a bedchamber fit for a prince. Oh, fairy cakes—what will they think of us when they see the state of the guest quarters?"

The castle had a small number of guest chambers filled with wide beds and old, dusty furniture, but these hadn't been used in so long that the king had converted the largest into a solarium just this past winter.

"Oh, and he's seen you!" Tildy moaned, her gaze falling upon the scrawny figure of the princess. "In that disgrace of an old dress, with your face unpowdered and all your freckles showing…"

"What's wrong with my freckles?" asked Ivy huffily. "I never wear powder, and they always show."

"At least you haven't been running about in the sun so

much this summer," Tildy went on as if she hadn't heard. "Your skin is a halfway decent color for once. No prince is supposed to lay eyes on you until he's slain the dragon and you're betrothed. That's the way things normally work." Her voice was dangerously close to becoming an unladylike wail. "You don't know the first thing about interacting with royalty, and your table manners are atrocious. Oh, what if you scare him off?"

But, for once in her life, the princess was determined to be on her best behavior. The arrival of Prince Romil in his bone ship was the most exciting thing that had ever happened in Ardendale. He looked just like the dashing princes from the storybooks in the library, and Ivy was sure that, like them, he had accomplished countless feats of daring. She couldn't wait to hear of his far-off kingdom and his many grand adventures.

That evening, the Great Hall bustled with more than a handful of people for the first time in the princess's life. Tildy had laced her up in one of her mother's old gowns, nothing of Ivy's being fine enough for dinner with a royal guest, but the dress was much too long, and there hadn't been time to hem it. The lovely blue fabric pooled on the floor like a small puddle that followed her wherever she went. She had to be careful not to trip over it.

The castle servants had spent the whole afternoon preparing the Great Hall, but Ivy couldn't help feeling that the drafty old room wasn't up to the task of a formal dinner. The long dining table was usually unadorned except for tall brass candlesticks that had seen better days. The king, in his carelessness, had stained all the tablecloths long ago, but Ivy noticed that one had been pulled out for this special occasion, with a couple of carefully placed vases of pink chrysanthemums from the castle garden hiding the worst of the stains.

The gray flagstones were bare of any type of rug or carpet and had been hastily swept clean just that afternoon. The ancient tapestry of damask roses draped across the southern wall was beautiful but a bit frayed at the ends. Time had faded the color of the roses to the barest hint of a blush.

Only the painting of the late queen, resplendent in her white brocade wedding gown, looked pristine and perfect in its cherished spot over the enormous fireplace. The king saw to it that the gilded frame was regularly polished and the canvas carefully dusted. The painter had captured every detail of the beautiful queen, from the delicate ridge of her high cheekbones and the long lashes framing her lovely eyes to the gold combs that pinned her dark hair beneath her veil and even the tiny pearls sewn onto the full skirt of her gown.

If the Great Hall was a little worse for wear, at least the food was worthy of a royal guest. Cook had outdone herself for this special meal, serving much finer fare than usual: hare stewed with sage and parsley, stuffed pheasant, pork dumplings, cabbage boiled in broth, and, for dessert, gooseberry tarts and roasted figs basted in honey.

"There are no trees in Glacia," Romil said when the king asked about his unusual ship. "The ground is frozen. Since we have no wood, we build our ships by carving whale and walrus bone. We even use the tusk of the unicorn whale. The sail and ropes are sealskin. A less resourceful people would have never come up with such an ingenious design, but we Glacians have always been of a superior mind."

"Are your buildings made out of bones, too?" asked the king.

"All of our buildings are constructed from sculpted ice," Romil said. "The palace is quite magnificent. There are one hundred and ten rooms, nineteen towers, and a bridge of ice that spans a garden of ice crystals and a giant frozen waterfall."

"Goodness," said the king.

Ivy's heart danced at the thought of this sparkling palace. "How do you keep it from melting?" she wondered.

"Ice never melts in Glacia," Romil said. "It never gets warm enough."

"So how do you cook your food?" asked Ivy. "If you light fires in the palace, your rooms would start to thaw."

"Princess Ivory, you shouldn't pester His Royal Highness with all these questions," Tildy scolded from the other side of the table.

"I am well aware that outsiders find Glacia a fascinating kingdom." The prince smoothed his white-gold hair with fluid ease, as if he had had a lot of practice making that particular motion. "It is only natural the princess would want to know more about it.

"We have large fire pits in the palace's courtyards, dug

very deep so that the heat of the flames never reaches the palace walls. All of our cooking is done there. That is also where we smoke our meat and tan our sealskins and pelts."

"It sounds so different from Ardendale," said Ivy.

"Quite," replied Romil rather brusquely. "I should have liked to have been king of Glacia," he confessed. "But I had the great misfortune of being my father's second son. My older brother was the one to inherit the throne when our father died last winter. But I've always known I was meant to rule, and I am determined to have a kingdom of my own.

"Ardendale is small and…*quaint*," he said, spitting out the last word as if it left a bad taste in his mouth, "but I suppose it will do."

"I'm sure once you've spent more time here, you will come to see Ardendale's many charms," the king said good-naturedly.

"This kingdom has possibilities, with my hand to guide it," said Romil. "And there *is* the dragon treasure. I must confess, I'm surprised you didn't use a portion of your own spoils from slaying the dragon to dress up the castle a bit. It's quite…rustic, isn't it?" He cast his frosty gray eyes around the room disdainfully.

"Well, we prefer a nice, modest existence here in Ardendale," said the king, looking nervous.

"Modest is right," Romil sniffed, wrinkling his nose as he poked at the meat on his plate. "I have a much grander look in mind for when I am king. There will be no sullied table linens or hideous tapestries cluttering the walls. And that ridiculously soppy painting over the fireplace will have to go, of course." He inclined his head toward the portrait of the queen.

The king looked crestfallen but managed a polite smile. "Of course, Ivy's husband will be the new king and may do as he sees fit," he said in a soft voice.

"It's a lovely painting," Ivy declared defiantly. "And I rather like it."

Tildy's eyes shot daggers at her. If the nursemaid hadn't been such a proper lady, she probably would have kicked Ivy under the table.

"Yes, I suppose someone with simple country tastes would." Romil looked down his nose at her, a scornful expression on the sharp features of his face. "Nevertheless, once I am king, it will be replaced. I must have a castle worthy of my royal status."

"You speak as if the castle were yours already," said Ivy, her growing dislike of the prince making her bold. "You must have a lot of confidence in your ability to slay the dragon."

"I am the best hunter in all of Glacia." The black stones set into the bear pendant around the prince's neck glinted in the firelight, as if to signal agreement with his words. "I have single-handedly brought down snow bears and bull seals. I once speared a whale so large there was enough meat to feed the entire palace for weeks on end. And even if I were not a huntsman of such remarkable skill, I would still have an advantage that no other prince could hope to possess.

"Long ago, there were dragons in Glacia," he explained. "They were the color of snow, and their scales glistened like ice. As I have mentioned, my people are of a particularly clever and resourceful nature. We have long known that a dragon's scales are harder even than the iron for which we trade with the lower kingdoms. When one of the beasts was slain, we did not let such valuable material go to waste. Its scales were used to make armor, for what better protection from a dragon's claws and fire than the nearly impenetrable plating of a dragon itself? The talons and teeth were used for spearheads, for they were far superior at piercing the defenses of a dragon than any weapon humans could hope to make.

"My own great-great-grandfather slayed one of the last dragons in Glacia, and I have brought with me the very armor and spears he used to do so. With my skills and such weapons, I am more than a match for any beast."

Ivy spent a long time getting ready for bed that night, for she was far too upset to go to sleep. How could she ever have thought Prince Romil dashing? He was so arrogant, so sure he would be the next king of Ardendale, and he didn't even like it here. What were these "possibilities" he saw for the kingdom? He was probably going to try to build his own glittery palace, Ivy thought bitterly, full of statues of himself spearing whales and slaying dragons. What kind of snooty, selfish king would he make? And what kind of husband?

Ivy peered into the mirror over her dressing table and glared at her reflection. The girl who glared back was thin and of middle height, with sandy brown hair that fell past her shoulders and set, stubborn brown eyes, bright with anger. A smattering of tiny freckles stood out on the bridge of her small, inelegant button nose.

Ivy didn't have Rose's fair, sunny looks, or Clarinda's soft, pretty features. She wasn't ugly by any means, but Ivy knew she would never in a million years be the great beauty that her mother had been. She would certainly never be the gracious and regal queen that Tildy hoped she would blossom into. And from that night forward, Ivy was determined that there was one more thing she would never be: Dragon Treaty or not, she would never be the wife of a certain prince whose heart was as icy as the frozen kingdom from which he came.

6

Frogs and the Plotting Princess

"Ivy, you wouldn't try to get out of being locked in the tower, would you?" Clarinda asked, sounding just a tad horrified at the thought.

"Of course not," Ivy said crossly. Having her father and Tildy lecture her on the importance of the Dragon Treaty was bad enough; she didn't need her friends starting on her as well. "Just because a prince has to save me from the tower doesn't mean it has to be Romil. I just have to make sure he's not the one who slays the dragon."

"How are you going to do that?" Clarinda wanted to know. They were huddled under the cover of an arched walkway leading into the castle courtyard, where they could speak without being overheard.

"I haven't figured that out yet," admitted the princess.

"Prince Romil is awfully handsome," Rose said dreamily from her perch atop a bale of hay set to one side of the walkway, no doubt destined for the stables on the west end of the courtyard. "Are you sure you don't want to marry him?"

"I told you, he's horrible," said Ivy, feeling queasy at the thought. "I don't care how good-looking he is, he would be a terrible king. Now help me think of a way to get rid of him."

"He sure practices a lot with his guards. He could break a leg or something and not be able to fight the dragon," Clarinda said hopefully.

Every day since his arrival in Ardendale, Romil and his guards had gathered outside the castle gate in the small stretch of meadow next to the pear orchard. Clad in his dragon-scale armor, which made him look as if he were encased in a glistening suit of ice, Romil sparred with his men and hurled bone-handled spears at a series of sealskin targets. From the times she had spied him from the castle windows or while strolling along the walk above the castle gate, Ivy had to admit he looked a most capable warrior.

"No, that's not likely," she said with a sigh. "He's much too coordinated to break any bones."

"I know—what about your fairy godmother?" said Rose. "Fairy godmothers are supposed to help princesses out of difficult situations."

"Drusilla? Maybe she would help me," Ivy said. "But I don't know where she is. I don't know anything about her, really, except that she's been godmother to all the princesses of Ardendale for as long as anyone can remember—and Tildy doesn't like her. Says she's as flighty as dandelion fluff, and the only time my mother acted the slightest bit improper was around her."

"My mother says the queen and Drusilla were as close as anything," said Rose, plucking delicately at stray strands of hay with one long-fingered hand. "And that Drusilla was more like her sister than her godmother. They always got kind of giggly around each other. If Drusilla cared about your mother so much, surely she would help you."

"But I have no way of finding her," Ivy pointed out. Discouragement and frustration welled up inside her, threatening to give way to despair. Then suddenly, a wonderfully devious idea began to take shape. "Wait a minute—the first day Romil was here, Tildy said something about being worried I would scare him off. What if I behave so badly he doesn't want to marry me? I'll be the worst princess ever. I'll stay dirty all the time—those Glacians seem to like everything so clean and perfect—and I'll have positively dreadful manners."

"I don't know, Ivy," Clarinda said uncertainly. "What if Prince Romil gets mad at you?"

"So what if he does?" said Ivy. "Then he'll want to leave. He'll realize that marrying me is the last thing in the world he wants, and he'll go searching for some other kingdom to rule."

Ivy wasted no time putting her brilliant plan in action. She arrived late for dinner in a plain day dress streaked with dirt. Her hair was wild and unkempt, and she had rubbed a generous dose of golden pollen on her nose, courtesy of the patch of yellow hog thistle growing in a ditch next to the castle. She looked as if she had just crawled through a hedgerow.

"Sorry I'm late, I've been out for a walk," she greeted the room cheerfully.

The king's counselors gawked at her as if they couldn't believe their eyes, and Tildy turned so pale that one of the serving maids ran to fetch the smelling salts, just in case. To Ivy's immense satisfaction, Romil, Gar, and the rest of the perfectly groomed Glacians looked thoroughly shocked. Romil's nose wrinkled and something close to disgust showed in his haughty gray eyes. Only the king seemed unaware that anything was amiss and chatted on happily with those around him.

"Oh, darling, there you are," he called when he spotted her. "You must try the roast partridge. Cook has prepared it in a cream sauce that is truly delightful!"

Tildy, of course, cornered her near the stairwell to her tower room as soon as dinner was over, dragging the unwitting king behind her.

"Your Majesty," she said sharply, "I really must insist that you say something to Princess Ivory about her shameful appearance. To arrive for dinner looking like an ill-bred farm girl, in front of important guests—why, it's absolutely scandalous. Just look at her dress, and that nose!"

"Is there something on Ivy's nose?" the king asked. He leaned in to take a closer look at his daughter. "There does seem to be a spot of yellow, doesn't there? Not to worry, Tildy. I'm sure Ivy will wash it off once she gets to her bedchamber, won't you, dear?" He gave Ivy a little pat on the head and a fond smile, and clearly considered that the end of the matter. Tildy could only look on bleakly.

Now that Ivy knew she could get away with looking as if she'd been raised by trolls, she made a point of doing so all the time. She even went so far as to rub dirt underneath her fingernails. Since Romil trained with his guards for a large part of every day, Ivy usually only saw him at meals. She made sure to use this time wisely. She chewed her food loudly, slurped her drink, and jostled her cutlery about, noisily dropping forks and spoons on the floor just in time to startle Romil if he happened to be pouring wine into his goblet or cutting his meat.

He scowled at her when this happened, and every once in a while she caught him throwing a dark glance her way when he thought she wasn't looking, but most of the time he seemed content to pretend that she didn't exist. He didn't talk much, unless it was about Glacia, to brag about how he had yet again bested one or another of his guards at practice, or to find fault with the food.

"The weather has been lovely lately, don't you think?" Ivy ventured to say to him one evening in between noisy slurps of lamb stew. She hoped to annoy him with pointless chatter. "I could spend the whole day outside."

"Yes, I can tell you like to spend a great deal of time outdoors...near dirt," the prince replied ungraciously.

"Well, I figure, why bother spending a lot of time washing it off when you're just going to get more on you?" Ivy said, smiling brightly.

"Indeed," sniffed Romil.

He turned his attention back to his stew, and that was the end of the conversation. Despite how displeased he always looked, day after day passed and he showed no signs of wanting to leave.

"How can he still possibly be interested in marrying me?" Ivy moaned to her friends one morning as they snapped bunches of shiny black elderberries off the low tree that grew to one side of the castle gate. The king had a keen fondness for elderberry wine; Cook kept a few barrels in the kitchen and a good stock of the sweet stuff in the cellar at all times.

"Perhaps he's madly in love with you and is determined to win your hand no matter what," said Rose, starry-eyed.

"It's more likely he's determined to win a kingdom no matter what," said Ivy in a sour voice. "And the only person he's madly in love with is himself. You should have heard him at dinner last night, carrying on about how he hasn't missed a single target in the last four-and-a-half years. His head is bigger than a pumpkin. I haven't done enough to drive him away. There's not much time left until my birthday. I'm just going to have to take more drastic measures."

That afternoon, with their skirts tucked up around their knees, Ivy and Rose caught nearly a dozen frogs from the overgrown lily pond in the castle garden, while a reluctant Clarinda stood by with an old sack from the stables. Ivy had noticed that as picky as Romil was about food, he had a particular fondness for bread, perhaps because there was nothing even close to wheat in the frozen reaches of Glacia. As was only polite, the king and Tildy saw to it the prince was always the first person to select from the bread basket at dinner.

Ivy hurried to the castle kitchen just before the evening meal and emptied the entire contents of the sack into the deep well of the bread basket, the green frogs plopping down among the small loaves of bread. She quickly covered the basket with its heavy cloth, hoping the frogs would stay put until it was removed by one very surprised Glacian prince.

"I didn't see that," chirped Cook with a knowing wink. Romil, who was used to eating fish and eel and something called blubber, constantly complained about her cooking. The castle staff didn't want him to be king any more than Ivy did.

The princess thought she would go mad waiting for dinner to be served that evening. She watched impatiently as dish after dish was carried to the table and set in its proper place. Finally the bread basket arrived, and, as usual, Romil was offered first choice.

He unfolded the cloth only to find himself staring down at a pair of bulging, round eyes attached to a small, bumpy, green creature. It opened its wide gape of a mouth to emit a long, throaty *"Ribbbbbbbbbbbbbit,"* that rolled about the drafty room like a small peal of thunder. Romil started at the sound and, with a very unprincely curse, dropped the basket as if it were a hot coal. One would have thought a man who had faced snow bears would have been a bit braver in the situation, but in all fairness to him, Ivy thought, he had probably never seen a frog before.

As soon as the basket hit the table, it toppled onto its side and rolled, spilling bread and frogs all over. The frogs immediately began to hop off in every direction. One knocked over a vase of flowers, which shattered loudly on the floor and drenched the flagstones with water. Tildy shrieked as another landed in the middle of her salad, and up and down the table people were jumping to their feet as frogs bounded across the tabletop, upsetting dishes and sending vegetables and bits of gravy flying in their wake.

"Well, don't just stand there," Tildy snapped at the serving staff. "Round them up!"

It was as if someone had kicked an anthill. Suddenly, the Great Hall was full of bodies in motion—the king's man-in-waiting grabbed a candlesnuffer and tried to herd a frog toward the window with it; several young maids tried to trap frogs underneath overturned bowls without actually having to touch them; and servant boys dived across the table, trying to snatch frogs with their bare hands. One particularly lively frog kicked over a candlestick, setting the tablecloth on fire, and a quick-thinking Glacian poured his goblet of water over it, dowsing the flames.

"For crying out loud, can't anyone get control of this situation?" barked Gar. His hawk eyes flashed angrily. He opened his mouth to say more just as an especially large frog leaped into the soup terrine. Carrot soup went flying everywhere, hitting Romil and Gar full in the face and shoulders, and splashing several nearby Glacians as well. Gar ended up swallowing a large mouthful. He coughed and sputtered in a most unseemly manner, orange soup dripping off the ends of his neatly trimmed beard. Romil wiped soup out of his eyes. His previously spotless tunic was now covered with thick, undignified orange splotches.

Ivy just couldn't help herself. She erupted in a fit of laughter. She had been planning to laugh all along; she wanted Romil to know it was she who had put the frogs in the bread basket. The stuffy prince certainly wouldn't want a wife who played practical jokes. But she really hadn't expected to enjoy herself so fully. The laughs just seemed to keep coming, ringing loudly through the hall, and even after she had clapped both hands over her mouth like a plug, a few muffled giggles escaped.

Romil and Gar glowered at her, their scowls so big it nearly split their faces in two, and Tildy shot her a seething look from where she had taken cover behind the high back of her carved wooden chair. As usual, only the king was unruffled. He sat calmly in his place at the head of the table, where he had watched the whole hullabaloo unfold with quiet interest.

"You know," he said thoughtfully, "I never knew that frogs liked bread."

A Perfectly Devised Plan

Tildy had had enough.

"I am going to speak to your father one more time," she fumed later that evening, pacing back and forth across the princess's bedchamber with quick, angry steps. "But I don't care what he says or does, I am not putting up with your childish antics any longer." Her eyes blazed blue fire, and her round face had turned a most unbecoming shade of scarlet. "I know you don't like Prince Romil, but he is a royal guest, and your behavior toward him has been deplorable. From now on, you will meet me in your bedchamber a half hour before every meal, and I will see to it that you are clean, properly dressed, and that there isn't a frog or any other disgusting creature in sight. Is that understood?"

"Yes, ma'am," Ivy said from where she sat on the edge of her bed, beneath a canopy of dusty and faded plum-colored draperies. She had never seen Tildy this upset and felt a stab of guilt at being the cause of it. She had long grown accustomed to falling short of her nursemaid's rather fussy expectations, but Tildy's disapproval stung nonetheless.

"Your mother would be so disappointed in you," Tildy said, giving the princess one last harsh look before departing.

That thought hurt as well, but at the same time, Ivy doubted that her mother would have wanted to see Arden-dale end up in the hands of such a haughty, selfish king, no matter how proper she had been. No, Ivy was doing the right thing by driving Romil away, and it was for the good of everyone in Ardendale, even if Tildy was too shortsighted to see that. She would just have to find ways to pester Romil outside of the Great Hall—when Tildy was not around—and she knew just the place to start.

Boggs and the stable boy, Owen, were having a lunch of cold meat pies under a crooked old oak tree the next afternoon, watching down the meadow as Romil skillfully wielded a broad-bladed sword in a practice duel against one of his men.

"Hullo, Ivy," Owen said cheerfully as she strolled up to greet them. He was a stocky boy who always had a friendly word and ready smile. His thatch of curls was as red as fox fur and had bits of hay sticking out of it, and his clothes were filthy from mucking out stalls. "I heard about the frogs in the Great Hall last night. I wish I could have been there to see the look on Prince Romil's face. It's about time someone put that fancy-pants in his place."

Ivy beamed, pleased with the praise.

"And hith men, too," lisped Boggs. "You thould hear them complain. They can't believe we don't have grander roomth or finer food." He gave an undignified snort. "You would think it wath them that wath the nobility, the way they grumble and carry on."

Boggs's gaze fell upon the furious sword fight taking place at the other end of the meadow. "But though I hate to admit it," he said, "that Printh Romil ith a forth to be reckoned with on the battlefield."

"Have you seen him throw a spear?" asked Owen. "I bet that ill-tempered icicle could spear a sparrow out of the sky from fifty paces away. And Boggs was just telling me what a clever idea it is to use spears against a dragon.

"You see, one has to be close to the dragon to use a sword, and when you're close, the beast can strike at you with its teeth and talons, burn you with its dragon fire, or slash at you with its tail. By throwing spears, Prince Romil can keep some distance between himself and the dragon, long enough to wound it before it can do any serious damage, anyway. A dragon would have a hard time getting out of the way of a spear sailing through the air. Dragons can't move particularly fast, seeing as they're so large."

"Romil ith good with a thword, too." Boggs inclined his head in the direction of the duel, where Romil had just deflected a swipe of his opponent's sword with practiced ease. "Onth the dragon ith injured, he can move in and finith it off with hith blade."

"One good thrust into the underbelly would do it," said Owen. "That's the most vulnerable part of a dragon, you know, since there are no scales there to protect it."

"The dragon would bleed to death," said Boggs. "Bye-bye, beathtie."

"Owen, can I talk to you for a moment?" Ivy broke in quickly, finishing off dragons not being a topic of conversation she cared to continue.

"Of course." The stable boy rose to his feet and followed her to the castle gate in lumbering strides, leaving Boggs to finish the rest of his lunch under the oak tree. "I really am glad you let those frogs loose in the Great Hall, Ivy. Boggs and I come out here and watch Prince Romil every day at lunchtime. That snow-swallower makes more noise than an ungreased cartwheel. He gloats when he gets in a good strike and loses his temper when he doesn't. I'd hate to be one of his men and have to put up with him. I don't think I'll care for it if he becomes king."

"I don't want him to be king," Ivy said. Tildy would probably say she shouldn't be quite so honest with a mere stable boy, but Owen had been so approving of her prank with the frogs, it seemed perfectly natural to tell him everything. "I'm going to keep playing tricks on him until he leaves."

"Smart girl," said Owen, giving her an encouraging smile. For some strange reason, that smile made Ivy's cheeks flush as if she had lingered too long by a winter fire. "So what can I do to help?"

"I wanted to know if you've seen any sneeze-seed lately," Ivy said.

Owen grinned. Sneeze-seed was a spiky, unpleasant weed that bore large, crusty seedpods late into the year. As its name suggested, the plant's fuzzy black seeds were notorious for causing watering eyes and lengthy fits of sneezing. They smelled terrible, like stale bog water, and made your skin erupt in itchy pink pustules.

"There's a patch of sneeze-seed behind Old Man Osbert's barn down the road," Owen said, a gleam in his eyes. "I just saw it this morning, on my way to get oats for the horses. The heads are near bursting, they're so full of seeds. If you'd like, I can get you some before I head back to the stables."

"If it's not too much trouble . . ." Ivy cast a grateful smile in his direction.

"Anything for you, milady," Owen replied with a playful bow. "And anything to get rid of His Royal Frostiness."

True to his word, Owen met the princess in front of the entry hall not half an hour later with a wooden bucket filled to the brim with smelly black seeds. Each was about the size and color of a horsefly and covered with tiny, sticky fibers that clung to cloth and hair like day-old porridge to the insides of a cooking pot. Ivy's eyes were getting a little teary just being near the bucket's malodorous contents.

"Be careful not to get any on you," warned Owen, "or you'll be up all night, sneezing your insides out. I had to wear my cowhide gloves to pick the pods and shake out the seeds. You'd best tie a handkerchief around your nose and mouth when you let them loose, just in case."

"Thanks, Owen," said Ivy. "I owe you for this."

"Just let me know how it goes," Owen said. His face broke into an impish grin. "Let's hope a nice rash on his lily-white hide is enough to send Prince Romil packing."

After Owen had set off for the stables, Ivy made her way up the stairs to the library, being careful not to spill any seeds along her way. Before heading off to bathe before dinner, Romil always sat on a stone bench in the castle garden to remove his greaves. It was right underneath Ivy's favorite library window. If she leaned out just a little, she could make sure the unsuspecting prince was showered with sneeze-seed from above and duck back inside before he could spot her. Although Ivy felt sure Romil would know who had doused him with the foul stuff, he would have no way of proving it.

Ivy could see that the prince's men had already retreated inside. Romil sat on the bench, his back to the window, unbuckling his dragon-scale greaves while Gar stood before him, looking as ruffled and ill-tempered as an old goose. Ivy grinned at her luck; she could get both of them with one shot.

She didn't have a handkerchief to tie over her mouth and nose as Owen had suggested, but she decided to risk it, anyway. The window was already open, and Ivy was careful not to bump the wooden shutters, lest they squeak on their rusty hinges and give her away. Below her, bright green vines twined up the castle wall. She could see the top of Romil's shiny blond head and Gar just steps in front of him, too busy rattling on to notice her. *Perfect*—she positioned the bucket just right and carefully began to tilt it.

"—don't know how you managed to keep your temper last night," Gar was saying to the prince, his voice tight with anger. "When that bratty bumpkin started laughing her head off, it was all I could do to keep from wrapping my hands around her throat and wringing her scrawny neck."

Ivy froze as Gar's words drifted up to her on the still afternoon air. Gar sounded positively furious.

"How can people live like this?" He swept a hand around to indicate his surroundings. Even from her height, Ivy could see his nostrils flare beneath his long nose. "What a pitiful little kingdom this is! The king is a muddle-brained old fool, the princess an utter abomination, and the castle little more than a crumbling heap of stones. The entire monstrosity could fit into one of the courtyards at the palace back in Glacia—one of the *smaller* courtyards. I don't know how much longer I can put up with this wretched place. They don't even have any decent guest chambers. And the kingdom is so unbelievably filthy—not at all like our sparkling white Glacia—all this dirt and dust and bits of greenery floating around in the air. It's all so terribly unhygienic!"

"Calm yourself, Gar," Romil said, his voice as cool as an ice floe. "I don't like being here any more than you do—and I'm the one who has to marry the blasted princess. But we must all make sacrifices for the greater cause. Things will soon turn in our favor, you shall see. The Glacian army is full of soldiers who favor me over that woefully unambitious brother of mine. As soon as I assume the throne of Ardendale, they will set sail for this little valley to pledge their loyalty and allegiance to me."

"Yes...yes, of course," said Gar, relaxing at the thought. "It is only a matter of time. The Fringed Forest stretches on for leagues and leagues. There are enough trees to make an entire fleet of wooden ships."

"Ships large enough to carry wooden catapults," said Romil, "which we will use to fling flaming barrels of tar at the Glacian palace itself. Fire is the greatest threat to a kingdom made of ice. My brother will have no choice but to surrender and hand the rule of Glacia over to me."

Ivy didn't need to see his face to know it was plastered with the hungry grin of a cat about to pounce on an especially plump and juicy sparrow.

"Up until now," he said, "our kingdom has never had the resources to reach its full potential, but once I have the entire Glacian army under my command and the wood and crops of Ardendale to support our conquests, just think of the kingdoms I shall conquer...."

"It is a perfectly devised plan, Your Highness." Gar's tone was as smooth as honey sliding off a wooden spoon. "Soon you will be ruling not only Glacia, but an entire Glacian empire."

"Yes." Romil's voice dripped with satisfaction. "For such a prize, we can put up with these backwater buffoons for a short while longer, don't you think?"

Ivy didn't hear Gar's reply. Her breath had caught in her throat, and her heart was thumping so loudly, she could hardly believe that neither Romil nor Gar could hear it. Prince Romil was even more horrible than she had thought.

It was one thing to be a selfish prince, but Romil was a tyrant in the making, determined to rule as much of the world as he could get his greedy hands on. He was even going to overthrow his own brother. The king had to know about this immediately.

Ivy's eyes suddenly drifted back to the bucket in her hands, and she was startled to discover it was still tipped at a dangerous angle, a handful of black seeds mere inches from spilling over the brim and raining down upon the scheming Glacian prince and his unscrupulous adviser. Stifling a gasp, she straightened it quickly. Then as quietly as she could manage, she pulled herself inside the window and backed away from it on shaky legs until she was safely out of sight.

I have to find Father, she thought frantically. Her heart still pounding as if someone were beating on it with a mallet, Ivy darted out the library door and down the hall. To her utmost surprise, her father was already waiting for her at the bottom of the stairs.

"Ivy, I have been looking all over for you," he said, a grave look on his weathered face. "I have just come from speaking with Tildy, and she has informed me of the most troubling news. She believes it wasn't mere happenstance that those frogs were in the bread basket last night, but that you actually put them there in an effort to vex Prince Romil. Is this true?"

Ivy had forgotten Tildy's promise to speak with her father about her little stunt.

"Well...yes...it is true," she admitted reluctantly. "But I have something much more important to talk to you about—"

"I think the Dragon Treaty is very important," the king said, and, indeed, these days, the Dragon Treaty seemed to be the only thing he still took seriously.

"Yes, of course it is," said Ivy. "But—"

"Is that sneeze-seed?" the king asked suspiciously, his gaze falling to the bucket in her hand, which she had forgotten in her distress. Her stomach plummeted.

"You were going to use that on Prince Romil as well, weren't you?" The king's voice was very, very low.

"Father, please listen to me," she said, deciding it was best if she didn't answer that question just now. "I've come from the library. Romil and Gar were talking outside the window. The only reason Romil wants to be king of Ardendale is for the wood and the crops. He's going to lay siege to the palace at Glacia, overthrow the Glacian king, and then move on to conquer other kingdoms. He wants to rule an entire empire."

The king raised a heavy gray eyebrow as he studied his daughter for a brief moment, his eyes colored with doubt.

"Young lady, I am not going to stand here and listen to you make up stories about Prince Romil," he said indignantly. "He is a man of noble birth, here purely to honor the age-old tradition of dragon slaying. He would never do such a terrible thing."

"But I heard him myself!" cried Ivy.

"Ivy, I am disappointed in you," her father said. "I thought you understood the importance of the Dragon Treaty, yet here you are, trying to get out of your obligations by playing pranks on a royal guest, and making up untruths about him on top of that."

His eyes were empty of their usual warmth. "You know I have never been much of a disciplinarian, but I'm afraid in this case I have no choice but to put my foot down."

Ivy's mouth fell open.

"You are to go to your room immediately and stay there until morning," the king ordered. "And you are not to go near any haystacks for an entire week." Ivy could see by the grim look on his face that he thought this was a dreadful and fitting punishment.

She felt as deflated as risen bread dough after all the air is punched out of it. A day ago she would have never thought her father could take her for a liar, but at this moment she didn't think there was a single thing she could say or do to make him believe her.

"Yes, Father," she mumbled feebly. Her shoulders slumped as she turned to make her way down the hall, the flagstones beneath her feet somehow looking even more gray and worn than usual.

8

Foul-Weather Friends and a Journey to the Fringed Forest

"That vile, conniving, rotten toenail of a swamp rat," Rose spat out angrily. She was pacing to and fro along the rocky strand beneath the castle. Ivy had told her friends everything she had heard between Romil and Gar the previous afternoon. Rose was fuming, and Ivy wasn't surprised by her friend's rapid change of heart toward the Glacian prince. Once people proved unworthy of her admiration, they fell out of favor with the high-minded, romantic Rose as quickly as clouds shifted course.

"Here I was, thinking he was so handsome and princely," she cried, "and he was nothing more than a worm-eating barley bug all along."

Clarinda winced at her friend's coarse words and cast a timid look in the princess's direction.

"Are you sure you heard him correctly, Ivy?" she asked for the third time. "Perhaps you misunderstood."

"For the last time, I heard him perfectly clear," snapped Ivy. Between uncovering Romil's foul plot and having the king accuse her of lying, she was in a thoroughly wretched mood. "But why should you believe me when my own father doesn't?"

"Ivy, I didn't mean it like that." Clarinda sounded stricken. "Of course I believe you. It's just that... well, I suppose part of me was hoping there was some way it wasn't true."

"Of course we believe you," echoed Rose, spinning on her heels in mid-pace to turn and face the princess. "You were right from the start. You can't marry that loathsome little wood louse. He'll strip the valley bare and put everyone to work building his fleet of warships. Our entire kingdom will be ruined."

A wave of gratitude washed over Ivy. At least her friends didn't doubt her, and she wasn't entirely alone in this terrible mess.

"I'll run away before I let Romil become king," she said. "I won't go into the stupid tower. He can't marry me if I'm not here."

Clarinda gasped. "Ivy, you can't break the Dragon Treaty," she protested in a weak voice.

"The kingdom would be better off with the whole valley full of angry dragons than with Romil as king," Ivy said. "At least we can fight dragons. There's no way we could stop our own king."

"No, Clarinda's right," said Rose. "It's too risky. There has to be a way to stop Prince Romil without endangering the treaty."

Ivy blinked. She knew things were bad when Rose started being the voice of reason.

"Besides," her golden-haired friend continued, glancing meaningfully at Clarinda, "there's something you should know. We've been poking around, seeing what we could learn about Drusilla and where she might have gone off to all those years ago. Yesterday, Cook asked us to draw water from the well, and Prudence and Wynne, the washerwomen, were there in the courtyard. We got them talking about the queen and Drusilla and what the two of them used to get up to, and they told us about Felda the Farseeing."

"Who?" Ivy asked.

"Felda the Farseeing—she's a fortune-teller." Clarinda's voice brimmed with excitement. "Or she was, anyway. A long time ago, people in the valley went to her when they wanted to learn of their future."

"Prudence said that the queen and Drusilla visited her all the time. The three of them would spend entire afternoons together," Rose said. "That's part of the reason Felda was so popular with the common folk. They figured if the queen thought enough of her to use her services, then she must be good."

"Tildy never said anything to me about a fortune-teller," said Ivy. "But then again, she doesn't hold with that kind of thing."

"There's more," Clarinda added. "They said after your mother died, the locals wanted nothing to do with Felda. People thought if she was such a great fortune-teller, she should have foreseen the queen's death and done something to prevent it. They stopped going to see her, and she became something of a recluse, shutting herself up inside her little house in the Fringed Forest."

"And Absalom the butcher says Felda still lives there." Rose's blue eyes shone bright with anticipation. "In that same house off the Inland Road..."

"And we thought she might know where your godmother went," Clarinda finished, "seeing as they spent so much time together."

Ivy was doubtful, and a voice in her head that sounded an awful lot like Tildy's was saying that someone who claimed to be able to see the future was not to be trusted for figs, but Rose and Clarinda seemed to think it was a good idea, and Ivy didn't have any others at the moment.

"I suppose it can't hurt to talk to her," she said, seeing the expectant looks on their pretty faces.

"Oh, I knew you'd think so." Clarinda clapped her hands, delighted she'd been able to help. "It's quite a ride to the Fringed Forest, however—all the way to the other end of the valley...."

"But we'd be happy to keep you company, if you'd like," Rose said.

Ivy could tell they had already planned this out, and, once again, she found herself very grateful to have such steadfast and loyal friends.

"We'll start early, then," she said. "First thing after breakfast tomorrow. I'll tell Tildy we're going on a picnic—I'm sure she'll be happy to have me out of her hair for a day. She won't have to worry about me doing anything to embarrass myself in front of the Glacians for once. Owen will ready some horses for us if I ask him to. We can follow the Inland Road all the way to the forest."

The Inland Road crossed the entire length of the valley, then wound its way through the hilly expanse of the Fringed Forest to the northern lands on the other side. It was the only route in or out of the kingdom, other than coming by sea, and would lead them straight to their destination. Ivy was surprised to find that she felt a little more hopeful already. Having a plan—any plan—was better than doing nothing.

"Oh, fairy cakes—I've just thought of something," Clarinda said, a frown furrowing her brow. "We'll have to pass the king's hayfields to get to the Inland Road, and we can't do that. Ivy isn't allowed near haystacks."

Ivy was usually pretty tolerant of her hopelessly obedient friend, but this time, she laughed right along with Rose as they dragged Clarinda back toward the castle.

The next morning, as the girls made their way through the valley on two well-behaved mares and a small gray pony, it was clear that autumn was well on its way. The riot of summer wildflowers was over, and the meadows they passed boasted only a few small handfuls of late-blooming stitchwort, yarrow, and purple betony. Hazelnuts were starting to darken in the stands of trees along the road, and blackberry brambles were bedecked with clusters of dark fruit. There was a slight chill to the early air that made Ivy thankful for the shelter of her cloak.

The ride was long but not unpleasant. They waved to a few farmers in their fields but met no other travelers along the road. Chatting with her friends in the fine autumn weather, Ivy almost forgot the desperate nature of their journey, but the all-too-familiar feelings of dread and dismay came rushing back the moment she spotted the dark line of bedraggled trees on the horizon. Before she knew it, the land grew high and rolling, and they were at the threshold of the Fringed Forest, staring into its dark depths where the road disappeared in shadow.

"Why would anyone want to live in there?" Clarinda asked, gazing at the stringy ropes of moss that dripped from the tree branches like oddly colored icicles. "It's such a spooky place."

"It's just a forest like any other." Rose tried to sound brave and unconcerned, but even she couldn't hide the touch of uncertainty in her voice.

"Well, come on, let's get on with it." Ivy took a steadying breath and urged her horse forward into the gloom beneath the trees. The sooner she got this over with, the better.

The Fringed Forest was not lush and lovely the way most forests are, although Ivy supposed it had its own eerie kind of beauty. The ancient trees were thick and tall with wide-reaching limbs but somehow seemed tired under their burden of scraggly moss. High above the girls' heads, the tangled canopy of branches, leaves, and moss was so dense that only the barest hint of dappled sunlight broke through. The forest floor was dim and cool, and although a few meager shrubs sprouted from the moist soil, was largely absent of the usual plants and ferns, which couldn't grow in such poor light.

It was strangely quiet in this gloomy place. The stillness was interrupted by occasional signs of life—the low chattering of squirrels or a snatch of birdsong—but these were always fleeting and quickly swallowed up by the sea of trees. Even the horses had slowed to a tentative pace. The unnatural quiet made the forest all the more unfriendly, as did the long cords of droopy moss, which were the sad gray-green color of lichen on a gravestone.

"Where did Absalom say Felda's house was again?" Ivy asked.

"Not that far into the forest," Rose replied. "Over the hill off the first curve in the road."

Sure enough, not half a league into the forest, the road swerved sharply to the east, veering around a small hill. The girls tethered their horses next to the roadside in the only stunted patch of grass they could find and made their way up and over the muddy rise. On the other side, they had to be careful as they trudged across the uneven ground, where ancient tree roots snaked in and out of the damp earth.

"Over there," said Rose, pointing excitedly.

Ivy didn't see anything she would typically describe as a house, but nestled in a nearby thicket was one of the largest trees she had ever seen. It wasn't all that tall, but it was as big around as a windmill, and some of the bends in the gnarled tree roots were so high, one could have seen right into the space underneath if they hadn't been blocked up with heavy, gray stones. One of the largest gaps in the roots had been fitted with a pair of wooden shutters, painted blue, and five earthen steps led down into the tallest gap, which contained a lopsided door, complete with brass knocker. On one side of the tree, a thick, low branch had been sawed off, so it was just a stump sticking out of the tree trunk. Apparently, it had been hollowed out and was now used as a chimney, since smoke was pouring from it like steam from the spout of a teakettle.

"Do...do you want us to go in with you?" Clarinda whispered, her voice trembling.

Ivy knew Clarinda and Rose would go with her if she asked, but she thought they had done more than enough on her behalf these past few days.

"No, I think it would be best if I spoke to Felda on my own. She may not be used to having visitors anymore." Ivy also kept her voice low, although she wasn't exactly sure why. Felda was an old acquaintance of her mother's, after all. Still, anyone who lived under a tree in this creepy forest had to be a little odd.

"Why don't you wait for me back at the road and have some lunch from the picnic basket Cook prepared for us?" Ivy said to her friends. "I'll try not to be too long."

Clarinda looked terribly relieved. Even Rose, for all her bravado, seemed happy to return to the road and the horses.

"Good luck," she said. "We'll see you soon."

Ivy would have felt better if Rose's voice hadn't been tinged with doubt, but she had come too far to turn back now. As her friends disappeared back over the hill, she gathered the courage to pick her way around a couple of currant bushes choked with moss and descend the short steps to the peculiar door.

She raised the heavy brass knocker, but before she could use it, a light and breezy voice that reminded her of wind chimes drifted from the other side.

"Welcome, Princess," it said. "Won't you please come in?"

9

Tea with Felda the Farseeing

The door in the tree roots swung open on creaky hinges. At first, Ivy didn't see anybody, and for a heart-pounding moment she thought the door had opened of its own accord. Then a woman's head, sporting a massive amount of wild hair, poked out from behind it.

"Well, come on, then," she said in the bright, musical voice Ivy had heard moments earlier. "I won't bite."

Ivy hesitantly stepped into the strange, sunken home. Felda the Farseeing shut the door behind her with a soft click, and, as she turned to face the princess, Ivy got her first good look at the mysterious fortune-teller.

Felda looked much younger than Ivy had expected. Even though she had been telling fortunes since before the princess was born, she didn't look a day over twenty-five. But even with her smooth skin and youthful complexion, Felda was one of the strangest-looking people Ivy had ever seen. She wore a drab brown dress, a bit frayed about the ends, a worn woolen shawl, and no shoes. Ivy had never seen anyone with so much hair. It was the color of wood ash and fell well below Felda's waist in thick, unruly waves that stuck out all over and reminded Ivy of a twisted mass of bindweed. Most of it was loose, but at least a dozen tiny braids were scattered among the wild tresses. They had been interwoven with long strands of the same moss that hung on the forest trees, giving Felda's hair the appearance of having gray-green streaks.

But the strangest, most noticeable thing about the fortune-teller was her eyes. They were a startling shade of pale violet, shining like gems, so deep and intense that they seemed to be gazing straight into Ivy's soul.

"Please come and sit down," said Felda in her silvery voice. With a gentle hand on Ivy's back, she swept the princess toward a spindly table in the center of the room that looked as if it had been made of twigs and tree branches bound together. Ivy carefully lowered herself into one of the small, rickety chairs.

While the rest of the forest was dark as a stormy day, the little hollow beneath the tree was surprisingly bright and cozy. It consisted of only one round room, the size and shape of the tree's trunk. In a small nook, a copper tea-kettle bubbled merrily over a crackling fire, the source of the smoke Ivy had seen outside. A straw pallet resting on a simple wooden frame suggested that the area also served as Felda's bedchamber.

"Aren't they fantastic?" Felda asked when the princess lifted her eyes toward the ceiling.

It was domed like an eggshell, obviously the underside of the tree. A number of roots crisscrossed the space like beams, and from them hung dozens of upside-down bundles of dried herbs—artemisia, lavender, thyme, marjoram, feverfew, and many others Ivy couldn't name. Red clay jars that undoubtedly contained even more herbs and spices sat like fat, happy cats upon rows of wooden shelves. It was no wonder the room was such a hodgepodge of pungent aromas—sweet, earthy, and a little tangy.

"I use them to make tea," explained Felda, plunking down in the wobbly chair across from the princess. "Wonderful stuff, tea. So many uses, so many possibilities: willow bark tea will bring down a fever, chamomile tea will soothe an upset stomach, and lavender tea will calm a frenzied mind. A nice mixture of dandelion, wood sorrel, and honey cures a sore throat faster than an arrow can fly. And did you know if you bathe in a special brew of chickweed tea, it will not only cure poison ivy but leave your skin as smooth as the finest silk gold can buy?"

"Um, no," said Ivy.

Felda leaned forward earnestly, and the pleasant scent of meadowsweet wafted across the table.

"Tea can also unveil the future—if you're fortunate enough to grasp the language of the leaves. That's how I knew you were coming today. I spied the figure of a young lady in my tea leaves this morning—a sure sign a visitor was on her way—and I sensed it would be you. I've always felt you would seek me out one of these days. The signs have been pointing to it for some time now.

"Oh, I'm so glad you came." Her voice danced like fairy bells, and her violet gaze lingered upon the princess. "My, how you remind me of your mother!"

"I do?" Ivy blinked back her surprise. She looked nothing like the beautiful woman in the portrait that graced the Great Hall.

"Yes, you do," Felda answered plainly. "You radiate a strong aura, just as she did—although yours is even more vibrant. She might not have been quite as venturesome as you, but she could still be rather plucky when she wanted. Most people avoid the Fringed Forest if they can, but your mother liked it here. She thought it was much more interesting and exciting than that dull old castle. She always did crave adventure, that girl."

"She did?" Ivy's wonder grew to astonishment. "But Tildy always told me she was a very proper lady."

"Well, she was," Felda said. "No one could ask for a more proper, regal, or well-behaved queen, at least not at the castle. But your mother had a whole other side to her that most people never saw. She wasn't exactly what one would call bold, but she had her opinions and liked to be a little more carefree when she got away from the watchful eyes of Tildy and the court. That's one reason she liked to come here with Drusilla. We'd drink tea, I'd tell her fortune, and we'd have a great many laughs. Your mother, godmother, and I were once as close as well-sewn stitches, you know."

"That's what I've been told," said Ivy, "and that's why I came. I was hoping you could tell me where I could find my godmother."

"Where to find Drusilla?" Felda looked surprised. "Why, I haven't seen that wayward slip of a fairy for years. As you must know, your poor mother didn't survive the night you were born, and I'm afraid her death hit Drusilla rather hard. Some people are not so good at accepting the hand dealt by fate.... You see, Drusilla loved the queen dearly. I think she felt terribly guilty that she couldn't save her. She up and disappeared when you were little more than a month old. I imagine she went home, back to her fairy realm, but I haven't the faintest idea where that could be."

With these words, it suddenly seemed as if Ivy's last hope had been dashed to pieces. Hot tears pricked her eyes and spilled onto her cheeks. She felt dreadfully ashamed to be crying in front of Felda, and this only made her cry all the more.

"I'm in t-terrible t-trouble," she said, sobbing. "Drusilla m-may be the only one who can h-help me."

"Oh, you poor, poor dear," Felda cooed, patting the hand Ivy had rested upon the table. She produced a square of dingy white cloth and passed it to the princess. "Why don't you tell me what's wrong?"

Ivy blew her nose on the handkerchief, which, like Felda, smelled of meadowsweet, and collected herself enough to speak. "Everything's wrong," she said ruefully. "I'm going to turn fourteen in a week, and I'll be locked in the tower." She proceeded to tell Felda all about Prince Romil and his awful plans.

"He's going to cut down the forest!" Felda exclaimed indignantly, her violet eyes blazing like beacons. "Who would do such a thing, destroy all these lovely trees just to build a fleet of warships? This prince must truly be a monster."

"He is," said Ivy. "And I have absolutely no idea how to stop him, since my father thinks I'm making the whole thing up to get out of being locked in the tower. I thought about running away. Romil can't marry me if he can't rescue me. But my friends think it will only bring trouble if I fail to fulfill the terms of the Dragon Treaty."

"When in doubt, it is always best to consult the leaves," said Felda. "The leaves never lie, and I have never known them to be wrong."

"Well, if you think it would help," said Ivy. She still wasn't sure she believed in fortune-telling, but if her own mother had set store by it, maybe there was some truth to it after all.

Felda rose and made her way to the rows of shelves. She seemed much more somber and serious now than when Ivy had first met her.

"Mint and lemon balm, I should think," she said, studying Ivy with her curiously colored eyes.

She took two small handfuls of dried leaves from jars on the shelves. Lifting the lid on the teakettle over the fire, she flung these into the steaming water. A few minutes later, she set a white teacup and saucer in front of Ivy and poured out the pleasant-smelling brew.

"Sip the tea and concentrate on what you want to know," Felda instructed.

Ivy sipped and, as the soothing, minty liquid flowed down her throat, found herself closing her eyes. *I want to know how to find my fairy godmother, Drusilla,* she thought. *I want to know if I should run away rather than let myself be locked in the tower. I want to know if everything will turn out all right.* When she opened her eyes again, she was surprised to find that only a very small amount of tea remained at the bottom of the cup, with clumps of tiny dark leaves dotting its surface.

"Very good," said Felda in her gentle, feathery voice. "Now take the cup in your left hand and swirl it around three times."

Ivy did as she was told, watching the still-warm tea whirl around the bottom of the cup.

"Set it upside down on your saucer," Felda said, "and we shall see what the leaves have to tell us." She waited for the last of the liquid to drain from the cup, then picked it up with a slender hand and peered into it intently. She didn't speak for several long seconds. Ivy felt her heart beating in anticipation.

"I'm afraid the leaves are somewhat vague," Felda said finally, frowning into the cup. "Sometimes they see fit not to reveal too many of their mysteries all at once. There are no definite signs of success or failure in your future—that remains to be seen, I suppose. It is quite clear, however, that time is running out for you to make an important decision. There is the prominent likeness of an hourglass in your leaves, the sand already half spent. I also see mountains in your cup—obstacles in your path—and they are calling to

you...yes, there is a line of fate leading straight to them...
certainly something you must soon face...."

Felda turned the cup slightly, as if to get a better look at
something.

"I see a shape, perhaps a box—no, a window," she said.
"It's a window, next to the cup handle, the answer you
seek."

"The answer I seek?" Ivy asked, puzzled. "How can a
window be the answer to something?"

Felda ignored her and continued to gaze fixedly into the
little teacup.

"I can discern only one symbol more," she said softly,
"and it's right next to the rim, which means it is in your very,
very near future. I'm afraid its meaning is quite obvious."

For the first time, she raised her violet eyes from the
cup.

"What...what is it?" Ivy asked, her voice quavering.

"A dragon," Felda replied sadly.

10

Into the Tower

So that's it, then, Ivy thought unhappily as she watched the sun set that evening from one of the arched windows that ringed the north wall of her bedchamber. She had asked the tea leaves if she should run away rather than enter the tower, and now she had her answer. Felda had seen a dragon in her immediate future, and what else could that mean but that it was her fate to be imprisoned in the white tower at the foot of the Craggies, guarded by the beast sent there to watch over her? To make matters worse, she was still no closer to finding Drusilla or getting rid of Romil. Maybe she should just ignore Felda's reading and run away after all. Perhaps, in the end, fortune-telling was nothing but a load of humbug and hogwash.

But Felda's word was good enough for your very own mother, pointed out a nagging voice in the back of Ivy's mind, *and she did know you were coming this afternoon....*

Ivy sighed heavily. Her head ached, and she felt as confused now as she had ever been. It seemed she had no choice but to play the part of a proper princess and dutifully enter the tower—and hope by some miracle that Romil's plans didn't come to pass.

Her remaining days of freedom flew by as swiftly as autumn leaves scattered by a breeze, and she found herself growing more and more dejected. A restless gloom settled over her like a stubborn fog, following her wherever she went and refusing to lift its dreary veil.

"Maybe there's still hope," Clarinda said to Ivy the afternoon before her birthday. "Maybe...maybe the dragon will defeat Prince Romil." She sounded horror-struck to be hoping for Romil's demise at the hands—or, actually, claws—of a dragon, but they all knew it was the only way out of this awful predicament. Ivy, however, had watched enough of Romil's target practices and duels with his guards to know that if anyone was a match for a dragon, it was the strapping, stone-faced Glacian prince.

"Promise me you'll watch over my father while I'm in the tower," she beseeched Rose and Clarinda. "And keep your eyes open for a way—any way—to convince him of Romil's guilt."

Her friends promised faithfully, but it did little to lighten Ivy's heavy heart.

The day of her fourteenth birthday dawned cool but clear, a gloriously golden autumn morning. Despite the lovely weather, there was to be no celebration or laughter or gifts, but instead a solemn procession from the castle to the white tower on the eastern edge of the kingdom. The dragon would take its post at sunset, and Ivy felt sure that Romil, who wouldn't waste any time, would arrive bright and early the next morning, ready to do battle.

At least I won't be in the tower for long, she thought, trying in vain to lift her sagging spirits. But she knew she would rather spend the rest of her life alone in the tower than marry Prince Romil of Glacia.

After a hasty breakfast of cheese and boiled eggs, a small company consisting of the king, the princess, Tildy, and a handful of the King's Guard set out to cross the low valley on horseback. When they passed weathered old farmhouses or clusters of thatched cottages, people abandoned their scythes and hearths and looms to line the sides of the road and watch the party go by. They bowed their heads reverently as Ivy's horse trod past.

"It's a gesture of honor and appreciation," Tildy said, looking very pleased. "For fulfilling your royal duty."

It was past midday when the group finally arrived at the tower. It stood in the shadows of the towering Craggies, tucked in a small recess between two jutting slopes of mountain. It may have been gleaming white at one point in time, but now the stone looked old and cracked and rather dingy. It was at least twice the height of the castle's own towers, a high, straight pillar crowned with a peaked slate roof. At the top, a lonely square window faced the valley. At the foot, a heavy oak door was set in the dull stone. Ivy's knees went a little weak when her gaze fell upon it, for a large iron bolt slatted ominously across the worn wood. Unlike the rest of the tower, the bolt was shiny and new.

They must fit a new one to the door for each new princess,
Ivy thought sourly.

The tower may have been tall, but it was positively
dwarfed by the jagged peaks of the Craggies, which loomed
behind it like waiting giants, rocky crevices covered in a fine
dusting of snow.

Once everyone had dismounted, Ivy's father gave her a
quick hug and a knowing wink.

"That Prince Romil is a born dragon slayer if ever I saw
one," he said in good cheer. "I have no worries about your
time in the tower. I think we shall be seeing you again very
soon indeed."

Tildy was the only one who followed Ivy across the
threshold into the foot of the ancient structure.

"I'm very proud of you, Princess," she said, enveloping
Ivy in a warm hug. "And your mother would be, too. I know
you've had misgivings about all this Dragon Treaty business,
but trust me, you're doing the right thing."

For a moment, wrapped in the warmth that was Tildy,
Ivy could almost believe everything would be okay. Then,
with a small wave and a half-rueful smile, Tildy was gone,
the door shut and bolted behind her. Ivy found herself alone
at the bottom of the tower, with only the lingering scent
of lavender to remind her that anyone else had ever been
there. After a few minutes, that, too, vanished.

And so the only way to go was up. The winding staircase
spiraled out of sight high above Ivy's head. She took the
steps slowly, one at a time, her footfalls echoing through the

airy column of stone. The sound was so empty and hollow, it filled her with a lonely ache.

When she reached the top of the stairs, several minutes later, she was pleasantly surprised by the chamber at the tower's summit.

"Oh my!" she breathed. Tildy hadn't been exaggerating—it was truly lovely.

Sunlight filtered through the large west-facing window, which was absent of any shutters or coverings. The stone here showed its age, like the rest of the tower, but a charming ring of painted roses and tendriling vines rimmed the high walls with bright colors.

The centerpiece of the room was an enormous canopied bed draped in reams of damask silk. The wide headboard was unlike anything Ivy had ever seen, an elaborate relief of a fire-breathing dragon encircled by a wreath of thorny briars. It was sleek and shiny from countless polishings with lemon juice and beeswax.

A paneled wardrobe of the same dark walnut stood next to the bed. Peeking inside, Ivy discovered that it was stocked with every imaginable type of garment: light summer frocks, warm woolen dresses, and cloaks of varying thickness and color, as well as nightgowns, underclothes, and stockings. There were even a few fancy gowns that would have made Tildy swoon. They were finer than anything Ivy had ever worn, although what she would do with them while locked at the top of a tower was beyond her. She supposed some princesses liked to dress up for their would-be rescuers.

Across from the wardrobe was a dressing table with a

delicate white basin and pitcher for washing. (According to Tildy, fairy nectar was good for that, too.) Mounted on the wall above was a small looking glass that could only be the magic mirror. The glass was framed by an intricate lattice of woven gold, embedded with tiny pearls and sparkling gems of every color. It was beautiful and obviously no ordinary mirror. When she wasn't staring directly at it, Ivy swore it glimmered just inside the edge of her vision.

She spotted the enchanted wishing table to one side of the tower's lone window. It would have looked very much like a normal table except for the glorious golden tablecloth draped over it. The glossy folds shimmered in the light like a scattering of stars. It looked as delicate as spun gold, but when Ivy rubbed the material between her thumb and fore-finger, she was surprised to find it as sturdy as sackcloth. The golden goblet sat in the center of the table like the jewel in a crown. Sparkling quartz stones the size of acorns adorned its rim. They were as white as apple blossoms and glistened like ice.

Realizing she was parched from her climb up the stairs— and knowing she'd have to face another before long, as the privy was back at the foot of the tower—Ivy cupped her hands around the goblet's golden curves, just as she had been instructed by Tildy.

Let's see if this thing really works.

Wondrously, as if being poured by unseen hands, liq-uid as golden and clear as apple wine filled the cup to its brim. The fairy nectar was as sweet as honey, but not half so heavy or rich. She could drink this heavenly stuff all day long and never once feel sick to her stomach. In fact, as it flowed down her throat, Ivy realized that she felt wonderful, as if she had just woken from hours of refreshing sleep and had enough energy to run the entire length of the king's hayfields without once losing her breath.

She decided to save the wishing table for later, since her stomach was too fluttery with excitement and nerves to be hungry, but the thought occurred to her that she might as well try out the magic mirror.

She stood before the dressing table and admired its luminous beauty once again. Although she knew she probably shouldn't, she just couldn't resist holding the exquisite mirror in her hands. It was small and lightweight, and she easily slipped it from its place on the wall. But what to say to make the mirror work? Could she simply tell it what she wanted to see, or did she need to use special words, like a spell of some sort?

"Um, hello, magic mirror," she said, "I'd like to see my father, if you don't mind."

Apparently that was good enough for the mirror. Its surface rippled the way a lake does when a pebble is dropped into its depths. Ivy watched as the misty, rolling waves twisted and distorted her reflection. When they cleared, she was no longer looking at herself, but at a stretch of the Inland Road winding through the valley. Her father was riding along in the afternoon sunshine with Tildy at his side. They were on their way home. In the background, Ivy could make out the band of King's Guard in their faded blue livery, following at a short distance. Her father looked so close, she could see every line and wrinkle on his face, and it seemed as if she only had to reach out to touch his tumble of gray beard.

"How nice it will be for our kingdom to have a young, new king," she heard him say to Tildy. He sounded as if he were not five steps away. "Since I have to give up the throne, I will be glad to see it in such capable hands. Prince Romil is most suited for the position."

"Oh yes, most suited," Tildy was quick to agree, but then her round face fell as abruptly as drifting clouds shadow the moon. "I only wish Princess Ivory were more taken with him. I don't know why the girl insists on being so difficult, but I'm sure once she grows out of this silly phase, she'll come to see just what a catch he truly is. Any other princess would count herself lucky to have such a husband. He's so strong and brave, with such a commanding presence—and handsome as a peacock! Just think how dashing he will look in his wedding suit."

"Yes, I suppose he will," said the king. "He is truly a right and proper prince. He has all the makings of a ruler. Only..." The king's voice trailed off uncertainly. "Only sometimes I wish he were ever the slightest bit more congenial," he admitted in a quiet voice, as if he didn't want anyone to overhear him saying such a thing. "I have offered to introduce him to Frederick three times, you know. I thought it would be nice for them to get to know each other, seeing as Prince Romil will soon be a member of the family, but he never seems inclined toward such a meeting."

"The prince is very busy these days, what with all his target practices and sword fights and the like. Perhaps after he's slayed the dragon, he'll have more time for niceties," Tildy said. She was trying to sound bright and hopeful, but did Ivy detect a tiny hint of doubt in her voice, as if she were trying to convince not only the king, but herself as well?

"Yes, yes, you're right, of course," said the king. "What an exciting time this will be for all of us. I'm not loath to share that I have the highest of expectations for our future king, and so does Frederick." The king's face brightened beneath his long beard. "Speaking of Frederick, I can't wait to return to the castle and see him. It would have been nice to bring him along on our little ramble, but I'm afraid his old bones just aren't up to such a long ride."

As the king continued to chatter happily about his beloved horse, the image of him and Tildy faded until Ivy was once again staring at her own lonesome reflection in the mirror.

She felt a little better for having seen them, but at the same time was heartsick at their hopes. How sorely Romil would disappoint them!

At least she knew the mirror worked. How strange and wonderful to be able to peer into other people's lives whenever she wanted. It filled her with a satisfying sense of power. Her thoughts drifted to Romil once more, and she wondered what the spear-slinging brute was up to at this very moment. The temptation was more than she could resist, and in an imperious voice she commanded the mirror, "Show me Prince Romil."

11

What the Mirror Revealed

The magic mirror rippled again, and this time when the waves cleared, there was Romil, sharpening his sword in a far corner of the vacant castle courtyard. Gar was nearby, looking as hawkish as ever as he slipped Romil's sharp-tipped spears into a large sealskin quiver for carrying.

"By this time tomorrow, I'll have that dragon's head mounted over the fireplace in the Great Hall," Romil was boasting. He ran his thumb along the edge of the blade to test its sharpness. "I'm rather looking forward to it. It's quite rewarding watching everything come together exactly as I've planned."

"It won't be long now before you're sitting on the throne of this filthy little valley. 'Your Majesty' has a nice ring to it, don't you think?" Gar gave Romil a mock bow.

"And the first thing I'm going to do as king of this

backwoods kingdom is lift that ridiculous ban on dragon slaying," Romil said, giving his sword one last scrape along the whetstone. "When my soldiers arrive from Glacia, they will want some challenging sport. It's not like there's anything else for them to do around here. Besides, I can't have those filthy beasts living so close to my new lands, now, can I?"

"Absolutely not," sneered Gar. "Maybe these rustics are content to share their border with dragons, but for the more civilized of us, it will hardly do.

"But, I wonder, Your Highness, about the blithering old king and your little horror of a bride-to-be. Even though you'll be the one in charge, don't you think they'll put up a fuss and make things a bit . . . difficult?"

Romil grimaced. "Not to worry, Gar. I have it all figured out. Shortly after my wedding, a terrible accident will befall the royal family of Ardendale. I think perhaps a fall from one of the castle's towers. My poor, clumsy, dim-witted father-in-law will lean a little too far out one of the windows, and his devoted young daughter will try desperately to save him, only to end up tragically falling as well. . . ."

"Brilliant, Your Highness! The last of our problems solved with a simple push, and then you're free to build your magnificent new empire."

"Indeed." Romil's eyes gleamed like polished stones. "Besides, rumor has it the queens of Ardendale bear only daughters, and once I am ruler of an entire empire, I will need a son and heir. In any case, can you imagine how humiliating it would be for an emperor to be saddled with that insufferable wench for a wife?"

"You'd never be able to show your face in polite society," Gar sniffed.

"This way, everything works out perfectly," said Romil. "Ardendale will be mine, and I can find myself a new wife worthy of being my empress."

Smash! Quicker than the blink of an eye, Romil's smug, pale face disappeared from view. With a start, Ivy realized the mirror had slipped from her numb fingers and shattered on the stone floor of the tower. Pearls and gemstones had jarred loose from the golden frame and now rolled like little beads in a noisy whirlwind about her feet. Ivy had just destroyed a priceless fairy relic, and she should have been mortified, but the princess only stared at the wreck of glass and gold without feeling.

She was thunderstruck. But in the space of a heartbeat, the shock receded, replaced by a much more powerful emotion. Somewhere in the back of her mind, Ivy knew she should be afraid, should fear for her life. But at that moment, the only thing she felt was anger—glowing, white-hot anger. It coursed through her like a river of molten lava, sweeping her up to ride its burning tide.

What kind of vile creature would plot against the king—a harmless, befuddled, kindhearted old man? Ivy felt her blood boil. Romil was in for a nasty surprise. Dragon Treaty or not, she'd be torn apart by wild dogs before she'd let him hurt a hair on her father's head.

I have to get out of here, she thought. But how? Her eyes

darted frantically around the room and fell upon the large window letting in streams of afternoon sun. *The window.* Felda had said a window was the answer she sought. Perhaps this meant it was the means of her escape.

But how would she get down the outside of the tower? What she needed was a rope. She was a fair climber. How many times had she spent the entire day in the old pear orchard, scrambling up and down trees until the palms of her hands were scraped raw? What was a smooth stretch of tower compared to rough bark and thousands of scraggily branches? All she needed was something to hold on to.

Carefully stepping over bits of broken mirror, Ivy made her way to the wardrobe and threw open its wide doors. The clothes were as fine as she recalled, the fabric of the highest quality. Ivy wasn't all that heavy; surely such well-made garments were strong enough to support her weight.

She dug her way through the trove of clothing. The light-weight frocks and flimsy underthings would tear too easily, but she pulled out the thicker cloaks and the heavier of the winter dresses and tossed them into a pile on the floor. She added the bed linens as well. That done, she set about tying the lot into one long chain, using a sturdy knot called the Lover's Embrace, which Boggs had taught her long ago. She knotted sheets to sleeves and skirts to necklines, not caring how roughly she handled the fine material. (Tildy would have had a fit!) She worked feverishly, and by the time she was done, she had a length of fabric so long it coiled around the room like a colorful sea serpent.

But Ivy hadn't realized how long the task had taken.

A glimpse out the window showed the western sky aflame with the descending sun. Thankfully, there was still no sign of the dragon, but she'd have to move fast to get out of here before the beast arrived at sunset.

Now I just need something to tie the rope to, she thought.

The huge bed was the heaviest thing in the tower. There was no way Ivy was strong enough to push it over to the window, so she simply tied one end of the cloth rope to a bedpost and stretched it across the floor. On the other side of the room, she dropped the remainder of the colorful cord out the window.

As long as it was, her makeshift rope still fell short of the ground. But Ivy didn't have time to add to it. She would just have to drop the last six or seven feet.

"It's nothing I can't handle," she reassured herself. "The orchard wall is higher than that, and I've fallen off it too many times to count."

She tucked up the sides of her long skirts. With a firm grip on the rope and one last breath to steel her nerves, she lowered herself out the window.

She clung tightly to the cloth with her legs; the knots she had tied made surprisingly good footholds. Hand underneath hand, she slowly slid down the length of fabric. She was making good time, and just as she had the satisfaction of thinking her plan was going to work, from somewhere above came the sound of ripping cloth. Ivy cried out as she felt herself drop several inches, but mercifully the rope held.

Cautiously, she lifted her head. Several garments up, the sleeve of a red velvet gown was tied to the tail end of a cloak.

It had torn at the seam and was slowly unraveling. Her heart lurched. There was no way it would hold until she reached the ground. She wasn't even halfway down. A fall from this height could easily kill her. What was she to do? The window was certainly closer than the ground, but if she climbed back up she'd be trapped yet again.

Ivy's head reeled, but before she could make up her mind, fate decided for her. With one last, horrific rip, the cloth rope tore in two. Ivy plummeted, and a terrified scream she barely recognized as her own pierced the cool evening air. Wind roared past her ears, and the brown earth beneath the tower rushed up to meet her at an impossible speed. She closed her eyes, preparing to hit . . . but the ground never came. She felt a sudden gust of wind, then something closed around her torso tightly, something that stopped her fall with a jolt so sharp, it forced the breath from her lungs.

"Oh dear, oh dear," came a trembly voice very near her right ear. "That was close!"

Startled, Ivy opened her eyes. Her vision filled with an expanse of shiny black skin, scaled like a fish, along with a golden eye as round and wide as the mouth of a soup bowl, which was studying her in distinct alarm.

"Good goat fur," said the owner of the large eye. "I do believe you're actually supposed to stay *inside* the tower."

PART TWO

The Dragon

12

Elridge

If Ivy didn't feel, high in her chest, the dull ache from having the wind knocked out of her, she would have thought all this a dream. She was grasped in the closed claw of a dragon, its talons wrapped around her rib cage so tightly they could have been a corset. Not that Ivy would ever wear a corset, of course.

"Oh my, I'm pretty sure this isn't normal," mumbled the dragon. It sounded rather nervous, its voice shuddery and not nearly as deep or full as Ivy would have expected. "No one said anything about princesses *falling* from the tower."

With a surprisingly soft plop, it landed on the hard-packed soil at the tower's foot. Sitting back on its haunches, the dragon held the breathless princess in front of its face as if she were a lady's hand mirror and it were carefully examining its own reflection.

"Um, you there, are you all right?" it asked hesitantly.

Ivy could see long rows of pointed teeth lining its mouth when it spoke. She was too stunned to answer.

"Um, hello?" The dragon gave her a little shake, as if she were a baby's rattle. "Hello, there? You do talk, don't you?"

Between her dizzying fall from the tower and the shock of finding herself face-to-face with a real, live dragon, Ivy wasn't sure she actually *could* talk at the moment.

"I'm . . . I mean . . . you, you're a dragon," she managed to stammer, words tumbling out of her like water over rocks in a stream. "You're *the* dragon, the one that's come to guard the tower."

The creature before her looked very much like illustrations of dragons she had seen in books—scaled skin like a lizard's, large batlike wings, a row of thick spines along the crest of its back and down its tail, and two slightly curved horns protruding from the bony ridge above its eyes. But pictures always showed dragons with eyes that burned with hatred and malice, while these dragon's eyes merely peered at her quizzically. And something else was different about this dragon. Ivy had read that dragons were as big as gate-houses or small barns, but this one was only slightly larger than elephants were said to be in the kingdoms of the east.

Without thinking, she blurted out, "Aren't you a bit small for a dragon?"

Apparently, she had struck a nerve. At once, the drag-on's friendly concern seemed to vanish. It bristled, the spines along its back and tail suddenly taller and straighter than before. Affronted, the dragon acted much less flustered. "You know, I think perhaps it's best if we get you back inside the tower," it said briskly. "I'll just fly up and pop you back in through the window, shall I?"

The creature unfurled its wings, ready to take flight.

"No, wait!" cried Ivy. "I'm sorry. I shouldn't have said that. I didn't mean to offend you. Please don't put me back in the tower—*please*. You don't understand—he's going to kill me!"

That stopped the dragon short.

"Kill you?" it asked, looking uneasy. "Who's going to kill you?"

"Prince Romil," Ivy all but wailed. "He's coming tomorrow to battle you, and you *have* to defeat him. If he becomes king, my father and I are dead. He's planning to murder us both—and he's going to lift the ban on slaying dragons," she added, thinking this would surely motivate the dragon. The creature might not care what happened to her and the king, but it would want to save the lives of its own kind. "I heard him. He has an entire army, and when they get here, he's going to let them start hunting dragons."

The alarmed look on the dragon's face faded. It raised an eyebrow skeptically, or to be more exact, it raised the part of its face above one eye where an eyebrow would have been, if it had had eyebrows.

"You wouldn't be making all this up just to get out of the tower, would you?" it asked. "It sounds a bit far-fetched."

"It is not far-fetched!" retorted Ivy. Why did no one want to believe her? Any remaining fear fled before a hot rush of annoyance and frustration. "It's all true, every last word."

Before Ivy knew it, she had told the wary dragon

everything—about Romil's plans, her visit to Felda, what she had seen in the magic mirror, and how she had tried to escape down the outside of the tower.

"Dear me…now that you mention it, I did see that bone ship when I was flying over the valley," admitted the dragon, who was starting to look troubled again. "It was anchored right off the beach. It was one of the strangest things I've ever seen, even for something built by humans…and I suppose you *would* have to be pretty desperate to try to scale the outside of that tower, without wings and all. Good goat fur, I'd never try something so risky if I were that small and couldn't fly. You could've been squashed like a bug."

The dragon shuddered at the thought, and Ivy felt her whole body tremble in its grip.

"So do you think you'll be able to defeat Romil?" she asked hopefully.

This dragon wasn't exactly what she had expected, but it was a dragon, after all. Terrorizing unsuspecting humans was what dragons did best. It may have been small for its kind, but it was still by far the largest creature Ivy had ever seen. It had claws and horns and could doubtlessly breathe fire, so maybe it was more predatory than it looked. Prepared for Romil's secret weapons, it just might have a chance. In the midst of her desperation, Ivy saw a small glimmer of hope, and she latched onto it like a limpet to a wet rock.

"Romil has those spears and that dragon-scale armor I told you about, but now that you know about them, maybe you could come up with some sort of strategy to defend yourself," the princess said. She started talking more and more rapidly. "I could even help. I don't know much about combat, but I'm willing to give it a try. If you can stop Romil, all our problems will be solved: my father and I will be safe, and the rest of the dragons, and the whole kingdom, really, since Romil won't be around to drag anyone off on those stupid conquests of his. What's wrong?"

The dragon had lowered its head like a puppy being scolded, a ridiculously timid action for a creature of its size and form. For a moment, all was silent except for the anxious shuffling of its clawed feet.

"About defeating the prince," it said at last, in a sheepish voice that seemed awfully small for a creature with a wingspan wider than most trees were tall, "you see...I'm not exactly what you'd call skilled at battle. Never been much of a physical creature. Too nervous for it, really. It's all I can do to catch a couple of wild goats now and then for a meal. And you were right before, I am slightly smaller than average for a dragon—especially a boy dragon. The other dragons tease me about it quite a bit." Its his voice faltered even more. "What I'm trying to say is...you see... this Prince Romil of yours sounds like a formidable oppo nent and I...I don't think I'll be much use against him," he finished lamely.

Ivy's heart sank. This dragon did seem awfully unsure of himself. What had she been thinking? Romil was a match for a full-blown dragon; surely he could defeat a meek and slightly-smaller-than-average one. If this dragon was truly as timid as he sounded, Romil would make a pair of dragon-hide boots out of him in no time. Or, considering how much hide the dragon had, several pairs of boots, a number of belts, and a matching satchel or two.

Even the dragon looked forlorn. "Oh, good goat fur—I'm not cut out for this, not cut out for this at all," he moaned. "It was just my luck the lot fell to me to guard the tower this time around. The other dragons thought it was hilarious. 'Might as well send a three-legged sand lizard,' they said. 'It would put up as much of a fight.' Gave them a real laugh, it did. . . .

"Oh, I knew something disastrous was going to happen—I just knew it! The one time I'm chosen to guard the tower, and a dragon-slaying super prince shows up with unstoppable armor and spears. This is just so typical—I can't *ever* get a break!"

The dragon was so distressed that he nearly dropped Ivy, and the princess let out a squeaky gasp.

"Sorry," the creature mumbled, tightening his grip. He drooped his head and stared at the ground, looking thoroughly disheartened.

"That's all right," said Ivy, who couldn't bring herself to be upset with such a pitiable creature. "It sounds like we're both done for, anyway."

"Oh, dear me, so it would seem." There was a long, unhappy silence. Then the dragon asked, "I . . . I don't suppose Felda said anything that could be of help during your reading? What did she tell you again?"

"Just what I said before," said Ivy. "That twaddle about time running out to make a decision and the mountains calling me or some such nonsense." The princess was feeling rather cranky toward Felda. So much for a window being the answer she needed. She didn't think anything could be the answer to her problems at this point.

The dragon, however, looked as if he was carefully considering Felda's words.

"The mountains calling you..." he mused. "Do you think she meant the Craggies? It would have to be them, since they're the only mountains around here...."

"Who cares?" Ivy said impatiently. "It was just drivel about some clumps of leaves in the bottom of a teacup. It doesn't mean anything."

The dragon looked shocked. "Dear me, of course it means something," he said. "Why, Felda the Farseeing wouldn't have seen it if it didn't."

"You know Felda?" asked Ivy, surprised. She wouldn't have thought dragons had much use for either tea or fortunes.

"Well, I've never actually met her," said the dragon. "But even us dragons know about her. She's a legend in these parts. She's been telling fortunes for nearly as long as this tower has been standing."

"But that can't be right," said Ivy. "The tower is hundreds of years old, and Felda looks so young!"

"Of course she does," the dragon said patiently, as if he were explaining something to a very small child. "She's a halfling—half-fairy, half-human. She ages much, much slower than a normal human, although she doesn't have the eternal youth of a fairy. She also doesn't have full-fledged fairy magic, but she was born with a gift for divining the future—in her own roundabout way. If she told you to go to the mountains, then that's where you should go."

Ivy slowly digested this new information. So that explained the unnatural color of the fortune-teller's eyes. If Felda really did have a gift for seeing the future, courtesy of her fairy bloodline, then surely it was safe to rely on what she had seen in Ivy's tea leaves. That fall from the tower hadn't exactly been fun, but she *was* alive and no longer locked up in its stony confines. In a way, Felda's reading had gotten her this far.

"Maybe a clue to finding this long-lost fairy godmother of yours is up there," said the dragon, nodding his head at the looming mass of mountains. "She is what you went to see Felda about in the first place."

Now who's being far-fetched? Ivy thought wryly. She couldn't imagine Drusilla having anything to do with the bleak expanse of the Craggies. She knew enough about fairies to know they were drawn to beautiful, magical places, not gigantic piles of ugly, bald rock.

No one *ever* went into the Craggies. Besides being so cold and rocky that not even the basest weed would deign to grow there, the towering mountains were the realm of trolls, and they certainly weren't going to be of any help to Ivy, unless she could somehow convince them to eat Prince Romil. *If they didn't eat me first,* she thought with a shudder.

"It doesn't matter," she said. "There's no way I could get up the Craggies in any case."

The creature's reptilian face brightened. "Why, I could fly you up," he said in an excited voice. "You're right—your scrawny little human arms and legs weren't exactly made for mountain climbing, if you don't mind me saying so. I may be small for a dragon, but I'm nothing if not a good flier—and much faster than the other dragons. That's the one good thing about being small: not so much weight to lug around."

"You'd actually fly me into the Craggies?" Ivy couldn't believe it. A dragon, help her—the very dragon sent to guard her?

"Well, if this Romil really is a threat to dragonkind, it's my duty to do whatever I can to stop him," reasoned the dragon. "My kindred may tease me a lot, but even they don't deserve to be slain by a bunch of fur-clad soldiers from the North. I know I don't have a fighting chance against Romil," he confessed, shamefaced, "and I'm not fortunate enough to have a fairy godmother of my own, but maybe yours could find a way to get us both out of this mess."

Ivy was still doubtful.

"Look, tomorrow is my first official day guarding the tower," the dragon said. "This Romil can't show up until sunrise at the earliest. So if we flew into the mountains tonight, no one would be the wiser, not as long as we're back by morning. My treasure should be safe in its hiding place for one night. We can always turn around straightaway if we don't find anything. It couldn't hurt just to have a look around, could it? Especially since it would appear that both our lives hang in the balance, not to mention your entire kingdom and all of my kind."

When he put it like that, how could Ivy refuse? Besides,

hadn't she promised herself to do whatever it would take to keep her father safe?

"All right," she said. Then a distressing new thought seized her attention. "Fairy cakes," she gasped. "It's already dark." Night had fallen while she and the dragon had held their unlikely conversation. Granted, the sky was clear and the moon round and full, casting a milky light upon the world below, but it was still night. Ivy could see little more than shadows and shapes outlined in the murky moonlight.

"Not to worry," the dragon said with a careless wave of his claw. "Dragons have excellent night vision. I can see almost as well as if it were broad daylight."

"I'm going to have to rely on you, then," said Ivy. She suddenly felt a strange kinship with the scaly creature before her. As unbelievable as it seemed, at the moment this dragon was the only ally she had.

"By the way," she added, almost shyly, "my name is Ivy."

The dragon gave her a wide, toothy grin that she would have found frightening only a few minutes earlier.

"I'm Elridge," he said.

13

Flight into the Craggies

Elridge seemed a curiously mild name for a dragon. Ivy would have expected dragons to be called something like Bonebiter or Bloodfury, or one of those other intimidating names dragons always had in old stories. But after a moment's reflection, Ivy decided she liked the name Elridge. It was a nice, trustworthy kind of name. Besides, it probably wouldn't have been a good idea to fly off into the Craggies with someone named Bloodfury, anyway.

"Are you comfortable like this? Shall I just hold you in my claw?" Elridge asked.

Now that Ivy thought about it, she wasn't at all comfortable in the dragon's stifling grip. "Well, actually, it's a little tight, and a bit hard to breathe," she said. "I don't suppose there's any way I could, er, maybe sit on your back?" She hoped this wouldn't offend the dragon. She didn't want Elridge to think she considered him the equal of a horse.

Her father might take this as a great compliment, but few others would.

Elridge, however, seemed to take the suggestion in stride. "I don't see why not," he said gamely.

He carefully set the princess on the ground. Released from the lock of his talons, Ivy took in several deep gulps of the refreshingly cool night air.

Elridge lay down on all fours so that the princess could scramble onto his back. She squeezed between two large spines at the base of his long neck, the fit snug but comfortable. She could even grip the tall spine in front of her to keep from slipping off, which would be an unfortunate fate indeed while flying along the steep mountainside.

"Elridge," she said, trying out the name, "do you think you could drop me off in the room at the top of the tower just for a moment? I want to grab a cloak, since I imagine it's going to be cold in the Craggies. Maybe I can find some other supplies for us as well."

"I've heard about you humans with your strange need to lug all sorts of objects with you wherever you go," said Elridge. He sounded amused, and Ivy realized he was teasing her.

With a powerful sweep of his scalloped wings, they lifted off the ground and soared through the chilly night air toward the dark square of the tower's window.

It was amazing. Ivy had seen much the same view through the window itself, but being surrounded by it, out in the open air, with nothing between her and the ground except for a lithesome length of dragon flesh, was really something spectacular. Elridge cut through the air as smoothly and deftly as a boat through water, the entire world stretched out beneath him.

"Dear me, you're not afraid of heights, are you?" asked the dragon, concerned at her sudden silence.

"No, no, not at all. I'm just awed by the view," Ivy assured him. "Heights don't bother me."

"I guess they wouldn't," said Elridge, "seeing as you were trying to climb down the outside of this tower just a few minutes ago."

The dragon came to a stop outside the window, flapping his wings lightly to hover in place.

"Um, we don't exactly have a lot of time," he hinted gently.

"Don't worry, I'll only be a minute."

As carefully as she could, Ivy slid down Elridge's scales to the window ledge and hopped into the familiar circular stone room. It felt even more empty and lonesome at night. Glass and gems from the shattered mirror littered the floor and crunched beneath her footsteps.

She lit the candle on the dressing table. In the flickering light, she saw that the upper part of her ill-fated cloth rope was still tied to a bedpost by a blue woolen cloak. Quickly, Ivy undid the knots. She flung the warm if slightly rumpled garment about her shoulders, tossing the rest of the rope aside.

She should take the golden goblet as well, she thought. It would come in handy if she got thirsty or needed a burst of energy somewhere along the way. It was really too bad she couldn't take the wishing table, in case she or Elridge fancied a snack. She was sure a magic wishing table could produce enough food to feed even a hungry dragon. At least she could make use of the beautiful tablecloth. It would be perfect to carry the goblet in, although she felt a bit guilty about using the finery in such a common way.

Even though she was rushed for time, Ivy couldn't help stopping for a moment to pick up the largest of the shards of mirror from the floor. It was nearly as long as her forearm. She handled it gingerly; its edges were sharp and glinted threateningly in the candlelight.

"Show me Romil," she commanded, doubtful that anything would actually happen. If only she hadn't been so careless, she'd still have the advantage of being able to see what the vile prince was up to.

But much to the princess's surprise, there still seemed to be life left in the magical glass. It misted over slowly, as if it was straining to obey her command, but the frothy gray mist just whirled endlessly and never cleared to reveal what was on the other side.

Maybe she would have better luck with it later. She rose with the shard still grasped in her hand. Then, upon second thought, she gathered up several of the smaller shards from the floor as well, just in case.

The golden goblet sat in the middle of the wishing table where she had left it. Ivy placed the mirror shards next to it and proceeded to bundle the entire lot within the shimmering tablecloth. By bringing the four corners together and tying them firmly, she was able to make something of a good-size purse. The gap beneath the knots even made a convenient handle that she could slip over her wrist, leaving both of her hands free.

All right, enough shilly-shallying, she scolded herself. *It's time to go.*

After a quick puff of breath to extinguish the candle's flame, Ivy was once again clamoring out the window, where Elridge waited patiently.

"I wanted to thank you for saving my life," she told the dragon as she took her place nestled between two spines. "That fall would have finished me." Ivy paused thoughtfully. "I hope this isn't a discourteous thing to say, but I wouldn't have expected a dragon to save me."

"Well, to be honest, most dragons probably wouldn't have," said Elridge. "As I'm sure you know, my kind aren't exactly fond of humans. But I never did seem capable of the kind of burning rage the other dragons have. When I saw you falling, dear me, it made my heart jump something awful. Catching you just seemed like the right thing to do. I didn't think twice about it." The dragon gave a loose shrug of his scaled shoulders. "Now, hang on tight." Elridge pushed away from the window and smoothly glided toward the jagged outline of waiting mountains.

As the dark peaks grew larger and larger in her vision, Ivy was again struck by a sharp pang of doubt. Was leaving the tower really the right decision? By breaking the Dragon Treaty, was she causing even worse trouble? *You're being ridiculous,* she told herself. *Nothing can bring more grief to the kingdom than Romil himself.*

The princess felt Elridge's massive head and shoulders slant upward and his body lift. The Craggies rose before them like a black challenge. The dragon skimmed low over the stony slopes, following the curve of the mountains higher and higher, carrying her off into the dark distance, farther from home than she had ever been.

14

Tunnels and Trolls

Ivy had never appreciated just how far above the valley's floor the giant peaks of the Craggies extended. The air grew colder the higher they climbed. Low clouds clung to the ragged slopes, and halfway up a whirling snow began to fall, stirred by a blustery mountain wind. "It's a good thing I stopped for the cloak," Ivy said, snuggling deeper into its woolen folds as she clutched the bony spine in front of her with both hands.

"Dear me, you humans must be awfully sensitive," said Elridge. "I don't feel a thing." Ivy figured his magnificent, diamond-hard scales shielded him from the worst of the cold.

This high up, the moon looked enormous. It seemed to hang just above their heads, peeking over a bank of dark clouds. In the silvery moonlight, the princess could make out shadowy ridges and an endless expanse of runneled rock, rushing by at an unnerving speed. Elridge himself would have blended in perfectly with the night sky if not for the glint of moonlight off his shiny scales.

"We're almost to the top." Elridge had to raise his voice so she could hear him over the wind. Before long Ivy could barely see through the flurrying snow. When the dragon's long body leveled out, she knew they had finally crested the jagged peaks. She strained to focus her eyes.

It was hard to imagine a more desolate landscape. A barren sea of rock stretched in all directions, with no sign that any tree or plant had ever grown there. The only thing that broke the monotony of stone was a thickening coat of powdery snow. Elridge flew low across the mountaintops, their points as sharp and ragged as the teeth of an old saw. His legs and belly grazed mere inches from the summits, and Ivy recalled with alarm what Owen and Boggs had said about a dragon's underside being its most vulnerable spot.

"Do you see anything yet?" she called over the roar of wind. She hoped Elridge was as sharp-sighted in the dark as he claimed.

"Not yet," the dragon called back, turning his head slightly in her direction. "But I've got my eyes peeled. I'm sure something will pop up any minute now—"

As if on cue, something large and long pierced the air next to them with a whoosh loud enough to be heard over the rumbling wind, missing the dragon's side by not three arm lengths.

"Good goat fur!" With a start, Elridge veered sharply

to his left. "Wh-what was that?" he choked out, his voice panic-stricken.

"I don't know," Ivy breathed. Fear rose as a hard lump in the back of her throat. This *was* a bad idea, after all. There was a reason nobody ever came to these mountains. Nervously, she gazed out into the darkness and the swirl of falling snow.

Then, from somewhere below, she heard another telltale whoosh. "Here comes another one!" she cried.

This time Ivy was able to make out the shape of a thin, oblong object as it whizzed by. She had let loose enough arrows in her time to recognize the familiar sound of a shaft slicing through air.

"Elridge," she yelled. "Someone's shooting at us!"

"What?" Elridge's voice cracked with fright.

"We have to land," Ivy said frantically. "Quickly—we have to get out of the air!"

"Oh, good goat fur, there's no place to land around here," said Elridge. The mountains were all sharply formed peaks and steep slopes, with no flat ground where they could set down safely.

"What are we going to do?" cried Elridge.

"Keep looking," said Ivy.

Elridge's head slid from side to side as he furiously scanned the mountains below.

Another arrow shot by close enough for Ivy to feel the draft of air in its wake, followed by yet another. The arrows were coming faster now; it wouldn't be long before one of them hit its mark.

"Over there!" Elridge shouted. "I think I see a ledge and an opening, like a cave."

"Fly for it!" Ivy screamed.

Elridge banked to avoid a volley of arrows and dived toward one of the dark peaks in the distance. As they drew closer, Ivy could see that it was much larger and taller than any of the others. Sure enough, near the very top there was a ledge fronting the dark "O" of a cave. It was just big enough to hold a slightly-smaller-than-average dragon.

Ivy had hoped they would be less of a target once they were out of the air, but even through the falling snow, moonlight glinted off Elridge's scales in a regrettably eye-catching way. As the dragon made a rushed and clumsy landing on the jutting lip of rock, yet another arrow flew by, this time right between two of his tail spines, embedding itself in the rock that rimmed the cave's opening. It was enormous—easily twice the size of any arrow Ivy had ever seen.

"Whoever's shooting can still see us. I—I think they're following us." Her throat tightened.

"Get inside!" shouted Elridge.

Ivy didn't need to be told twice. She slid off Elridge's back and scrambled through the mouth of the cave, the frantic dragon right behind her. She found herself in a long, rocky corridor, and she could dimly make out flickering light at the far end.

"Hurry! Keep going," Elridge urged. His large body almost filled the entire circumference of the corridor. They had been lucky he could fit inside at all.

The light grew closer and closer until the tunnel

emptied into an enormous round cavern. It was so large, even Elridge could move about comfortably. Ivy quickly spotted the source of the dusky light. The floor in the center of the cavern was level and flat, as if worn smooth by centuries of plodding feet, but the outskirts were still littered with boulders, outcroppings, and sharp stalagmites. Scattered here and there among this rocky debris were small, sputtering fires. Wood was undoubtedly hard to come by in these stark mountains, so the residents of the cavern had taken to burning waxy blocks of a yellowish-white animal fat, a crude form of tallow. Some of these blocks burned in little hollows on top of boulders, which appeared to have been carved out for this very purpose. Some of the burning blocks were even impaled on the points of stalagmites, dripping long rivulets of oily, smelly wax down the sides of these most unusual candleholders. The tallow burned poorly, releasing a sickly yellow half-light and black smoke that smelled of burnt meat.

All around the cavern, tall openings pitted the stone walls. More tunnels, no doubt, just like the one they had come from, except these appeared to lead not to the surface, but deep into the heart of the mountain.

"What is this place, and where do you suppose all those tunnels go?" Ivy wondered aloud as she took in their shadowy surroundings.

"It doesn't really matter," rasped a throaty voice that seemed to issue from the very core of the mountain itself. "Seeing as the only place you're going is inside a very large cooking pot, with a dash of feldspar fungus for flavor."

Five hulking figures emerged from the dark maw of a tunnel on the other side of the cavern.

"Trolls!" cried Ivy.

Elridge seemed to have lost the ability to form words; he made only a squeaky choking sound in reply.

The trolls were massive—each was at least seven feet tall with the broad body of a bear. But instead of being covered in hair, they had sinewy skin the pasty gray color of a turkey's head. Their black eyes were large; their hooked noses even larger. Their clothes were roughly made from some type of fuzzy white animal fur. Since their feet were bare, Ivy could see their crooked, gnarled toes that stuck out at all angles like tree roots.

"It's been such a long time since I've had anything but cave crawler," one of the trolls said longingly. "I've heard human flesh is much more tender, especially young human flesh. . . ."

"And no one in our tribe has had dragon in generations," said another, looking at Elridge hungrily. "Boulders, this will be a treat!"

It was then that Ivy noticed the trolls were armed with very crude sets of bows and arrows. One of the trolls also had a nasty-looking club made of stone.

"It was our good fortune to spot the pair of you flying over our mountains," the troll with the raspy voice said. He sounded so hoarse, Tildy would have said he had a frog in his throat. "We were getting low on meat."

"Oh no, oh dear, oh dear," squawked Elridge, managing to get words out at last. "Ivy, run!"

The dragon himself bolted for the nearest tunnel, but he didn't get very far. The trolls were already on the move. Surprisingly quick for their size, three of them darted across the stone floor in time to block Elridge's path. Now the dragon was surrounded, with trolls in front of him, and trolls behind.

"Can we skewer the scaly critter?" one of them asked, nocking an enormous arrow with a tip of sharpened stone.

"No," Froggy Throat barked. "You know the Guamp likes meat as fresh as possible. Now that we're nice and close, we can use webbing to bring the beast down."

Much to Ivy's surprise, Elridge actually tried to put up a fight. The dragon lashed about wildly with his tail. He managed to knock down the pair of trolls behind him before they could clear out of the way. Then he whipped around in the opposite direction, the second bunch of trolls receiving a sweep of his tail that sent them sprawling like chess pieces.

Ivy would have found the whole thing comical if not for the fact that Elridge was fighting for his life—and hers.

"Ivy, get out of here!" he shouted.

Ivy hated the thought of leaving him, but she knew she had even less of a chance against the trolls than her dragon friend, who at the very least could use his size to his advantage. The princess quietly slipped into the mouth of the nearest tunnel, desperately hoping she would think of a way to save Elridge before he became the trolls' next meal.

A Tangled Web

The sounds of the skirmish in the cavern were growing more and more ferocious.

"What's the matter with you lumps of leadstone?" Froggy Throat croaked. "Back on your feet!"

"We're trying—honest we are," one of the trolls said plaintively.

"Watch the tail—here it comes again!" shouted another.

"Where is the human? I don't see her anywhere."

"Never mind, we'll worry about her later," Froggy Throat snapped. "For now, tie down that dragon!"

The tunnel Ivy had chosen turned sharply to the left just inside the opening, creating a corner of sorts where she could press up against the wall, hidden from the trolls' view. But she couldn't see what was happening out in the cavern and was desperately worried about Elridge. Things didn't sound good out there. If only there was some way she could see what was going on. . . .

With an inspiration born of panic, Ivy thrust her hand into the gap at the top of her tablecloth purse. She dug around frantically until her hand closed over one of the smaller fragments of broken mirror. Inching as close to the tunnel's opening as she dared, Ivy held it up to the corner, angling it so that she could see around the bend in the mirror's crystalline reflection . . .

. . . and hurriedly stifling the gasp that rose in her throat. Elridge seemed to have done a good job of keeping the trolls off their feet, but Froggy Throat had crawled out of range of the dragon's lashing tail. Elridge was facing the opposite direction, too busy dealing with the other trolls to notice. The troll with the stone club managed to get close enough to give Elridge a solid whack on the shin. The dragon yowled, and Froggy Throat used this moment of distraction to aim an arrow unseen behind Elridge's back. He was going to shoot the dragon after all.

"Elridge, behind you, look out!" shrieked Ivy.

The dragon froze, startled by the sound of her voice, and before he could recover, Froggy Throat let the arrow fly.

Ivy bit back a scream, but instead of striking the dragon, the arrow arched neatly across Elridge's back and over his head, trailing a thick, gossamer strand behind it.

"Wh-what is this stuff?" Elridge sputtered as the lustrous, not-quite-white thread settled onto his scales. The dragon shook his head furiously from side to side, then his body and tail, trying to dislodge the stubborn strand, but it clung fast to its unwilling host.

By this time, Froggy Throat had another arrow at the ready and launched a second strand over the flustered dragon.

"Stop that," pleaded Elridge. "Leave me alone!"

But the trolls surrounded the dragon from all sides, firing more of the filmy threads until Elridge was trapped under an entire web of sticky netting. The troll with the stone club ran in large circles around the dragon, looping a length of thread about Elridge's scaly ankles. When Stony Club pulled the thread tight, the dragon's ankles snapped together beneath his large body. Top-heavy and unable to stay balanced, Elridge toppled onto his side like a felled tree.

"Ouch!" he exclaimed as he hit the ground hard. "That hurt!"

"Good work, you lot," Froggy Throat grunted. "Finish bundling the creature up so we can drag it back to the Guamp. You," he indicated Stony Club, "get the human girl. Her voice came from over there."

With horror, Ivy realized Froggy Throat was pointing a meaty finger in the direction of her hiding place. For a moment, her heart went still and she stood as if frozen to the spot. Then she flung the mirror shard back into the table-cloth purse and took off down the dark length of tunnel as fast as her wobbly legs would carry her. But without any light, not even the faint glow from the cavern, it soon grew too dark to see. She had to slow her pace considerably and feel her way along the corridor by keeping one hand on the rocky wall. Her heart nearly burst out of her chest when a sudden, yellowish light flickered to life behind her, and she realized that Stony Club was inside the tunnel and had struck up some kind of flame.

"Don't run, little human." Stony Club's mocking voice rolled down the corridor, as ominous as a peal of thunder. "Tonight we feast on dragon, and you're going to be the dessert."

His light was just bright enough to illuminate the tunnel in front of Ivy, and without having to worry about tripping or colliding with a wall, the princess began to run once more.

"Wait up, you!" Stony Club's voice rang through the passage, followed closely by his heavy footfalls as he started after her.

With his wide feet and long legs, the burly troll covered a lot of ground. The circle of light that stretched before her grew wider and brighter, and Ivy knew the troll was gaining on her.

Up ahead, the tunnel made a sharp "U" as it rounded a bend. Without pausing to think, the princess swung blindly into the turn.

"Aaaggghhh!"

Something silky and a little slimy was stretched across the tunnel like a fisherman's net hung out to dry. It stuck to her skin and put an abrupt stop to her frenzied flight. Desperate, Ivy tried to pull away from the gooey mess, but the more she struggled, the more entangled she became.

Stony Club rounded the tunnel's curve far more carefully than she had, avoiding her sticky fate. Light came with him, and Ivy could now see she was caught in something that looked like a giant spider's web stretched across the entire width of the tunnel.

"Well, rollicking rockslides," Stony Club chortled with delight. "The little human has gone and got herself snared in the web of a cave crawler. Just like a human—rock dust for brains. But I shouldn't complain." He set down his torch and drew out a knife that was little more than a roughly sharpened stump of metal. "It saved me the trouble of having to chase you down, didn't it? I'll just lop off a bit of web, and you'll be well on your way to making a nice stew. Luckily, you don't have to have too many smarts for that."

Ivy was about to spout a very unflattering reply (surely even Tildy would agree there are some situations where politeness and decorum just aren't called for, enduring the taunts of a troll who has just chased you deep into the belly of a mountain and planned to eat you as soon as he cut you out of a giant spiderweb being one of them) when a sudden clicking sound caught her attention. It came from somewhere above her head, up in the shadowy recesses near the tunnel's ceiling. Stony Club heard it, too.

"Pesky creepy-crawly," he grumbled.

A movement in the shadows caught Ivy's eye, then something large, white, and fuzzy descended into view on the tip of a gossamer string. Coming to a stop directly in front of the startled princess was the most enormous spider she had ever seen. Its full, round body was the size of Cook's largest soup cauldron, with the tuft of a head and eight long, crooked legs poking out of it. A lifetime in these sunless caverns had left the spindly-legged creature as white and colorless as a ghost.

The ghastly thing had eight eyes, divided into two short rows. All were as black as orbs of obsidian. The clicking noise, Ivy realized, came from two fanglike appendages in front of the spider's hairy mouth, which were closing and opening like pincers, as if the horrible creature were chewing.

Ivy suddenly knew how it felt to be a fly. The spider scuttled toward her until it was so close she could see her own reflection in each of the creature's black eyes. She could also see the moist, pointed tips on the ends of the spider's fangs, beading with little drops of venom. She watched as eight separate Ivys opened their mouths to scream... but no sound ever came. The scream got caught somewhere deep in the back of her throat. She desperately wanted to look away as the spider opened its dripping fangs wide, but she was too terrified to make even that tiny movement.

Whack! The powerful swing of a stone club sent the white spider hurtling backward through the web, tearing at threads as it went. The creature hit the cave wall with a thump and slid, dazed, to the floor. Giving off a whimper like a wounded puppy, it scurried away into the darkness.

"I wasn't about to let that bothersome beastie have you," Stony Club said, thumping his club against the palm of his free hand and looking thoroughly pleased with himself. "You're to be part of *our* dinner."

In a bit of a daze herself, Ivy dimly wondered why everything in these mountains was so confoundedly hungry.

Stony Club set about cutting her loose from the jumbled

web. Instead of freeing her entirely, he cut around in a wide circle, making sure Ivy stayed tangled in the mess of threads in the middle. When he finally separated her from the rest of the web, he wound all the extra dangly ends about her. She was now so tightly wrapped in sticky strands that she could barely move.

"Time to go."

Tossing his bundled-up prisoner over one shoulder, Stony Club trudged back up the passage toward the cavern.

The princess's bindings were nothing compared to what the ambitious trolls had done to poor Elridge. The dragon looked as if he were trapped inside an enormous cocoon. She could still see his frightened face, which poked out of the wad of netting, although his snout had been clamped shut with more of the sticky spider silk. He lay on one side as he had fallen, but now his legs and tail were pinned uselessly against his body. He had been completely immobilized.

"The girl managed to get herself tangled in a crawler's web," Stony Club informed Froggy Throat cheerfully. "After that, catching her was easier than turning a roasting spit over the fire."

But Froggy Throat shared none of his companion's glee. From where she hung limply over Stony Club's shoulder, Ivy noticed the scratchy-throated troll studying her very carefully, almost suspiciously.

"Toss her onto the pile," he rasped finally, nodding to the mass of webbing that contained Elridge. "We'll haul the two of them to the Guamp."

16

The Guamp's Great Challenge

It was no small feat to drag a nearly cocooned dragon into the underground depths of the Craggies, but the trolls managed. All five of them took up stray ends of the strong thread that bound Elridge and heaved away, dragging the trussed-up dragon and princess along behind them. It was lucky for Ivy that she had landed near the top of the sticky heap, so that no part of her body actually touched the ground. Elridge's hard scales withstood being scraped along the rocky cave floor better than her soft human skin would, even with a cushion of spider silk.

"Elridge, are you okay?" she whispered with concern.

Unable to speak, the dragon had to settle for nodding rather pathetically, barely managing to bob his head up and down because so much webbing was wrapped around his lengthy neck.

"If we get out of this, I'm marching straight back to the

Fringed Forest and giving Felda a piece of my mind," Ivy growled under her breath.

The insides of the mountain were a labyrinth of tunnels and caves. Ivy lost track of time as the trolls dragged them up one stony passage and down another. At one time, their path wound along the bottom of a cliff wall, its sheer face dampened by hundreds of tiny trickles of water. A little farther along, they crossed a stone bridge over a gorge so deep that Ivy couldn't see the bottom.

It soon became obvious just how much the trolls depended on the cave crawlers that inhabited this underground world— and not just for meat. Now that Ivy had encountered one of the giant spiders herself, she recognized where the trolls got the fuzzy white fur that clothed them and, of course, all the sticky thread. Why, even the smelly tallow for their fires probably came from the spiders. The trolls' torches were long, jointed spider legs, burning from the thick end. The trolls basically lived off the gangly creatures. No wonder they were so eager to have something else to eat for a change.

Finally, after several hours, the trolls lugged their cargo into a huge cavern lit with smoky, sputtering fires. It looked as though an entire community of trolls lived here, bent busily over cook fires or pounding at lumps of metal, shaping them with tools made of stone. There were even young trolls, only as tall as Ivy herself, kicking round stones like human children playing ball. An excited buzz ran through the multitude as they caught sight of their companions' impressive catch. With a sinking feeling in the pit of her stomach, Ivy noticed some of the watching trolls licking their lips.

Froggy Throat and his friends dragged their prisoners to the far end of the cavern, where an enormous stone throne had been carved out of a tall boulder.

"Your Mighty Guamp-ness," Froggy Throat croaked to the large, decorated figure seated there. "I think you will be very pleased. We have brought the tribe a delightfully tasty offering."

The Guamp was the biggest of the entire bunch and sat importantly on his high throne, draped in long, fuzzy white robes. His gray hair, thick as a horse's mane, fell past broad shoulders. Instead of a crown, he wore an ugly headdress made out of a stuffed cave crawler. The crawler's pouf of a body sat atop the Guamp's enormous head like a hairy hat, and its spindly legs, bent like the corners of a picture frame, squeezed against the sides of his head, four on the left and four on the right.

He surveyed the bound dragon and princess before him with shiny, eager eyes.

"You have indeed had an exceedingly successful hunt," he said, his voice booming. "The tribe will eat well tonight."

A happy cheer went up among the trolls, who had left their fires and makeshift forges to gather around the throne and enjoy the spectacle. Froggy Throat, however, didn't look pleased at all. "Um, if I might be permitted to speak, Your Magnificent Hairiness," he said hesitantly. "The dragon will undoubtedly make for good eating, but about the girl..." His gruff voice trailed off uncertainly.

"Yes?" said the Guamp, with a touch of impatience. "Whatever you want to say, spit it out."

"It's just that...well...I'm not sure we should eat her," Froggy Throat said.

"What?" The Guamp looked incredulous, and a murmur ran through the assembled crowd. "Of course we should eat her. How often do we get the chance to eat a nice tender young human, or a nice tender young anything? Or anything at all other than *cave crawler?*" The Guamp spat out the last two words as if they left a foul flavor in his mouth, and he scrunched up his nose disagreeably. Ivy suspected cave crawlers didn't taste very good.

"That is all very true, Your Most Fearsome Fierceness," Froggy Throat agreed readily. "But I fear there is some wicked magic about the girl. After all, she *was* traveling with a dragon, actually riding on its back as it flew over the mountains, and everyone knows that humans and dragons absolutely loathe one another. Why, the dragon even tried to protect her when we attacked. There's only one explanation for such behavior—that dragon is under some sort of magic spell!"

The cavern filled with the low rumble of uneasy voices.

"And there's more," said Froggy Throat, aware that he now had the crowd's undivided attention. "While we were dealing with the dragon, the girl ran off into one of the tunnels, around a corner—yet right before I launched an arrow at the beast, she screamed out to warn it. How did she know I was going to shoot? How could she see what was happening? It was magic, I tell you, some kind of terrible magic. Mark my words, that scrawny girl's a witch or sorceress. She bespells dragons and sees through walls, and who knows what manner of horrible things will befall us if we eat her?"

The Guamp looked thoughtful.

"Your Snappy White Robed-ness," said Stony Club, "if I might be so bold, that is the biggest load of cave rot I have ever heard." He shot Froggy Throat a defiant look. "If that girl is such a powerful magic-doer, then how come she got caught in a crawler's web and how come she hasn't escaped from us? Surely a great sorceress would use her powers to set herself free."

"She's a young thing yet, Great Roaster of Cave-Crawler-on-a-Stick," Froggy Throat said stubbornly. "Perhaps she's still learning her evil tricks. It doesn't mean she's not dangerous."

"I say we eat her and not let good meat go to waste!" declared Stony Club. There were enthusiastic shouts of agreement from some of the onlookers.

"Always knew you had the sense of half-crumbled rock," Froggy Throat croaked at his companion.

"Dripstone!"

"Boulder-brain!"

"Pssst—Ivy." Startled by this new voice, the princess glanced down. Elridge had managed to loosen the spider silk around his snout and was whispering out of the corner of his mouth. "Tell them they're right—you've got magic powers," he hissed. "You'll hurt them if they try to eat us."

Of course! thought the princess. *How clever!*

"Your friend is right," she shouted to Stony Club from her high perch. "I *am* a sorceress, and my talent lies in, uh, brewing magical potions. I mixed one powerful enough to bespell this dragon. I slipped it into the spring from which he drinks, and now he obeys all of my commands and flies me wherever I choose.

"What's more—before we came to these mountains, we both drank a very special brew." She paused dramatically for effect. "We'd be deathly poisonous to anyone who tried to eat us."

Many of the trolls looked shocked and disappointed by this news, but Stony Club merely scoffed. "Most Artful Arranger of Rock Gardens, the girl would say anything to get out of being eaten. For all we know, that dragon captured her. I haven't seen it obey any of her commands."

"Of course he obeys me." Ivy tried to sound offended that they doubted her. "Dragon, thump your tail."

Elridge thumped his tail upon the ground the best he could under wads of sticky webbing.

There were a few gasps, and a low murmur of consternation ran through the throng of trolls. Ivy was pleased to note that even Stony Club was starting to look a bit nervous.

"There you go," she retorted. "As you've said, what dragon would listen to a human if he wasn't under a magic spell?"

"Enough." The cavern fell silent at the Guamp's sharp command. He turned toward Ivy, and it seemed as if she not only had the eyes of the ruler fixed upon her, but those of the cave crawler mounted upon his head as well.

"I know a way in which you can prove beyond all doubt your abilities as a sorceress and master potions-brewer," said the leader of the trolls. "I will set before you a challenge, one that none of my trolls has been able to accomplish, and one that is particularly close to my own heart.

"At the base of these great mountains is a mudhole of a swamp," he explained. "It lies on the opposite side of the mountains from the kingdom called Ardendale. For all I know, no human has ever set foot there. We trolls call it 'Wrathful Swamp,' for it is haunted by an entire host of angry, vengeful spirits. By and large, our tribe avoids this unpleasant place as surely as we avoid causing cave-ins. But every so often, a particularly brave or foolhardy soul will set his mind to venture there. Most never come back."

The Guamp looked very sorrowful at these words, and it was a moment before he spoke again.

"Wrathful Swamp is the only source of wood available to us trolls. You have surely noticed that no trees grow in the mountains themselves. Each of our bows and arrows, every scrap of wood in our possession, was retrieved by those few trolls who have managed to return from this deadly swamp. But they also returned with terrible stories, of voices and strange lights, luring trespassers to drown themselves in the muddy waters. The spirits even lay curses upon some of the outsiders who dare to enter their realm, and this is what happened to my poor son." Grief shone in the Guamp's eyes, and Ivy felt an unexpected pang of pity for the large, imposing ruler.

"Two days ago, the venturesome youth had it in mind to gather wood from the swamp," said the Guamp. "He was determined to have a bow and arrows of his own. I would have never allowed it if I had known what he had planned. I don't know what befell him in that accursed place, but he crawled back to this cavern, covered from head to toe in welts and sores, and quickly fell sick with fever. Obviously, it is some form of powerful dark magic. None have been able to heal him, not even my most skilled medicine-makers, and he will surely die if a cure is not found shortly.

"Of course, healing him should be no trouble for one as skilled at making potions as you claim to be," said the Guamp. "If you can restore my son to health, I will believe all you have said and you will be free to leave these mountains. If not, I will take you for a liar and tonight my tribe shall hold a great feast as planned.

"You two," the Guamp waved at Froggy Throat and Stony Club, "cut her down and take her to my son's sickbed."

Froggy Throat and Stony Club managed to pry Ivy loose from the mound of webbing. With short, blunt knives, they cut and stripped away the threads that bound her. It stung a bit, having the gooey strands pulled from her skin.

"But... I don't have any ingredients," Ivy protested, panic rising in the back of her throat like bile. The trolls would be furious when they discovered she was about as magical as a butter churn.

"I will have my tribe's entire medicine trove brought to you," the Guamp replied evenly.

"Move it, girlie." Froggy Throat seized her by the back of her cloak and half dragged her along, Stony Club marching behind.

Ivy turned to glance at Elridge. The dragon looked absolutely wretched in his silken binds, his golden eyes wide and frightened. She was suddenly very reluctant to leave him.

"What about my dragon?" she called to the Guamp.

"You may have him back when my son is well," said the ruler.

Ivy gave Elridge an apologetic look and wondered if she would ever see him again.

So much for being clever, she thought ruefully.

17

False Sorcery

Froggy Throat and Stony Club hurried Ivy to a dark corner of the vaulted cavern where a boulder as tall as a bookcase rested against the wall. With a grunt, Stony Club rolled the boulder to one side, revealing a troll-size opening behind.

"Go on, get in." Froggy Throat gave the princess a shove that sent her stumbling into the waiting hole and left her sprawled on her knees on the other side. "I'll bring the medicine trove." He strode away, leaving Stony Club to guard the gaping entrance.

Ivy found herself in a small, dim cave, no bigger than her own bedchamber back in the castle. A dripping lump of tallow burned in one alcove, and Ivy could faintly make out a raised stone slab on which a short figure lay. Rising to her feet and moving closer, she saw the figure was a young troll boy, flat on his back and sleeping fitfully. He looked terrible.

The only piece of clothing he wore was a tattered pair of trousers, ripped at the knees, and every inch of exposed skin was covered with raised bumps the size of ripe chestnuts. They looked like enormous bug bites. The boy was positively red with them, and his face and limbs were unnaturally puffy and swollen. Angry purple bruises splotched his body. He looked as if he had been attacked by a swarm of giant mosquitoes. Ivy shuddered at the thought. Giant spiders were bad enough.

Froggy Throat returned, carrying a large, rectangular block of stone. He deposited this next to the bed.

"The medicine trove," he croaked, nodding at the block. "And don't even think about trying anything funny, little witch. We'll be right outside."

He plodded out of the cave, and Stony Club rolled the boulder back over the opening as firmly as if he were shutting a dungeon door. Ivy gulped nervously. It was not a pleasant feeling, being trapped in the confines of this cave with only a sick, insensible young troll boy for company.

In the quiet that followed, Ivy could hear the poor boy's labored breathing. The sheen of sweat on his face and chest glistened in the firelight. Ivy didn't need to be a trained healer to know he was very ill, probably dying.

She ventured a glance at the so-called medicine trove. She had expected something along the lines of an apothecary's chest, but, of course, the trolls didn't have the wood for such a luxury. The block of stone had round grooves carved in the top, each containing some type of powdery substance. There were white, gray, and greenish flakes that looked to be dried fungi and lichen. The rest of the grainy powders were undoubtedly ground-up rocks and minerals of some sort. Ivy recognized none and didn't have the first idea what to do with any of them.

"What was I thinking?" she said, sinking to her knees beside the stone slab. "Listening to a fortune-teller, running off with a dragon, trying to deceive trolls? Stupid, stupid, stupid!"

Dejected, she let her head fall against the edge of the troll boy's bed—which was a very bad idea, seeing as the bed was made out of solid rock.

"Ouch!" Ivy cradled her forehead, positive a nasty bruise was forming even as she did. "Oh, I should have stayed in that stupid white tower," she moaned, "with that stupid magic mirror and stupid wishing table and stupid golden goblet—"

The golden goblet! Ivy suddenly remembered the magnificent chalice was tucked into the tablecloth purse at her wrist. It was imbued with fairy magic to refresh and revive whoever drank from it. Would it be able to revive someone even from the brink of death?

Ivy fished the goblet from the golden folds and cupped it in her hands. As before, the goblet immediately filled with sparkling fairy nectar. Tilting the troll boy's head slightly, Ivy poured the cloudless liquid down his throat in a steady stream until not a drop was left. This was fairly easy, seeing as his wide mouth gaped open limply. On a whim, Ivy filled the cup a second time, then a third, drenching the boy on the outside by pouring nectar over all of the bruises and ugly red sores.

For several moments, nothing happened. Then, just as Ivy become convinced that the goblet's magic was just not strong enough, the fiery red of the boy's sores started to fade. They shrank, closed, and healed, leaving no sign that they had ever been there. His bruises lightened. Before Ivy's eyes, the troll boy's swollen body returned to a normal size, and his skin turned a healthy pasty gray—well, healthy for a troll. Even his breathing became calm and regular. It was nothing short of a miracle.

Then the troll boy opened his eyes.

"Um, hello," Ivy said uncertainly, leaning over him from above.

The troll boy began to screech like a frightened cat. He bolted into a sitting position and proceeded to scream his head off.

"Um, it's okay, really, I'm only here to help," said Ivy, backing away nervously.

"What's going on in there?" Froggy Throat's gravelly voice demanded from the other side of the boulder. In a trice, he and Stony Club had moved the rock aside and rushed into the dark shelter of the cave. "The boy!" Froggy Throat gasped, staring in astonishment at the perfectly healthy young troll wailing away on his stone bed. "He's okay."

"It's all right, young one," said Stony Club, laying a comforting hand on the boy's shoulder. "You're safe now."

"I h-had a dream that a h-human girl was h-hovering

over me like a cave crawler d-dangling from a web," the young troll said.

"It was no dream," replied Stony Club. "That human girl is a powerful sorceress, and she just saved your life."

The Guamp was unspeakably pleased. He had ten trolls set to work cutting Elridge free as soon as word reached him that his son was well.

"Your dragon won't hurt anybody once it's loose, will it?" he asked Ivy a bit sheepishly.

"Of course not," said the princess, and she thought this was most likely true. Elridge didn't seem like the kind of dragon to hold a grudge.

"I am forever in your debt," the Guamp said as she patiently waited for Elridge to be disentangled from his prison of spider silk. "If there is ever anything I can do to repay you, you only have to ask."

"Well, I am looking for my fairy godmother, Drusilla," said Ivy. "I don't suppose you know where I can find her? I thought she might be somewhere near these mountains."

"Near these mountains, huh?" The Guamp looked thoughtful. "I know little of the fairy kind, but it has long been rumored that a fairy mound lies on the far side of Wrathful Swamp. It is said that once, before the spirits took up there, trolls used to enjoy crossing the swamp to spend an afternoon at the mound, for it is ringed with stones that sing and make the most beautiful music mortal ears can hope to hear."

"Stones that sing?" Ivy asked, wonderingly.

"Yes, they were called the Mumbles—no, the Mutters. No, that's not right." The Guamp scratched the side of his head, which looked terribly odd since he actually ended up scratching the side of the stuffed cave crawler perched there, making its legs twitch as if it were still alive.

"The Murmurs!" The Guamp snapped his fingers. "They were called the Murmurs, and it is said they mark the entrance to an entire underground fairy kingdom. Perhaps that is where you will find your godmother."

Ivy sat up eagerly. "So to get to these Murmurs, all we have to do is cross the swamp?"

"That is correct," said the Guamp. "But I'd advise against it. You've seen firsthand what the spirits are capable of."

An image of the sick, swollen troll boy flashed across Ivy's mind like a warning. But then she thought of her father, of Ardendale, and of what lay in store for the entire kingdom once Romil assumed the throne.

"I need to find Drusilla," she said stubbornly. "It's a matter of life and death. I'm willing to risk it."

The Guamp looked resigned. "There is only one exit from these caverns on that side of the mountains, and it opens directly into the swamp itself," he said. "It is not far from here. I will show you the way myself, if you wish."

By this time, Elridge had emerged from his wrappings like a butterfly from a cocoon.

"Elridge, you're loose!" Ivy had to resist the urge to throw her arms around him in delight—not that her arms would have fit around the dragon.

"Good goat fur, it feels nice to get that gunk off me,"

Elridge said, shaking the last shreds of spider silk from his scales. "I heard what the Guamp was telling you. Ivy, are you sure you want to go into this Wrathful Swamp? Dear me, it sounds awfully dangerous. Maybe we should go back the way we came. Once we're out of these caverns, we can fly over both the mountains and the swamp."

"Elridge, we don't have time," the princess pointed out. "Dawn is just hours away. Romil will be at the tower at sunrise, remember? We need to be back with Drusilla by then. We don't have time to backtrack through all those tunnels. Besides, you can take off as soon as we reach the swamp, and we'll fly away so quickly those spirits won't even know we're there."

The Spirits of Wrathful Swamp

"So this golden goblet of yours actually healed the Guamp's son?" Elridge asked in amazement. "I wondered how you managed to pull that off."

"I guess it's lucky I thought to bring it with me," said Ivy. "You know, due to my strange need to lug all sorts of objects with me wherever I go," she added with a smile.

Elridge gave her a wide, toothy grin in return.

True to his word, the Guamp himself had escorted them to the tunnel that led to Wrathful Swamp. "If you should ever have need to fly over our mountains again, tie this to your dragon's tail," he had said, giving Ivy a long strip of fuzzy white spiderskin. "If my trolls spot it, they will know to let you pass. No one will try to shoot you down."

There was no room for the Guamp's gift in the tablecloth purse, so Ivy tied it about her waist like a sash.

"And you must take one of our torches with you, my

friends," the Guamp insisted, handing the princess one of the long, bent spider legs. "So you can see your way in the dark."

"Eww," Ivy squeaked, gingerly grasping the end of the hairy limb with the tips of her fingers. "I mean, thanks."

Now she and Elridge were making their way down the long, winding tunnel that emptied into the swamp.

"Do you hear that?" Elridge stopped and tilted his head to one side, listening intently.

"Chirping." Ivy could just make out the busy sounds of crickets and other night insects. She raised the burning spider-leg torch above her head and peered down the tunnel. "We must be getting close to the swamp."

"The *haunted* swamp." Elridge shuddered. "Ivy, I think you should get on my back so we can take off as soon as we get outside."

Ivy found it a bit difficult to climb onto the dragon's back with the torch in one hand, but she finally managed to settle herself in place near the base of his neck. In a few minutes, they arrived at the mouth of the tunnel and were met by fresh, cool night air.

"Hang on tight." Elridge darted out into the open, spreading his wings wide.

As they lifted off the ground, Ivy gripped a dragon spine with one hand and clutched the torch with the other, but the quick getaway she had hoped for was clearly impossible. The trees of the swamp were unbelievably dense, and, as Elridge flew higher, branches clawed and scratched them both. They slapped at Ivy's face and arms and grasped at strands of her hair. Branches tore and broke in the wake of Elridge's frantic flight, but they soon became so thick that the dragon could fly no higher. Even in the middle of autumn, the swamp seemed exceedingly leafy and alive, and Elridge couldn't break through the profuse canopy.

"Too many branches," he complained, spitting out a mouthful of leaves.

"Try somewhere else," Ivy urged. "Maybe you can find a thin spot."

The princess was growing nervous. She knew Elridge could see perfectly well at night, but she was almost stone-blind in this dark, swampy wood. In the short cast of her torchlight, all she could make out was an endless tangle of branches, a profusion of leaves, and columns of thick, straight tree trunks. Below was the black glint of water.

Then, suddenly, there was something else.

"Elridge, do you see those lights?" she asked. Off in the distance, something flashed like blinking stars. A flurry of lights dotted the darkness beneath the trees: purple, blue, and green. "What do you think those are?"

"Fireflies?" Elridge suggested hopefully, his voice much higher and squeakier than usual.

"They would have to be the biggest fireflies ever," Ivy said with doubt.

"Well, we saw big spiders," Elridge said.

"They're coming this way," cried Ivy, and, sure enough, the strange lights came zipping through the night air, straight for the hovering dragon.

"Oh no, it's the spirits!" Frantic, Elridge tore off in the opposite direction, flapping his wings madly. He plowed through the maze of tree trunks in the space above the water but beneath the leafy canopy, coming dangerously close to colliding with random trees.

"Elridge," Ivy yelled. "Slow down! We're going to crash!"

"If I slow down, they'll catch us!" Elridge swerved sharply to maneuver around a large tree trunk, and Ivy, who was holding on with only one hand, felt her fingers starting to slip.

"Elridge, help!"

With a last desperate grab, the princess slid from her seat and tumbled through the air. Luckily, the swamp water broke her fall. She took a good dunking, which promptly extinguished her torch, and came up sputtering cold, scummy water.

"Elridge!"

The dragon was nowhere to be seen, but Ivy thought she heard him crashing through the trees somewhere off to her left. *I'm sure he'll come back for me once he's calmed down a bit,* she thought. She was beginning to shiver in the cold water and figured she'd better make her way to some low bough or tree root to rest on while she waited for Elridge to return. The spider-leg torch was soaked and useless, so she let it slip from her grasp into the dark water. She planted her feet on the squishy bottom and trudged toward the murky outline of a nearby tree.

"Nooooooo," buzzed a strangely airy but beautiful voice next to her right ear. "That's not the way you want to go. You want to go the other direction, deeper into the water."

She turned toward the voice, curious but not scared. How could one be scared of such a lovely sound? There was one of the lights, floating in the air over her shoulder, glowing the most beautiful blue Ivy had ever seen, like a tiny sapphire sun.

"Yes, deeper," hummed another voice, equally charming. A green starburst took its place next to its blue companion. "The water is so lovely, you want to go deeper, you want to lose yourself in it."

Suddenly, the air was a chorus of alluring voices, and Ivy found herself surrounded by so many glowing lights it was as if half the stars in the sky had decided to fall into the dark swamp at the same time.

"Come. Come deeper."

The lights moved away ever so slightly, and Ivy felt a stab of fear and longing. The thought of losing sight of them filled her with overwhelming sorrow. She took a hurried step forward.

"The water, lose yourself in the water, lose yourself beneath the water."

Ivy took several more steps and water brushed the tip of her chin.

"That's right," the voices beckoned. "Now that you have us, you need nothing else in this world. You don't need to run; you don't need to escape. You certainly don't need that bumbling dragon."

Something pricked at the back of Ivy's mind. She tried to shake it off, tried to focus on the mesmerizing lights, but it pushed its way to the forefront of her thoughts: *Elridge*. Elridge was supposed to come find her. If she went off following lights, how would he know where to look? And how would he know if she lost herself beneath the water?

Ivy came back to herself with a jolt. Why would she want to lose herself beneath the water? Wouldn't she drown?

"What *are* you things?" she lashed out angrily at the swirling lights, paddling away from them into more shallow water. "Just what do you think you're trying to do?"

"Drat," swore a blaze of purple in a squeaky, high-pitched voice very unlike the lovely ones Ivy had just heard. "We've lost her."

"Ack, the girl must have a strong will," said another little light, this one blue. "I hate the ones with strong wills."

Ivy peered closely at the nearest burst of color. It wasn't a light at all, but a tiny glowing person, small enough to fit inside one of Felda's teacups, and clad in a garment of moss and mud, with rainbowed wings like a dragonfly. Ivy didn't know why she hadn't noticed the itsy-bitsy beings before.

"You're water sprites," the princess exclaimed. "But I thought water sprites were kind and gentle, and protected lakes and ponds and kept them beautiful."

"We're *swamp* sprites," one of them corrected in an exasperated voice. He sounded as if he had had to explain this many times before. "And you'll find we're not nearly as soppy and sweet as our little lakeside cousins. We believe in taking a more aggressive approach to protecting our lovely home."

"We make sure the trees in our swamp grow big and strong and beautiful the whole year through," said another tinny voice. "Then daft mortals like you trample in and mess them all up!"

"Those ugly trolls are bad enough," said another. "They tear big strips off our poor trees and leave such nasty scars. And now we have to worry about humans and dragons to boot. That big lizard you flew in on did tons of damage. There are torn branches all over our beautiful swamp. We're going to take care of him next, just as soon as we're through with you...."

"It really is too bad you didn't just drown like a good, weak-minded little human," said a roguish green sprite. "It could have been so easy for you, but now we have to do things the hard way."

"The hard way?" Ivy backed up several steps, acutely aware there was really nowhere for her to go. "What do you mean?"

The little sprite grinned at her wickedly, exposing two long, fanglike front teeth. In a blink, he zipped over and sank the needle-sharp points into the soft flesh of Ivy's arm.

"Ouch!" Ivy swatted him off, but her arm burned where he had bitten her. Looking down, she noticed a large red bump already starting to swell upon her skin. So this is what had happened to the unfortunate young troll boy, she thought. His sores *were* bites, just as she had imagined, only not from giant mosquitoes....

"Get her!" one of the ill-tempered sprites shouted, and it was as if a battle cry had gone up. Sprites descended upon Ivy like a swarm of angry bees, biting and snapping and punching and kicking. Some even yanked on her hair, pulling out tiny fistfuls. Ivy screamed and flailed her arms wildly, trying to fend off the attacking creatures, but there were just too many of them. As she stumbled through the waist-deep water, she felt burning stings all over and didn't know how much more of this torture she could bear.

"Get off me, you little winged monsters!" she cried, burying her face in her hands as if she could hide from this nightmare. "Get off, get off, get off!"

"You heard her," came a huffy, indignant voice from out of the darkness. "I think it would be best if you stopped what you were doing."

The sprites were so startled they actually did stop what they were doing and looked around in confusion.

Ivy cautiously peered through her swollen fingers. Beneath some nearby trees, she could vaguely make out the silhouette of a large creature with folded wings and tightly bristled spines, the glow from the sprites' bodies glinting off its shiny, black scales.

"Elwidge!" she cried, faint with relief.

"It's that dragon," spat one of the sprites.

"Do somefink, Elwidge!" Ivy shouted, finding it difficult to talk around her swollen lips and cheeks. "Attack! Breave fire!"

"Fire?" The dragon looked uneasy. "Dear me, I don't think there's any need to resort to fire. I'm sure these good sprites will listen to reason—"

"You'll pay for what you did to our trees!" One of the sprites pointed a tiny finger at him. "Get that swamp-wrecking salamander!"

The sprites gathered into a giant glowing ball of light, as if preparing to launch a massive attack.

"Chawge, Elwidge—you're bigger dan dem. Chawge!"

Comprehension dawned on Elridge. Looking more than a little nervous, the dragon lowered his head, horns forward, and charged like an angry bull. He plowed headfirst into the swarm of sprites, and with little squeaks and squawks of dismay, they scattered before him like startled birds.

The dragon ground to a stop before Ivy, sending up a spray of swamp water.

"Oh, ugh, I hate getting wet," he complained, staring at his soaked scales in disgust. "Ivy, can you make it onto my back?" he asked, eyeing her with concern.

"I dink so," she mumbled. The princess clambered onto the dragon's back as fast as her tender arms and legs would allow.

"I'm going to try to get us out of here," said Elridge once she had gingerly nestled herself between two spines. "Hang on as best you can."

With a powerful flap of his wings, they were in the air once more.

"Da dwees," Ivy reminded him, remembering their failed attempt to leave the swamp earlier.

"We don't have to fly through the treetops." Elridge glanced behind them to see if the sprites were following. "I found the edge of the swamp. It's not far from here. Oh drat—those pesky little insects are coming after us."

Turning her head on a stiff neck, Ivy saw the sprites had indeed regrouped and were racing after the fleeing dragon like a shower of shooting stars. Elridge flapped his wings even faster, darting around tree trunks, but the mob of colored lights drew closer and closer.

"Don't those pests ever give up?" he asked, his voice aggravated. "Why are they so angry, anyway?"

"Dare upset dat we damaged da dwees."

"The trees, huh?" Elridge's voice was unusually low and calculating. "All right, then, let's see how they like this."

Gliding by a young alder covered in catkins, he gave its trunk a solid whack with his tail. The tree didn't uproot all the way, but it tipped precariously to one side, in grave danger of toppling over.

"Oh no!"

The air was suddenly awhirl with squeaky gasps and horrified voices.

"Quickly, save that tree!"

Ivy's last view of the sprites was of a constellation of lights surrounding the tilting tree, trying to push, pull, and tug its lopsided trunk upright once more. When she turned to face forward, she saw that the trees in front of Elridge were starting to thin considerably, then the dragon burst through the last of them in a miniature explosion of branches, twigs, and leaves. Stretched before them was an open, endless, moonlit plain.

"Whew," Elridge breathed, setting down in the stunted autumn grass. "I think we're safe now. I don't think those sprites will leave the swamp to come after us."

Ivy didn't reply. In the light of the full moon, she saw she was covered in purpling bruises and hundreds of painfully swollen sprite bites. She suddenly felt very weak and out of breath, and the world spun around her like a child's top.

"Ivy? Ivy, are you all right?" Elridge swung his long neck around to look at her.

"I...dohn't...peel...well," she mumbled feebly. The last thing she remembered as her fingers lost their grip on the dragon's spine was a flash of dark scales before her eyes, then the ground came rushing up to meet her.

A Misty Morning Conversation

Something flittered like a white moth on the edge of Ivy's awareness, a sound distant, lovely, and oh-so-familiar.

Birdsong, she thought happily.

She wanted to open her eyes and have a look, but this proved more daunting than she expected. Her cheek rested against a cool, soft surface, and her skin felt so comfortably warm. The muted red glow behind her eyelids told her some friendly light watched over her from above, blanketing her with its golden rays. She was sorely tempted to stay just as she was.

I'll open my eyes for a moment, she finally decided. *Just long enough to see where I am.*

And where she was, she discovered when she tentatively cracked open first one eye and then the other, was lying on a bed of grass in the middle of mist so thick it looked as if she could scoop it out of the air with her hands. Above this sea of white, a buttery sun was spreading itself across the hazy gray sky. Off in the distance, a happy meadowlark was singing its heart out.

Bewildered, Ivy sat up and looked around. She was in the center of a crescent formed by a ridge of rocks—but no, not rocks after all. It was Elridge's curled body, neck, and tail. His scales glinted in the light, even through the heavy mist.

Memories of the swamp rushed back to her like a douse of cold rainwater from a barrel.

"Elridge," she called urgently.

The dragon, who had been staring off distractedly into the swirling white tendrils, immediately lifted his head. Relief washed across his long, scaly features.

"Ivy, thank goodness! I was so worried. How do you feel?"

"I feel...fantastic," Ivy said, surprised. She was at a loss to explain it, but she had never felt so refreshed. Glancing down, she was astonished to find that her arms, which had been a ravaged mass of bruises and sprite bites, were now completely free of bumps or blemishes of any kind. All of her aches and pains had miraculously disappeared. With both hands, she carefully felt her lips and cheeks, pleased to discover they were just the size they should be.

"I can talk again," she laughed delightedly. "I mean, like someone who doesn't have a mouth full of marbles and cheeks the size of puffball mushrooms."

"That golden goblet is really something else," said Elridge. "After you fainted and fell off my back, I dug it out of your bag. I was afraid it might not work for dragons, but when I wrapped my claws around it, it filled right up. I poured nectar down your throat and splashed it all over you, just like you did for that troll boy. I think your dress and hair are still a bit wet," he added apologetically.

"So they are," Ivy chuckled, running fingers through her dampened hair. "I feel so good I didn't even notice."

What she did notice, with playful curiosity, was that Elridge's scales were not black as she had always believed. Rather, they were the color of a ripe plum—so purple they were almost black, and certainly looked so at night or within the depths of poorly lit caverns. But here in the sunlight, a purple sheen danced off them in the same dazzling way that light plays off peacock feathers.

Here in the sunlight. Ivy froze as the meaning of this sank in, and her good mood promptly vanished.

"Elridge," she gasped, horrified. "The sun is up!"

"I know," the dragon said miserably. He looked away, his face guilty. "You've been asleep for several hours. I thought about carrying you in my claws and flying back to Ardendale, but you were still unconscious and I was afraid to move you. I didn't know if you were okay."

"But that means Romil has been to the tower—and he knows that we've left," cried Ivy. "We were supposed to be back before sunrise. Oh, everyone's going to find out I've broken the treaty. The whole kingdom is going to hate me!"

"I'm sure word will get back to the Dragon Queen, too. She's not going to be happy," Elridge gulped, "and that's not a pretty sight."

"Elridge, what are we going to do?" Ivy suddenly felt uncomfortably warm and unclasped the blue cloak from around her neck so she could get some air.

"I've been thinking about that while you've been asleep," said Elridge. "Ivy, we have to keep going. We've come this far. Drusilla must be in that fairy kingdom the Guamp told us about—Felda the Farseeing wouldn't have sent us all this way if she wasn't."

"I'm beginning to think Felda is a few berries short of a pie," Ivy said crossly. "She sent us straight into troll territory and into the teeth of those rabid swamp sprites."

"Just because her predictions aren't easy doesn't mean they're not true," said Elridge, sounding a tad cross himself. "You need to wake up and smell the tea leaves. It's thanks to Felda that we even know where the entrance to the fairy kingdom is."

Ivy didn't say so, but she wasn't at all convinced this was Felda's doing. Finding out about the fairy mound could have just as easily been mere happenstance.

"Fairy cakes! My father's going to be so worried he'll go out of his mind—I mean, even more than usual," moaned the princess. "And Tildy—Tildy's going to be heartbroken."

"Ivy, we can't go back now," Elridge said. "No good will come of it. You'll just get locked in the tower again. I'll be forced to stand guard—and this time the Dragon Queen will see to it that I stay put, even if she has to station an entire troop of dragons there to guard *me*. Drusilla is the only chance we've got—we *have* to find this fairy kingdom."

Ivy was not convinced. What if her father, Tildy, and

the entire kingdom thought she had simply abandoned them because she was too selfish to stay in the tower? What if Romil hurt her father before she could warn him about what a black-hearted villain the prince really was? What if the valley was attacked by a horde of angry dragons, furious that a human princess had seen fit to break the Dragon Treaty? There were so many things that could go wrong. It hardly seemed the right time to run off in search of a fairy kingdom.

The princess's stomach rumbled loudly, and she realized that the last time she had eaten was almost a full day ago.

"I'm starving," she complained, more to fill up the awkward silence than anything else. "I wish I had a couple of Cook's almond cakes, the kind with strawberries and mountains of sweet cream on top. I'm so hungry I can even smell them."

"I can, too," said Elridge, who was so puzzled by this he seemed to have forgotten he was cross with her. He sniffed at the air with his melon-size nostrils and leaned down to nuzzle Ivy's tablecloth purse, which was lying by his side. "It's coming from in here."

Ivy undid the small bundle. In its center sat the golden goblet and the fragments of mirror as she had expected, but there was also a wonderful surprise—three small, pleasantly browned pastries, crowned with red berries and thick whirls of cream.

"It wasn't that old table in the tower that was magical," Ivy said in astonishment. "I thought it looked awfully ordinary. It was the golden tablecloth all along—it's a wishing cloth."

She snatched up one of the desserts and took a huge,

cream-filled bite. It was as warm as if fresh from Cook's oven.

"D'ya want somethin'?" she mumbled to Elridge, before thinking to swallow. "It doesn't have to be almond cakes. The wishing cloth will conjure up whatever you'd like—watch this.

"I wish I had a sausage pie," she said decisively, to no one in particular. "Nice and hot," she added for good measure, "and dripping with extra gravy."

Ivy couldn't have said exactly how it happened. One moment, the tablecloth was empty except for the goblet, pastries, and pieces of mirror, but the next there was a lovely flaky pie near the center of the sparkling fabric. Steam poured from it in delicious wafts, and brown juices bubbled through cracks in its golden crust. The famished princess was tickled by this feat of magic. Elridge, however, didn't look impressed.

"I'm not hungry," he said flatly. "I had a couple of wild goats a few days ago. Dragons only need to eat about once a week or so. We have big meals, so it takes us a long time to digest our food."

"Elridge, isn't there anyone back home who will worry about you?" Ivy asked, taking another bite of almond cake (she would have to work her way up to the sausage pie). It occurred to her that she still knew very little about this anxious young dragon. Maybe there was a reason he wasn't as eager to return home as she was.

"No one will worry," sniffed Elridge. "Although I'm sure they'll blame me for botching things up like I always do."

"That can't be true. You must have a family that cares about you," Ivy said. "Parents, brothers or sisters?"

"My mother thinks I'm a disgrace of a dragon," Elridge said bitterly, "and I only had one older brother. His name was Boldris, but he died."

"Elridge, that's terrible," said Ivy, feeling genuinely sorry for him. His life sounded so lonesome, and it must have been horrible to lose a brother.

"Well, we weren't very close," said Elridge, but he lowered his face and looked away. "He ridiculed me as much as all the other dragons. I think I embarrassed him, you know, because I'm so small and nervous all the time. I can't even find my fire."

"Find your fire?"

"Breathing fire is a chemical reaction for dragons," explained Elridge. "It takes a certain amount of willpower and ferocity to make it happen. Most dragons can breathe fire not long after they're hatchlings, but me... well, I've never been able to manage it. Can't seem to get a spark. The other dragons give me no end of grief about it."

No wonder Elridge hadn't tried breathing fire in the swamp, thought the princess. Poor Elridge. She had never heard of a dragon who couldn't breathe fire.

"Boldris was everything a dragon is supposed to be, and everything I'm not—big and ferocious and fire-breathing. Even if he was ashamed of me, it's sad to think he's gone. He was my brother, after all."

"What happened to him?" Ivy asked. She didn't like to stir up bad memories for Elridge, but her curiosity had gotten the better of her. She didn't think dragons died easily, especially when they were young.

Elridge looked extremely uncomfortable, and for a moment Ivy thought he wasn't going to answer.

"He was the last dragon chosen to guard the tower," he said finally, a miserable look on his reptilian face.

"The tower? But that means..." Ivy's voiced trailed off, a clump of cream catching in her throat. It suddenly tasted dry and flavorless, like a lump of sand. The princess swallowed hard. "The dragon my father slayed was...your brother?" Ivy felt stricken. It was a moment before she could speak again, and her voice was so choked she could barely get the words out. "Elridge, I don't know what to say...I'm so incredibly sorry."

"It's not your fault." Elridge sighed heavily, resigning himself to this unpleasant topic of conversation. "It's not your father's fault, either. I mean, he was just doing what princes do when they come to the tower. Boldris was something fierce. He had already finished off a good number of princes before your father turned up. If your father hadn't slayed Boldris, then Boldris would have made mincemeat out of him. It was going to be one or the other of them."

An icy chill descended upon Ivy. What a horrible thought—that one of them had had to die, that Elridge's brother had met such a terrible fate at her father's hands. That same fate awaited Elridge, this most unthreatening dragon who had just saved her own life. And his slaying would only be the first of Prince Romil's awful deeds.

"You're right," she said softly. "We have to keep going,

even if my father and Tildy will worry. We have to find Drusilla and stop Romil."

"I'm glad you think so," said Elridge, although his expression was anything but glad. "Ivy, I owe you an apology. If I hadn't gotten spooked by the lights in the swamp, you would have never gotten attacked by those sprites. Good goat fur, those winged mites could have killed you. And I was so scared I didn't even realize you had fallen—not until I looked back and you weren't there.

"I'm such a pathetic excuse for a dragon. I can't do anything right. No wonder my mother is so disappointed in me."

Ivy thought of Tildy with a pang. "I'm a disappointment, too," she said.

Elridge looked surprised. "You?"

"Yes, me," said Ivy, a little annoyed at his disbelief. "Do you think princesses usually try to climb down the outsides of towers?"

"I suppose not," said Elridge. "I never gave princesses much thought before."

"Well, my nursemaid thinks about them all the time," Ivy said sourly, "and what a sorry one I am."

"Good to know I'm not the only sorry creature around here." Elridge drooped his scaly shoulders. "I don't know how I manage to get myself into these messes. I mean, my brother would never have let himself be captured by trolls or scared by water sprites—water sprites, for crying out loud!"

Ivy didn't think this was the right moment to point out they were actually *swamp* sprites.

"Well, my mother would never have left the tower and

run off to the Craggies with a dragon," she said, "but I'm not my mother." She would always feel badly about causing Tildy distress, but if she had been the type of princess who never set so much as a toe out of line, she would never have met Elridge—and she found she rather liked this fainthearted, slightly-smaller-than-average dragon.

"And you're not your brother," she told him, "and I'm glad for that. Any other dragon wouldn't have bothered to save me if they saw me fall from the tower; you said so yourself. I'm guessing any other dragon wouldn't have offered to fly me into the Craggies, either. And you did come back for me in the swamp, and that was before you even knew the spirits were only sprites.

"You've been very brave, Elridge," she declared firmly. "You're a very special dragon, and I like you just the way you are."

Elridge suddenly looked exceedingly embarrassed. He still wouldn't look her in the eye, but there was a pleased half smile on his face that he just couldn't hide. Ivy thought he would be blushing, if dragons could blush.

"Come on," she said. "Let's find this fairy kingdom and have a chat with that godmother of mine."

The Murmurs

"I see it—I see the fairy mound!" exclaimed Elridge. "And those stones, the Murmurs. I knew they couldn't be far from here. I thought I saw a hill in the distance when we landed last night, before all this icky mist rolled in, but I was too worried about you to pay much attention."

The mist may have been thick, but luckily for Ivy and Elridge it was also low, clinging to the grassy plain like a layer of unspun cotton. When Elridge stood on all fours, his neck and head rose well above the banks of white, and he could scan the surrounding area with his keen dragon eyesight.

"What does it look like? How far is it? Can you tell if the stones are singing?" asked Ivy excitedly. Unlike the lofty dragon, she remained well below the mist-line, so the only thing she could see was, well, mist.

"Climb up and have a look for yourself," Elridge chuckled.

Ivy, her belly now comfortably full of almond cakes and sausage pie, scrambled onto his back. With one hand on his long neck to steady herself, she carefully stood on the ridge of his back and stretched up on tiptoes until her head peeked above the mist.

She could now see that it surrounded them entirely in every direction, like a sea of clouds. The ground was completely hidden by white, and the only things Ivy could make out were the treetops of Wrathful Swamp at their backs and, in front of them, in the distance, the rounded cap of a large hill that rose out of the mist like an island. A ring of tall standing stones encircled its crest like a crown, and Ivy knew these could only be the Murmurs the Guamp had told them about. She guessed the mysterious fairy mound was no more than a league away, although she couldn't see the base of the hill where it met the ground.

"That has to be it, all right," she said. "Shall we fly?"

"Um, I'd actually feel better if we walked," the dragon said, looking sheepish. "It's not that far, and if someone or something happens to be waiting there, we'd be better off if we sneaked up quietly in the mist."

Ivy had to suppress a smile. Elridge really was very cautious for a dragon. "Suit yourself," she said.

The walk was actually a very easy one, for the plain was as flat as a reed mat. The only unpleasant thing about being on the ground was that Ivy had to rely on Elridge to lead the way.

"Elridge, do you mind if I ask how old you are?" She was careful to speak quietly due to the dragon's apprehension that something might be lying in wait for them. She had been thinking of what Tildy had once told her about dragons living for hundreds and hundreds of years. Curiously, Elridge seemed no older than she. Everything about him spoke of youth, from the tightness and gloss of his scales to his rather timid nature. He frightened as easily as a young child, but Ivy had a suspicion this had nothing to do with age.

"Of course not," Elridge said, keeping his own voice low as well. "I'm a hundred and one, by human years."

"A hundred and one!" Ivy exclaimed, remembering too late that she was trying to be quiet. "Sorry." She lowered her voice. "It's just that I don't know anyone that old, not even my father, and he always says he's older than the dirt in the fields."

"A hundred and one is actually pretty young for a dragon. I'm the youngest of all my kindred," said Elridge. "But I've heard humans are notoriously short-lived. How old do you usually get, about eighteen or nineteen?"

"A bit more." Ivy laughed. "We're not *that* short-lived."

They continued to pick their way across the mist-shrouded plain. Ivy felt very comfortable in the sunlight that filtered through to the ground. She had left her blue cloak behind, finding it too heavy now that they had left the snow-swept mountains and not having room for it in her tablecloth purse. Before tying up the tablecloth once more, she had taken the opportunity to try out what was left of the magic mirror. She had asked a shard to show her Romil, but like before, it had merely fogged over uselessly. With a heavy heart, Ivy realized the enchantment of the mirror might be truly broken.

"Dear me, I hope my treasure is okay," Elridge said worriedly. "Maybe I shouldn't have left it in the rocks by the tower. You don't think Romil found it, do you? Maybe he didn't even look. Maybe he figured since there was no dragon, there'd be no treasure."

"My father says that dragon treasure...isn't what it used to be," said Ivy. She wondered if Elridge's treasure was as small as the one the king had claimed from Boldris.

"It's not like it was in the days before the Dragon Treaty," admitted Elridge. "Since my kindred stopped attacking humans, we've had no one to steal treasure from. We had a nice stash built up in the Smoke Sands, of course, but it's dwindled over the years, and my kindred have terrible fights over what little is left.

"Of course, I don't much like fighting, so I just sort of get what's left over once the other dragons are done battling it out. It's not much, but I've never been that taken with gold and gems, anyway, so I guess it doesn't really matter."

"Wait a minute—if your treasure isn't gold or gems, then what is it?" asked Ivy.

Elridge suddenly looked extremely embarrassed. "Well... it's...sort of...an old book," the dragon finished lamely.

"A book?" Ivy's eyes widened in surprise.

"It was at the bottom of a chest of coins," explained Elridge. "None of the other dragons wanted it. They wanted to burn it, in fact, thought it was some silly human artifact, but I took it when no one was looking. It's my treasure—the only treasure I've got."

"I didn't know dragons could read," said Ivy.

"I can't," said Elridge. "But it's full of pictures, Ivy—wonderful pictures of castles and sailing ships and walled cities, of minstrels and maidens—and even dragons. They're so colorful and full of life. I like looking at them and imagining what their story is, what the words say." Elridge hung his head. "I know it's not a very dragonly thing to do. It makes the other dragons laugh. You probably think it's pretty laughable, too." He looked away, shame written across his scaly face.

"No, of course not," said Ivy, giving him a gentle smile. "I like books, too. There are some fantastic ones in the castle library. When we get back to the kingdom, I can—" The princess stopped herself. She had been about to say she could show them to Elridge, but, of course, that was a ridiculous thought. Even if they managed to stop Romil, she would still have to go back in the tower. And sooner or later, another prince would come along, sure to make short work of poor Elridge....

"Ivy." The dragon's voice interrupted these unpleasant thoughts. "Do you hear that?"

The princess turned one ear in the direction of the mound. Drifting through the mist on a light breeze was the loveliest music she had ever heard. A collection of haunting, reedy notes trilled on the morning air, like a dozen fairy flutes being played all at once.

"It's beautiful," Elridge said, mesmerized. "That must be the stones singing. We're very close now."

Sure enough, a few minutes later the fairy mound loomed into view, and the wondrous music grew louder the closer they drew to its slopes.

"Be careful," whispered Elridge. "Fairies can be mischievous creatures. They're not above toying with mortals for fun."

"But I'm Drusilla's goddaughter," Ivy whispered back. "Surely they wouldn't do anything to me. I mean, I'm practically family."

They climbed the hill slowly, rising from the mist out into the open sky. Despite all of Elridge's caution, it seemed as if they were very much alone. At the top, seven oblong stones stood in a stately circle, each one taller than Ivy. It was from these that the music originated. The surface of each stone was punctured with a scattering of apple-size holes. Some were so deep, they went all the way through the rock and you could peer through them like windows. On their lofty perch at the hill's crest, the stones were left to the whims of the fickle wind. It blew across and through the holes, weaving a beautifully random flutelike melody in the air, one that no human musician could hope to rival.

Ivy understood at once why the stones were called the Murmurs. The music they produced was soft and rolling, yet chatty, like a number of brooks flowing together to form one gently babbling stream.

"So, if this is the entrance to the fairy kingdom, how do we get in?" Elridge asked, looking around. "I don't see a door or anything, do you?"

Ivy shook her head. For the next several minutes, they combed the hilltop, looking in and around each of the seven stones, and even scouring the ground for some sort of hatch or hole.

"Maybe there's something at the bottom," said Ivy.

The pair trudged back down and circled the base of the hill.

"Ivy, look at this," said Elridge. "It kind of looks like a door, don't you think?"

He indicated the side of the mound, where there was the definite outline of an arch in the damp earth. It looked as if someone had sliced out a sizable piece of hillside, then tried to stuff it back in. The fit was imperfect, the same way you can never put a slice of pie back with the whole and have it look like a normal, uncut pie again. There was a noticeable crack, through which feathery tendrils of mist were seeping.

"All this mist is coming from inside the mound," marveled Ivy. "There has to be something in there."

"So how do we get inside?" Elridge asked.

Ivy slipped her fingers into the tiny crack on one side of the massive arch and pulled for all she was worth. The giant earthen door didn't even budge.

"Do you think you can get it open?" she asked Elridge.

But even the strength of a dragon was no match for the stubborn fairy portal. Elridge clawed, tugged, and pushed at the chunk of hillside for several minutes to no avail.

"I don't think...outsiders...are meant...to get in," panted the dragon. He started to say more, but something caught his attention. He cocked his head to one side, listening intently.

Ivy heard it, too. The music had changed ever so slightly. A new instrument had joined in with the song of the stones.

It played the same ethereal melody, but sounded distinctly different—more solid and real than its airy counterparts. There was also the low tinkling of bells.

Ivy clambered up the hill to investigate before the wary dragon could stop her. As she gained the top, a spot of white moving across the hazy sky drew her eye. Sailing over the ocean of mist was what appeared to be a young man on a white horse. He had delicately handsome features topped with a shock of midnight-black hair, the only dark thing about him. His clothes were gleaming white, as was his fairy steed, which trod through the air on polished hooves as easily as a non-magical horse might run through a meadow. Its bridle and snowy mane were adorned with hundreds of tiny silver bells, which jangled pleasantly with the creature's every move.

"Oh, good goat fur, it's a fairy," muttered Elridge as he reluctantly trailed Ivy up the rise. "I hope we're not in for trouble."

But, amazingly, the rider of the flying horse didn't even seem to notice they were there, although Ivy would have thought a dragon on top of a hill would be hard to miss. The carefree youth sat sideways in his saddle rather than astride. A pipe was at his lips, and he was utterly absorbed in re-creating the stones' intricate tune. Eyes closed, head thrown back, he swayed slightly to the music as he played, completely oblivious to the world around him.

"Is it me, or did it just get even mistier around here?" Elridge asked the princess in a puzzled voice.

Looking down, Ivy saw this was indeed the truth. The

mist cloaking the bottom half of the hill had risen a good measure in the last few moments. Glancing at the entrance to the fairy kingdom, the princess saw why.

"It's the door," she said. "Elridge, it's opening!"

The large slice of hill was slowly lowering into the earth, like a portcullis that retracted down rather than up. Billows of escaping mist prevented Ivy from seeing what was on the other side.

"Of course, the music is like a key," said Elridge, realization lighting his golden eyes. "You match the stones' song, and the door opens. Oh, we'd best slip inside with our fairy friend. Music like that is not something us mortals can make, even if we had instruments to play."

"I don't think he's going to let us waltz into the fairy kingdom just because he's opened the door," Ivy said. "And you're much too big to slip in unnoticed. But maybe if we ask, maybe if I explain that I'm Drusilla's goddaughter, he'll help us find her.

"Hello," she shouted at the approaching rider, cupping her hands around her mouth to carry the sound. "Excuse me—can you help us please?"

But the fairy piper showed no sign of having heard her. He continued to blow fervently on his pipe, not once opening his eyes.

"Hello," Ivy called again, a little louder this time. "Hello! Excuse me!"

Like a honeybee into the folds of a flower, the white horse slipped into the hole in the side of the hill. Its preoccupied rider didn't look back. The music from his pipe began to fade within the misty depths of the mound, and the earthen door started to rise once more.

"Oh no," cried Elridge. "We have to move quickly!"

Ivy was about to make a mad dash for the bottom when the dragon leaped off the hillside in one fluid motion and spread his wings wide. Almost as an afterthought, his tail whipped out and wrapped tightly around her waist, jerking her off the ground and towing her through the air behind him. He shot like a dart through what was left of the shrinking opening.

On the other side, the mist was so thick the only thing Ivy could make out was the black hair of the heedless rider in front of them, swiftly disappearing from view as his magical horse carried him away.

"Wait!" Ivy shouted desperately from where she bobbed behind Elridge like a hooked worm on the end of a fishing line. "Please wait! I need to talk to you. I'm looking for my godmother, Drusilla."

But it was no use. With one last trill of warbling notes, the fairy piper was gone, swallowed whole by the waiting white.

21

The Underground Lake

The earthen door slid into place behind them with a soft but distinct *click*, which echoed through the airy passage ominously. There was no leaving the fairy mound now. Ivy had expected it to go dark, but it remained bright as day in the strange underground realm, even if the only thing she could see was mist as thick as good egg custard.

Elridge landed carefully and released her from the coiled grip of his tail.

"That fairy completely ignored us," said the princess. "It was like we didn't even exist." She was stunned and more than a little insulted. She recalled Tildy describing Drusilla as flighty. She had always dismissed this as one of Tildy's endless complaints—the nursemaid was so fond of complaining, after all—but what if this time she had been right? What if all fairies were that way? Would Drusilla ignore them, too? Hadn't she run out on Ivy when the princess was a newborn baby?

"I can't believe he just let us stroll into the fairy kingdom," said Elridge. "Well, okay, more like dive desperately, but still, you'd think they'd guard it a little better. And you'd think it would look nicer, too," he added, eyeing the persistent white mist with distaste. "Dear me, it's worse in here than out on the plain."

"So what do we do now?" asked Ivy.

"That flying horse was taking his rider somewhere," Elridge reasoned. "I say we head in the same direction." He nodded toward the drifts of white into which the fairy youth had disappeared. "I just wish we could see where we were going," he said uneasily.

It was an unnerving journey for both the princess and the dragon. Ivy had to hold on to the tip of Elridge's tail to avoid losing him in the mist. After bumping into hard stone walls on either side, they determined they were in a rather narrow passageway, and the only way to go was forward. Before long, the ground began to slope downward. Ivy fervently hoped they didn't walk straight into a pit or off the edge of a cliff. Trudging very slowly, venturing even deeper underground, they walked and walked and walked until, suddenly and without warning, they walked straight out of the mist, and a panorama of the world beneath the mound opened before them.

"Oh no, not another cavern," Elridge groaned, "and this one has water in it to boot."

They stood in a vast underground cavern at least ten times larger than anything they had seen in the trolls' domain inside the Craggies. Stretched before them were the murky waters of an immense underground lake. It reached so far into the distance, Ivy couldn't see the other side. The water was a strange milky green color, undoubtedly tinged with minerals and rock salt leached from the surrounding cave walls. Since she couldn't see the bottom, there was no way of telling how deep the waters ran.

Only a whisper of mist remained here, skimming the surface. The rest of it had apparently drifted away from the lake and collected in the confines of the narrow passageway near the door, where it leaked out of the mound and into the world above.

For the first time, Ivy could see why there was light so deep underground. The cave walls were splotched with a silver-gray lichen that actually glowed, emitting a soft, constant light that brightened the subterranean world as surely as the sun. Patches of mushrooms flourished here and there among the lichen, and these, too, glowed.

The cavern's ceiling was low and uneven, dripping with stalactites. Some of them were so long, they bored into the surface of the water and disappeared beneath. There was space enough for a horse to fly over the lake, but certainly not a dragon.

"The only way our fairy friend could have gone was across the water," said Ivy, studying the seemingly boundless lake before her with a growing trepidation. "There's no way I could swim that far. What about you, Elridge? Can dragons swim?"

"Of course we can," said Elridge, a bit indignantly. "We just don't like to. Dragons are creatures of fire, not water. Well, most dragons, anyway. As you know, I'm not one for fire myself. I mean, it *is* rather hot and unpredictable—"

"Elridge," Ivy broke in, "you're going to have to swim us across the lake."

"What?" Elridge started to protest, but gave in as soon as he saw the unyielding look on the princess's face. "Oh, all right. I guess we have no choice. But I hate getting wet. That blasted swamp was bad enough."

The water was cold but not unbearable. Sitting astride Elridge's back, Ivy found that her ankles dangled into the lake on either side. She tucked the skirts of her dress about her knees to keep them as dry as possible. She was sure that Elridge, with his thick plating of dragon scales, felt very little of the cold.

Despite the dragon's reluctance to get in the water, he made good time in crossing the lake. He cleaved the water like a small but sturdy ship, paddling with his powerful limbs and using his wings like oars to propel himself forward. His tail served as a rudder; he swished it from side to side, steering around low-hanging stalactites covered in luminous lichen and mushrooms.

It wasn't long before Ivy lost sight of the shore behind them and something new came into view in the distance.

"Elridge," she said with a gasp. "Do you see that?"

An island unlike anything Ivy had ever seen perched on the horizon like a promise—or a dream. It reminded her uncannily of a pedestal. It was perfectly round and rose high into the air, its sides solid white cliffs all the way down to the water. The plateau at the top displayed an entire sparkling white kingdom. Ivy could see turrets and spires and lofty walkways, elegantly arched windows too numerous to count, and peaked rooftops capping buildings that must have been at least ten stories high. The buildings grew higher closer to the middle of the island, so the whole kingdom resembled a mountain, with its summit a spire at the very center, flying a long white banner. Every edifice was constructed of crystal or sparkling white quartz, and the entire island gleamed like a jewel in the sun. It was the most beautiful place Ivy had ever seen.

"Good goat fur, that's a fairy kingdom if I ever saw one," Elridge said, awestruck. "Which, of course, I haven't," he added after a moment's thought.

"The cavern really opens up around the island," observed Ivy. She had noticed that the cavern's ceiling became high and vaulted to accommodate the tall island and its buildings. "If we can get out from under this low part, you could fly us up those cliffs."

"I just wish we knew what was waiting for us at the top," Elridge said uncertainly, but he began paddling toward the white island all the same.

"What was that?" he said suddenly, stopping dead in the water and glancing around nervously.

"What was what?" Ivy asked.

"I felt something brush against my leg," the dragon said uneasily.

"Seaweed?" Ivy guessed.

"In a *cave?*" said Elridge disbelievingly. He started violently. "I just felt it again," he hissed in an urgent whisper. "Ivy...I think something's in the water."

The princess sighed inwardly. She was sure Elridge was jumping at shadows yet again. He had probably swept past an underwater boulder or a school of fish or something completely harmless, and was now convinced they were in mortal peril.

"I don't see anything," she said impatiently.

"Over there!" Elridge yelled.

Turning in the direction the dragon was looking, Ivy spotted a large, long shadow gliding just beneath the surface of the murky water, heading straight for them. Little bubbles began to break the surface as whatever-it-was drew nearer.

"Elridge, we have to get out of here, quickly!" Ivy shouted.

But she needn't have said anything at all, for the dragon had already started in the opposite direction as fast as he could go, his limbs, wings, and tail all paddling furiously.

"Oh dear, oh dear, oh dear!"

Elridge was no match for the underwater creature, who seemed able to propel itself across the lake at amazing speed. In a matter of moments, the shadow had slid directly beneath the fleeing dragon, and a giant white tentacle shot up out of the water. It was lined with two rows of large circular cups, which suctioned onto Elridge's scales as it wrapped around the dragon and squeezed tight.

"Omphf," panted Elridge. "Get off me, you...you...big squid!"

The dragon flailed wildly and tried to pry himself from

the creature's grasp, but the tentacle only closed around him tighter. Several others snaked out of the water, and soon the dragon was at the center of a writhing mass of grappling, clutching, and clinging octopus arms.

A much smaller target than Elridge, Ivy managed to stay free of the questing appendages, ducking as they twisted and coiled around the struggling dragon. She grabbed the nearest tentacle and tried to wrench it from Elridge's scales, but it held as if stuck with a batch of Boggs's boiled rabbitskin glue. She slapped at it hard and screamed in frustration when this seemed to make no difference.

In the water next to them, the octopus's pale, bulbous head emerged to examine its prey, an enormous unblinking eye at the center.

"Ivy, help!" Elridge yelled. "This thing is trying to pull me under!"

Sure enough, Ivy felt herself sinking into the water and realized Elridge was slowly being dragged down into the depths of the lake.

"Ivy, do something," implored the dragon.

The princess looked around desperately for something—anything—she could use against the giant octopus, but they were in the middle of a lake, and there wasn't even a handy stick she could try to beat it off with. All she had were the few items in her tablecloth purse, and they wouldn't do her any good. Unless . . .

"Ivvvyyyyy . . ." The rest of Elridge's plea was lost as his head was pulled beneath the waves.

Ivy had to move fast. Her mind made up, she thrust one

hand into her tablecloth purse and drew out the largest of the shards of broken glass. She leaned toward the octopus's giant head and, in one swift movement, drove the pointed shard directly into the center of the creature's single eye. It exploded in a river of white pus and sticky blue blood, coating Ivy's hand. The octopus wailed like a banshee, so loudly that Ivy's ears rang, and it thrashed about in pain. Its arms recoiled like springs, setting off a series of loud pops as the suckers detached. The creature dived beneath the waves, desperate to get away. Its cries faded as it disappeared into the unseen depths of the lake.

Elridge shot up out of the water so fast, Ivy was thrown from his back. She landed in the lake with a splash and heard him taking in big, heaving gulps of air. The ties of her tablecloth purse had apparently loosened when she rummaged through it for the shard, for she felt it come undone and slip from her wrist. She tried to grab for it, but with the weight of the golden goblet, it sank fast, out of her reach almost as soon as she realized it had broken free. She focused on treading water instead.

"Elridge, are you all right?" she asked the dragon, who was now completely drenched and still laboring to catch his breath.

"I...hate...getting...wet," he wheezed grumpily in reply.

22

The Gatekeeper and His Gargoyles

Elridge offered to help look for the tablecloth purse before they continued on to the island, but Ivy quickly waved away this suggestion.

"I don't think we could find it even if we had the time to look," said the princess. "For all we know, this lake could be as deep as the Speckled Sea."

So much for the tower's enchanted objects, she thought bitterly. Not only had she broken the magic mirror, but now the golden goblet and the wishing cloth were lying at the bottom of an underground lake, never to be seen again. If nothing else, she would have the distinction of being the princess who single-handedly managed to destroy the tower's entire collection of magical treasures while also breaking the Dragon Treaty.

She still clutched the large shard of mirror she had used to stab the giant octopus. The lake had rinsed both princess and shard clean of the disgusting blue blood. She tucked it into the spiderskin the Guamp had given her, which was still wound tightly around her waist.

They moved on once Elridge had sufficiently recovered his breath and Ivy had reseated herself on the ridge of his back. There was only a little way to go before they reached the part of the cavern where the ceiling heightened enough for Elridge to fly. The dragon watched the water nervously, keeping an eye out for more giant octopi or other possible threats lurking beneath. As soon as he was able, he spread his wings and launched himself into the air, setting off a shower of water droplets that dimpled the surface of the lake and pattered like rain. It was a wobbly takeoff that required extra effort on his part, since he had no solid ground from which to push off.

"Good-bye, monster-infested lake," he said with relief as he took to the air.

In only a matter of moments, they had crested the white cliffs that encircled the island and were soaring about the airy heights of the fairy kingdom.

"It's incredible," sighed Ivy, who found the quartz towers and crystal spires even more beautiful up close.

There appeared to be some sort of celebration going on. The walkways and quartz-cobbled roads positively bustled with fairies—all handsome young men and beautiful young women swathed in tunics and gowns of white. Ivy could see they had violet eyes like those of Felda the Farseeing, only deeper in color and even more brilliantly gemlike. Each fairy had the same impossibly fair skin, although their hair color varied from golden to sunset auburn to black as coal. They were as jubilant as children—laughing, feasting, and dancing. A good number had musical instruments in hand; Ivy saw pipes, lutes, harps, even a hurdy-gurdy. White peacocks wandered the byways or perched on rooftops watching the festivities, their enormous tails spread out behind them like lacy fans. Everything in the kingdom sparkled, down to the peacocks' frothy white tail feathers.

If any of the revelers noticed a dragon with a human girl on its back circling their crystalline city, they showed no sign of it.

Elridge searched for a place to set down, but as soon as he got within a pebble's throw of one of the tall spires, he recoiled forcefully, as if he had flown straight into a wall and bounced off. Ivy held on tightly as the dragon stretched his wings to either side as far as he could, straight as a stick, trying to slow their backward reel through the air.

"What happened?" she asked once Elridge had managed to regain control.

"Good goat fur, there's something there, a wall of some sort, I think," the dragon said, shaking his head as if coming out of a daze. "You can't see it, but I flew straight into whatever it was. Oh, I knew these fairies would be trouble—I just knew it!"

"Try again," Ivy said. "But a little more carefully this time."

Elridge reluctantly approached the white heights of the fairy kingdom once again, this time very slowly and cautiously, one claw extended before him, palm out. Ivy heard a soft thump as the claw met with something solid. Elridge flew a short distance to one side, then the other. Both times his claws found the same unseen barrier.

"It's like an invisible dome around the entire kingdom," he said in an amazed voice. "It must be some type of fairy magic to protect the kingdom from unwanted guests."

"Do you think there's another way in?" asked Ivy.

Elridge continued his flight around the island. A few wispy strands of mist clung to the creviced cliff walls, but it was nothing compared to what they had traipsed through to get here.

"Elridge, look!" shouted the princess.

They had reached the other side of the island, where a thick finger of rock peeled away from the cliffside like a gigantic tree branch, creating a long shelf that jutted out over the water. An arched gateway of pure crystal perched here. It was bigger than the castle gate back home, tall, delicately carved, and beautiful, with four chiseled crystal gargoyles guarding its opening, two on either side. Oddly enough, the gate seemed to open onto nothing, for the only thing on the other side was the deep chasm that separated the rock shelf from the main island. A short fairy with fiery red hair stood before the entrance. He wore a pointed cap with a golden tassel at the tip, and an impish expression. Ivy assumed he was the gatekeeper, although he seemed rather small and unimposing for the job.

There were two fairies lined up before him, as if waiting to pass through the gate. The gatekeeper and the first fairy were having a rather animated conversation. The stunning young woman appeared to say something that greatly disappointed the gatekeeper, and with an airy wave of his hand, he stood aside to let her pass. In a burst of sparks, a white rainbow arched from the base of the gate, growing longer and longer until it spanned the void to reach the island at the other end. It shimmered with a sheen like ice. Looking delighted, the fairy woman dashed across the rainbow bridge.

"Did you see that?" Elridge gasped. "Good goat fur, I'm not sure I like having all this fairy magic around. It makes me nervous. The whole place is crawling with it."

The dragon landed just as the second fairy, a handsome but worried-looking young man with hair the color of ripe wheat, was about to step forward. There was a beautiful white mare by his side, and Ivy figured he must have just flown in.

"Excuse me," she asked hesitantly. "Is this the way onto the island?"

She half expected him to ignore her, but he seemed not only willing but perfectly happy to chat.

"Of course it is," he replied in a friendly voice, "if you can answer whatever nonsense the gatekeeper decides to throw at you. I don't see why we can't have a normal gatekeeper that just waves people in and out of the kingdom. I'm useless at riddles, you know. Sometimes it takes me four or five tries to get inside."

He didn't seem to find it strange that a dragon and a human girl wanted to enter the fairy kingdom. In fact, he acted as if this were an ordinary, everyday conversation, and

Ivy wondered if he had even noticed that they *were* a dragon and human girl at all.

"Riddles?" she asked, puzzled by this, but before the young fairy could say more, the gatekeeper sang out impatiently:

"Befuddle and perplex, I'm ready—who is next?"

"I better get on with it, then." The fairy youth sighed and turned away.

It was then Ivy noticed the rainbow bridge had disappeared once again. The golden-haired fairy reluctantly approached the gatekeeper, who began to recite in a high, singsong voice:

> *Welcome to the fair Isle of Mist,*
> *To cross this hold, answer me this:*
> *What has no hands, but arms, legs, and feet,*
> *A slender back but a well-padded seat?*

"That's easy." Elridge bent his long neck so he could whisper into Ivy's ear. "It's a chair. Even I can figure that out, and dragons don't even use chairs."

But the young man was apparently as bad at riddles as he claimed. He brooded over the gatekeeper's question for a full minute or two, only to scratch his head, looking baffled.

"Is it a spotted newt that's grown arms?" he asked hopefully. "Arms without hands on them, I mean."

"Dance and song, that's woefully wrong!" crowed the gatekeeper. He looked thrilled that he had managed to stump the none-too-bright fairy, and he snapped his fingers sharply. The gargoyles on either side of him jumped to life at once and eagerly advanced upon the young man. Laughing uproariously, they hoisted him high over their bald crystal heads.

"Oh bother, I hate this part," the fairy grumbled.

Without a moment's hesitation, the gargoyles trotted to the edge of the rock ledge and chucked the young man over the side.

"Whhhhhoooooaaaaa…"

Stifling a scream, Ivy dashed to the edge just in time to see the fairy's body hit the waters of the lake far below with a splash and disappear beneath the surface.

"WHAT HAVE YOU DONE?" she shrieked at the gatekeeper, but the little red-haired fairy was laughing so hard, tears coursed down his face, and he bent over, clutching his belly. The gargoyles chortled uncontrollably like a pack of hyenas. They could barely stay upright and had to lean against one another for support. They seemed to find the demise of the unlucky riddle-solver hilarious.

Horrified and disgusted, Ivy peered down at the water once more. Miraculously, the head and shoulders of the young man emerged from the waves, and he bobbed in the water as if he had no more than taken a leisurely dip. A human would have been lucky to survive such a plummet, but in her shock the princess had forgotten that fairies were immortal. She released a breath she hadn't realized she'd been holding. The white mare, looking as if she had done this many times before and knew the routine, stepped off the rocky outcrop and flew toward the water, undoubtedly on her way to collect her master from the lake.

"Maybe we ought to think twice about this riddle thing," Ivy said, her voice faint and her heart still drumming furiously against her rib cage.

"Ivy, don't worry," said Elridge. For once, the dragon sounded completely sure of himself. "That riddle was as easy as cornering a blind goat in a gully. I'm sure we'll have no problem answering the next one."

"I'm not sure I want to risk it," said Ivy. "A fairy might be able to survive a fall like that, but if I go over the side of that cliff, I'm not coming back."

"Ivy, you're forgetting I can fly." Elridge lifted one wing as if to remind her he had them. "I promise to catch you if someone throws you over the edge."

Ivy didn't find this particularly comforting, but she knew she would have to take the chance. Drusilla could well be on the other side of that bridge, so the princess had to play the gatekeeper's brutal game.

By this time, the gatekeeper had managed to pull himself together. He straightened up and wiped the tears from his eyes, and the gargoyles resumed their posts on either side of the gate. Unmoving, they looked like harmless statues, but now Ivy knew better.

"Daylight is fading," the gatekeeper chided. "Don't keep me waiting."

"No, wouldn't want to do that," Ivy muttered under her breath.

With one last uncertain look at Elridge, who smiled and nodded reassuringly, she stepped forward to receive their challenge.

The Crystal Kingdom

The gatekeeper lost no time setting his riddle before them. In an overly grand voice, he proudly warbled:

> *I can bring light where before there was none,*
> *But lock me up tight and away with the sun,*
> *A bird in flight or a moon on the wane,*
> *An ever-changing sight, but always the same.*

Elridge's jaw dropped so low, Ivy thought it might hit the ground.

"Huh?" he croaked weakly. "But...I mean...couldn't we answer the one about the chair?"

"Lace, linen, and ribbon, you'll take the riddle you're given," said the gatekeeper crabbily.

"Fine," the dragon muttered.

"Elridge, I thought you said this was going to be easy." Ivy didn't try to keep the accusing tone out of her voice.

"It will be, it will be," Elridge said. "We just need to look at this logically. It's something that brings light and has something to do with birds and the moon, and it changes but always stays the same."

"Right, because there are lots of things that change but always stay the same," snapped Ivy. She had warned Elridge this was a bad idea! Now she wondered how long the gatekeeper would wait before setting his gang of gargoyles upon them.

"So first let's try to think of things that bring light," Elridge continued, as if he hadn't heard her. "There's the sun, fire, candles, lanterns...."

"None of those things have anything to do with birds or the moon," Ivy said impatiently.

"You should be hasting; time is a-wasting," warned the gatekeeper. Both the princess and dragon roundly ignored him.

"Well, the sun is the opposite of the moon, and birds like the sun," said Elridge.

"The sun is already part of the riddle, remember?" said Ivy. " 'But lock me up tight and away with the sun?' Weren't you even listening?"

"Look, there's no need to get prickly about it," said Elridge. A touch of agitation was starting to creep into his voice now, as well. "You're not helping matters. Just try to stay calm."

Maybe it's easy for you to stay calm, thought Ivy resentfully. A fall from a cliff was no big deal to a dragon with a set of wings. She was in much more danger.

"Fine," she said. "Let's just try to think. We need an answer."

"We need an answer," echoed Elridge. His brow furrowed. "Why do I feel like I've heard that before?"

"Bell and chime, you're out of time," announced the gatekeeper gleefully.

"What? We barely had any time at all!" Ivy protested, but the keen little fairy snapped his fingers and the gargoyles sprang to life once more.

Two of them seized her joyfully, laughing with pure abandon.

"Elridge, help me!"

Her friend started forward, only to be restrained by the other two gargoyles. Each one placed himself to one side of the dragon, grasping a front leg with one brawny arm and a wing with the other. They were heavy and surprisingly strong, and they weighed Elridge down like manacles, even as he struggled to put up a fight.

"Let...me...go," he rasped. He could neither fly nor move more than a few steps in any direction. "Ivy, no!"

"Patience, my friend, don't be vexed. Wait your turn, you can go next," the gatekeeper crooned to the dragon, a wicked grin splitting his face.

Ivy struggled as she was dragged toward the cliff's edge. Panic rose, a bitter taste in the back of her throat.

"Elridge, do something. *Please!*"

But the dragon had completely lost his composure. He squeezed his eyes tight, as if he couldn't bear to watch, and was mumbling frantically to himself under his breath.

"We need an answer...we need an answer...we need an answer...."

The gargoyles reached the sheer drop at the edge of the rock shelf.

"ELRIDGE!" Ivy screamed.

But the dragon was still mumbling, words that made no sense to the petrified princess.

"...the answer we need...the answer you need...the answer you seek..."

Ivy was lifted into the air high over the gargoyles' heads. Her heart clenched painfully in her chest as her gaze fell upon the waters of the lake far, far below.

"Tee-hee, tee-hee, on the count of three!" The gatekeeper was practically dancing in anticipation as he began his deadly countdown. "One...two..."

Elridge's eyes sprang open. "It's a window!" he cried. "The answer is a window."

With a groan of extreme disappointment, the gargoyles set Ivy down and shuffled back to their gateside positions. The two clutching Elridge did the same. The dragon all but sagged in relief.

"That is right; that is true," the gatekeeper said, rather grumpily. "You may pass; inside with you." With a wave of his hand that might as well have been a dismissal, he stepped to one side, leaving the entrance to the gate wide open. The magical rainbow bridge once again arched across the fissure.

Ivy was stunned, then elated. For a moment, she was tempted to ask the gatekeeper if he knew where she could find Drusilla, but he seemed rather impatient for them to be off, and she didn't want to give him an excuse to set the guffawing gargoyles on them once more.

"Come on," she urged Elridge.

The pair of them hurried across the gleaming white bridge without so much as a glance back.

"Of course, a window lets in light," said Ivy, her heart finally starting to slow to a normal pace. "And the view from a window is always the same, but little things about it might change, like a bird flying by or the moon moving across the sky." She was greatly impressed with her dragon friend. "I would have never figured that out. How did you know?"

"A stroke of good fortune," Elridge grinned. When the princess merely gave him a puzzled look, he added, "Your tea-leaf reading? Don't you remember—you told me about it back at the tower?"

With his words, a memory came rushing back to her: a heavily scented room, a cup of mint-flavored tea, and a silvery voice like wind chimes. *It's a window, next to the cup handle, the answer you seek.*

Ivy was dumbfounded. She had taken a window being the answer she sought to mean that the window was her escape route from the tower, but all along it had been an answer in a much truer sense of the word—the answer to a riddle.

"You were right, Elridge," she laughed. "I guess Felda the Farseeing *does* know what she's talking about after all."

On the other side of the bridge, the island swarmed like the insides of a crystal beehive full of amazingly beautiful bees. The city was a dizzying whirl of sound and movement; Ivy would have certainly been lost in the churning press of bodies had not Elridge's lumbering form cut a steady path through the merrymakers. The fairies here were afflicted with the same strange obliviousness that Ivy had noticed before; they paid the dragon no more attention than if he were a terrier trotting down the street.

"This place is a madhouse," Elridge mumbled. "Fairies must really like to celebrate."

Large silver flagons mingled among the crowd, floating through the air as if borne by unseen hands; they tipped and poured cascades of golden fairy nectar into jeweled goblets that flew up to be filled and then flitted away again, presumably serving themselves to the raucous fairies.

Ivy was just thinking she could do with a cold drink when one of the goblets zipped over and thrust itself into her hands. Not about to let such a welcome gift go to waste, Ivy drained the cup in one long, satisfying gulp. Immediately she felt the pick-me-up effect of the nectar work its magic. The aches and pains of having traversed a cavernous underground realm and tangled with a giant octopus melted away. She felt supremely rested and refreshed. Impatient to be off, the now-empty goblet tugged itself loose from her grip and darted away, eager to be refilled so that it could serve some other thirsty soul in need of refreshment.

"How are we supposed to find your godmother in all this?" Elridge called over the babble of music and laughter. Someone nearby set off a shower of white sparks that rained down upon the crowd to a general murmur of approval and pleasure. "Do you know what she looks like?"

"No, I haven't seen her since I was a baby," said Ivy. "Maybe we could ask someone?

"Excuse me," she said to the nearest fairy, a towheaded lad banging on a tabor drum strung over his shoulder on a strap. "I'm looking for my godmother, Drusilla. Do you know where I can find her?"

He smiled at her brightly but didn't stop rat-a-tatting on his drum long enough to give her an answer.

Ivy approached three more fairies without luck, although one showered her with crystallized flower petals and another snatched her into his arms and whirled her around in a dizzying kind of waltz before she managed to get away.

Even Elridge, so much bigger than everyone around him, couldn't hold the attention of anyone long enough to get a reply.

Finally, Ivy encountered a pretty little fairy with dusky red ringlets whose eyes lit up when she heard Drusilla's name.

"Oh, you're one of Drusy's girls?" she squealed excitedly. "And here I thought she had gone and given up that whole godmothering business, I mean, after what happened to that last queen who was her goddaughter. Tragic, that was. Poor dear blames herself, you know, and it's nothing but a load of fiddle-faddle. There was never a more loving, dedicated fairy godmother than our Drusy, no matter what she may say to the contrary."

"The last queen?" Ivy asked. The last queen had been her own mother. Ivy supposed dying in childbirth *was* pretty tragic, but had it really been enough to drive Drusilla to give up godmothering altogether? Drusilla had lived at the castle in Ardendale for hundreds and hundreds of years. Surely she had seen people die before, seen generations of princesses and queens come and go.

"Oh, it was so sad, so sad," murmured Red Ringlets, raising one hand to her heart forlornly. She seemed lost in memory and emotion, and didn't say more.

"Um, yes...well...do you know where I can find Drusilla?" Ivy asked.

But just then a troupe of giggling fairies danced by, sweeping up Red Ringlets as they passed. She seemed to recover from her bout of melancholy with amazing speed and pranced away with her gleeful friends.

"Argh, can't anyone in this kingdom have a conversation that lasts more than ten seconds?" Ivy complained over the heads of the crowd. As she turned to make her way back to the dragon, she felt her right foot come down on something soft, furry, and warm.

"Ouch! Watch where you're putting those enormous stompers," came a high-pitched, nasally voice.

"Sorry." Glancing down, Ivy saw the tiniest goat she had ever seen. It was only about the size of a lapdog. The little creature was pristine white—like just about everything else in this sparkling kingdom—with a round little body and four short, stubby legs. The goat glared at her resentfully. Its tawny eyes had those strange, rectangular pupils that even goats in the human world have.

"'Sorry,' she says, 'sorry,' as if that makes everything roses and rainbows. Well, I'm *sorry* to inform you that 'sorry' doesn't get the ugly footprint off my rump, now, does it?" the goat snapped. She turned on her delicate hooves and tromped off into the crowd, her stump of a tail raised indignantly.

"I guess the goats here can talk," Elridge said drily as he watched her go. He didn't sound surprised.

"More than the fairies seem to," said Ivy, frustrated. "They have the attention span of goldfish. Don't they think about anything but music and celebrating?" Tildy had been right; fairies *were* a flighty breed.

A sharp bleat caught her attention. The little white goat had returned. She emerged from the mass of bodies and legs like a fawn from a forest. This time, she was followed by a stunningly beautiful fairy in a white gown.

"You need to set this clumsy oaf of a girl straight," the goat grumbled, nodding her head at Ivy. "I heard her tell Nathalia that she was your goddaughter." She said this last part with a note of accusation in her voice, as if clearly Ivy must be lying.

"My goddaughter?" The fairy peered at Ivy with a curious violet gaze. She had the same air of lazy unconcern that marked the other fairies of the kingdom and actually seemed a bit confused for a moment. Then, all of a sudden, the haze lifted from her eyes, and she looked very much alert and present as she beheld the scrawny, freckle-faced girl before her.

"Princess Ivory?" she asked with a soft gasp.

PART THREE

The Fate of the Kingdom

24

Drusilla's Confession

I vy heard the ripple of a snicker at her side and shot Elridge a narrow-eyed glare to let him know she didn't share his amusement.

"Sorry," said the dragon, trying to look contrite and not quite succeeding. "I didn't know your name was really Ivory."

"Are you really her, then?" Drusilla asked softly, her tone a mixture of hope and disbelief. Like Felda, her voice was lovely and tinkly, sounding of bells or coins jingling inside a bag of treasure. "Are you really Ivory?"

"Yes, although everyone calls me Ivy these days. Well, everyone except Tildy, that is."

With this, Drusilla's shock seemed to fade a little; her face softened, and a wry smile blossomed on her lips. "That sounds like Tildy, all right." Her laugh was a warm, pleasant sound, a summer breeze rippling through leaves.

Immediately, Ivy sensed she was going to like this good-natured fairy, even if she had never seen anyone who looked less like a godmother. Drusilla was tall and willowy and even younger-looking than Felda the Farseeing. Her fair skin was radiant, glowing with a pearly light. Despite her apparent youth, her hair was as white as winter's first snow, flowing to her waist in soft waves. The cascading tresses shimmered as she moved, like facets of quartz catching sunlight. Violet eyes shone as if two gems had been set into the delicate features of her face. Drusilla was all sparkle and light, and extraordinarily beautiful, even by fairy standards.

"You mean, she really *is* your goddaughter?" squeaked the goat, sounding rather disappointed. Ivy got the distinct feeling that the little creature had been looking forward to watching her get a good telling off.

"Yes." Drusilla beamed at Ivy. "This is Princess Ivory— Ivy, I mean—my goddaughter from the kingdom of Ardendale."

"A bit of a mess, isn't she?" the goat said, eyeing Ivy up and down disagreeably. "I would have thought they took better care of princesses topside."

For the first time Ivy realized how she must look—her clothes and hair still damp from her dunk in the underground lake, her dress full of little rips and tears made by swamp sprites, and a length of spiderskin tied haphazardly about her waist. Why, she must look as if she had gone half wild—certainly an absolute fright compared to the lovely fairies in this pristine, perfect kingdom.

"Yes, well, I'm sure it wasn't easy getting here," Drusilla

said kindly, giving the princess another smile, "and I can't wait to hear all about the journey. Ivy, this is my pixie goat, Toadstool." She gazed fondly at the grumpy-looking goat. "I called her that because she loves mushrooms."

"Yes, I do," said Toadstool in her shrill, squeaky voice. "And there's a whole platter of stuffed slippery jacks on the banquet table, so we'd best be going before they're all gone."

"Not just yet, Toadstool," Drusilla murmured gently, as if she were talking to a very small child. "Ivy and I have a bit of catching up to do first."

The goat sat down with a loud "Humpf" that made the princess suspect she was not used to being told no.

"This is my friend Elridge." Ivy introduced the dragon, who gave a polite nod in Drusilla's direction. "He helped me get here. You see, I came to find you because I—that is, we— need to talk to you about something rather important."

"It's a pleasure to meet you," Drusilla said brightly to Elridge. She extended a dainty hand but blanched a bit when his vicious-looking claw all but swallowed it in a friendly handshake. "Oh my, you must forgive me. It's been a while since I've seen a dragon up close. I'd forgotten how clawed and scaly you all are, not that there's anything wrong with claws and scales. I bet they're downright useful in a lot of situations." She turned back to Ivy. "However did the two of you meet? As far as I remember, dragons don't come to Ardendale, unless it's to..." Her already fair face paled noticeably.

"...guard the tower," Ivy finished for her.

"Has it really been almost *fourteen* years since I last saw you?" asked Drusilla. An expression of bleak understanding came over her beautiful features. "So you're actually supposed to be in the tower right now"—she looked at Ivy—"and you're supposed to be guarding it?" Her gaze shifted to Elridge.

"Yes." The princess suddenly found herself examining the quartz cobblestones so as not to meet her godmother's questioning eyes.

"Sounds about right," Elridge said guiltily.

"Oh dear," said Drusilla. "We're going to need to find a quiet place where we can all talk."

"Does this mean we aren't going to eat?" whined Toadstool.

"And I thought the goats aboveground were irksome little creatures," Elridge leaned in to mutter to Ivy under his breath. "Don't think I'm going to care much for the underground variety, either."

From what she had seen of the island, Ivy wouldn't have thought there was such a thing as a "quiet place" anywhere, but Drusilla led them to a small, shady arbor in a garden near the city's center that was surprisingly empty. It was the best they could hope to do. Elridge was too large to fit inside any of the buildings. He couldn't even squeeze into the arbor but managed to join in on the conversation by sticking his head through the thick screen of surrounding branches. Even the trees in this kingdom sparkled. The leaves were tiny crystal drops, and several fell and shattered like ice when Elridge poked his head through.

"It's too small in here for dancing and merrymaking," Drusilla explained, settling herself on a white marble bench. "So nobody will think to come."

"What is everyone celebrating, anyway?" asked Elridge. They could still hear laughter, music, and the buzz of the happy crowd in the streets and alleyways all around them.

"Oh, it's lunchtime," Drusilla said offhandedly.

"Lunchtime?"

"Well, music and dancing go so well with food," she said. "It would be a shame to waste the opportunity. They'll calm down in about an hour or so, at least until dinner."

"We had a little trouble finding you," Ivy told her. "It seemed like no one here wanted to talk to us or tell us where you were."

"Sorry about that," said Drusilla sheepishly. "Fairies love a good time, and we tend to get a bit caught up in ourselves, especially when a big group of us get together. The Isle of Mist is a place where you can lose yourself very easily. Fairies tend not to worry about things like outsiders or dragons or finding godmothers, or anything else that could interfere with our fun. I've kind of let myself go here," she admitted, looking uncomfortable at the thought.

Toadstool had curled up at Drusilla's feet with her legs tucked under her belly and appeared to be dozing off. In this kingdom of beauty and pleasure, the little goat had probably never had a care in her entire life, Ivy thought with a twinge that was half envious, half scornful.

"I heard the gatekeeper call this place the Isle of Mist, too," she said.

"Yes, you might have noticed, we get a lot of it around here," Drusilla replied with a laugh. "Luckily, it doesn't hang around the island. Most of it blows away."

"Yes, we know," said Elridge bitterly, obviously remembering the persistent mist that had dogged their journey to the fairy kingdom. "We had to walk through all of it to get here."

"Speaking of getting here," Drusilla said, her voice shifting to a businesslike tone, "tell me why you've come all this way."

At once, the entire story gushed from Ivy like water from a mountain spring. She told Drusilla everything, from Romil's plans to rid himself of his soon-to-be wife and father-in-law and wipe out the dragons of the Smoke Sand Hills, to her visit with Felda the Farseeing and her desperate journey with Elridge to find the long-lost fairy godmother they hoped would help set things straight.

As she finished her tale, Ivy felt an old fear rise to the surface. Despite all their trouble to find her, Drusilla might not agree to help them. She seemed nice enough, but what fairy would want to leave this carefree existence to battle an evil prince in the less-than-sparkling mortal world? After all, if Drusilla had really cared about her goddaughter, she wouldn't have left Ardendale so long ago with no word for nearly fourteen years.

"I know you don't really do godmothering anymore," the princess blurted out in a rush of panic, "and I wouldn't expect you to stay in Ardendale for good or anything like that. I know I make a lousy princess, and that was probably pretty obvious even when I was a baby. But if you could just help me this one time, to sort out this mess with Romil, I swear I'll never bother you again for as long as I live."

Drusilla looked hurt by this sudden outburst. "Ivy, I never *wanted* to leave you," she said.

"You didn't?" Surprise and relief flooded Ivy, mingled with a touch of confusion. "But, then, why *did* you leave?"

"I...I thought it would be best," Drusilla stammered. Her face clouded with emotion, and her voiced sounded choked. "I thought you'd be better off without me, after all that had happened."

"You mean my mother dying?" Ivy asked, remembering what Red Ringlets had said. "But there wasn't anything you could have done. I mean, her dying is my fault, really. She died giving birth to me." Her voice strained as a familiar feeling of guilt and loss that was never far from the surface welled inside her chest.

"Oh, Ivy, you must never think that," cried Drusilla. "You were just a baby; you didn't do anything wrong!" Tears pricked her gemlike eyes, making them brighter and more brilliant than ever. "Don't you know?" she asked softly. "Hasn't anyone ever told you what happened the night your mother died?"

"Well, not in detail or anything," Ivy answered awkwardly, not sure why Drusilla would ask such a thing. Her mother had died, had been taken from her forever. What more was there to know?

"It's about time you heard the story, then." Drusilla sniffled, dabbing at her eyes with the bell-shaped sleeve of her gown. "I suppose it's fitting that I be the one to tell you."

She took a deep breath, as if to steel herself to go on.

"Your mother, Felda, and I were all very good friends," she began in a low voice. "Your mother and I often made the long trek to the Fringed Forest just to have tea with Felda."

"I've heard about that," Ivy said, remembering what Rose and Clarinda had told her on the beach back in Ardendale in what had seemed like half a lifetime ago.

"Your mother loved going to see Felda," said Drusilla. "You see, away from the castle, she was a little more free to be herself, to laugh and joke and not always be so prim and proper. The three of us would have a grand time. Your mother thought having her fortune told was most entertaining— and informative. Sometimes the signs in the tea leaves were crystal clear, sometimes very vague, but they were always right in the end, as sure as salamanders. Like many mortals, your mother came to put a lot of stock in what Felda discerned in the leaves.

"Even once she got big with you, she insisted on visiting Felda. We'd tell Tildy that we were going shopping in one of the villages, or having a picnic on the beach, or some such excuse. What we'd really do was load your mother into a hay cart from the stables and set out for the Fringed Forest. Your mother was too far along to be riding a horse at that point. Tildy would have died from the scandal if she had found out—the expectant young queen being dragged across the countryside in the back of a dusty old cart." The ghost of a grin twitched at Drusilla's lips, as if all these years later, this small act of defiance was still a sweet satisfaction.

"Your mother was very excited to be having a daughter,"

the fairy said, "and one day when the time for your birth was drawing near, she asked Felda to read the leaves to see what the future held in store for you.

"I could tell something was wrong the moment Felda gazed into your mother's teacup." Drusilla's face held so much sorrow, Ivy didn't know how she managed to keep her tears from spilling over. "Her face went as white as wool. She tried to change the subject, tried to distract your mother, but the queen insisted upon hearing the reading. She could be very stubborn when she wanted. Finally, Felda was forced to reveal what she had seen in the leaves: the castle itself, alight with flames and surrounded by a horde of shadowy, clawed monsters. In the language of the leaves, monsters represent enemies. Felda thought the symbols unmistakable: the princess-to-be was going to bring a great enemy to the castle, and destruction and ruin would rain down upon its walls."

Ivy's stomach gave a massive lurch; this was *her* they were talking about. Out of the corner of her eye, she thought she saw Elridge cast a startled glance in her direction.

"Your mother was inconsolable," Drusilla said sadly. "As I mentioned, she had come to rely heavily on Felda's fortune-telling. Felda and I tried to comfort her the best we could. We pointed out that fortunes didn't always come to pass in the way you expected; sometimes they weren't nearly as bad or good as you might think. But, as you can imagine, it was kind of hard to throw any kind of positive light on 'destruction and ruin.' The queen was nearly hysterical, convinced that her daughter was destined to bring terrible misfortune to the kingdom.

"That night, after everyone in the castle had gone to bed, there was a pounding at my bedchamber door. It was the queen, and she was there to ask for my help. She wanted to run away. She wanted to leave that very night and get as far away from Ardendale as possible before the baby came. She was determined to make it to one of the northern kingdoms and raise the princess as a commoner. No one would ever know her true identity, not even the girl herself, and Ardendale would be saved from whatever dark fate the princess would bring upon it.

"Of course, I tried to talk sense into her," Drusilla said, looking helplessly at her delicate hands. "I pointed out that she could hardly expect to travel in her condition, that it would take weeks to get to the nearest kingdom and the baby was due any day now. I told her we would face whatever lay in store together, that I'd help her and the baby princess in any way I could. I thought I had convinced her, had made her see reason, but I was so horribly wrong." Tears shone bright in Drusilla's eyes once again.

"After she left my bedchamber that night, your mother sneaked down to the stables and saddled herself a mount. I suppose she had decided that if I wasn't going to help her, she would just have to leave the kingdom on her own. It was well into autumn, so the weather was chilly and there was a storm rolling in off the Speckled Sea. Your mother had packed herself a small bag, and she set off on horseback down the Inland Road, planning to follow it through the Fringed Forest and north to the other side.

"But the storm grew worse. The rain and wind picked

up, and then the lightning started. It was not a night for anyone to be out, certainly not a fraught mother-to-be. The queen had only made it about halfway to the Fringed Forest when a bolt of lightning came down right next to the road. The horse spooked something awful, and your mother was thrown into a ditch beside the roadway.

"Back at the castle, the storm had awoken one of the stable boys. He knew the stable roof leaked when it rained, so he got up to set out some buckets to catch the drips. When the horse your mother had been riding showed up at the castle gate, fully saddled but without a rider, he knew something was wrong. It wasn't long before it was discovered that the queen was missing. Everyone at the castle went out to look for her, of course. I'm sorry to say that she was not in good shape when a couple of the King's Guard found her. She had been in the cold and rain for hours, and had been hurt very badly in the fall. The shock of everything that had happened seemed to have started the baby coming as well. The queen was rushed back to the castle. I did everything I could for her, Ivy, truly I did, but fairy magic has its limits. Your mother lived just long enough to bring you into this world."

A dreadful silence hung over the arbor with the end of Drusilla's story, broken only by the fairy's deep breaths as she tried to hold back a sob. Ivy felt as if her own breath was trapped in her throat.

"If only I had handled things differently," moaned Drusilla. "I never thought she'd actually try to run away. I thought she was just a little emotional on account of the baby. If only I had taken her more seriously that night and agreed to help, I might have been able to keep her safe, the way a fairy godmother is supposed to." Drusilla was openly crying now, tears coursing down her lovely face.

"So you see, Ivy, it's not your fault that your mother died," she told the princess, her voice anguished. "It's mine."

25

Mirror Talk

Ivy couldn't speak; her throat felt like a reed that had dried beneath the summer sun—hollow, cracked, and useless. Learning one terrible secret about herself would have been bad enough, but Drusilla had presented her with a small catalogue of shocking revelations: Felda had predicted she would bring destruction and ruin upon the castle, her mother had died trying to prevent this from coming to pass, Drusilla had been overcome with guilt and grief, and so many other lives had been forever altered in the wake of the queen's death.

"So that's why you left?" Ivy finally managed to croak out, sounding every bit as hoarse and raspy as Froggy Throat the troll.

"You...you were barely a month old." Drusilla's voice was little more than a whisper. "The longer I stayed, the more I became convinced you were better off without me.

Godmothers are supposed to look after their charges, protect them from harm. But I was a failure; I had let your mother down. I was certain as soon as you grew old enough to realize what I'd done, you'd hate me for it."

"But I don't hate you!" Ivy's voice returned with a vehemence she wouldn't have thought possible only moments earlier. "It's not your fault my mother chose to run away that night. You loved my mother; everyone says so. You were like a sister to her, and I know you would never do anything to hurt her, not if you could help it." Ivy's voice broke ever so slightly. "If anything, you're the one who should hate me. I'm a curse upon the kingdom, what with that terrible fortune Felda saw, and my mother died trying to get me as far away as she possibly could. I wouldn't blame you if you didn't want anything to do with me."

"Oh, Ivy, a million bad fortunes couldn't make that happen," Drusilla cried, a fresh wave of tears spilling onto her cheeks. "Leaving you was the hardest thing I've ever done. I'm... I'm so glad you came to find me!"

Ivy didn't know exactly how it happened, but suddenly Drusilla's arms were wrapped around her, and the princess was crying now, too, enveloped in an embrace as welcome and warm as a favorite quilt, for all her godmother's crystalline appearance. Even Elridge sniffed loudly from his vantage point among the glistening tree branches, although he turned his enormous head away from them to try to hide it. Only Toadstool remained unaffected by any of the goings-on around her. Her eyes were closed into tiny slits, and Ivy believed she had succeeded in falling asleep.

"I always planned to check up on you, you know," said Drusilla, when she and the princess finally broke apart. "I thought I could pop up topside and find out from Felda how you were doing, but I never made it back to the Fringed Forest. It was something that was always in the back of my mind, something I always meant to do, but I just sort of... forgot. This place will do that to you. Time passes differently for fairies, and until I saw you today I hadn't realized it had been fourteen years."

"So will you help us?" Ivy asked, trying, with difficulty, to keep the desperation out of her voice.

"Yes, of course I'll help you." Drusilla chuckled at the princess's eagerness, but her mood quickly grew somber again. "It's not going to be easy, however. I can't just whisk away your problems, you know. Fairy godmothers are on a rather low rung when it comes to magic. Most of my spells are fairly domestic in nature—making torn seams mend themselves, enchanting furniture and household objects, tinkering with the weather so a picnic doesn't get canceled, and things like that.

"And I'm not sure how welcome my assistance will be at the castle," she added worriedly. "I imagine your father and Tildy aren't thrilled that I up and left without so much as a good-bye. I just couldn't bring myself to face them at the time. Your father might understand that, but Tildy won't easily forgive me for walking out on you."

"I'll stick up for you, no matter what they say," Ivy promised. But worry gnawed at her. "Drusilla, what about Felda's prediction?" she asked. "I really, really don't want to bring destruction and ruin upon the castle." A shocking thought suddenly besieged her. "Oh no, what if I already have? Maybe leaving the tower was a big mistake. What if Romil has already done something to my father?"

"Ivy, I'm going to tell you the same thing I told your mother all those years ago," said Drusilla, laying a hand on the princess's shoulder and looking her full in the eye, "and I sincerely hope you'll listen to it better than she did: you can't live your life based on some shapes at the bottom of a tea-cup. Felda's predictions are ... well, unpredictable. Who can say how they'll unfold? You can't hide from them, and you can't spend all your time constantly worrying about what will happen. The only way to face life is as it comes."

"I'd like to believe that; honestly I would," said Ivy, wringing her hands nervously. "But I would feel better if I knew my father was safe. Oh, I wish I had another magic mirror like the one in the tower, so I could see him and make sure he was all right." Ivy thought dejectedly of the useless fragment of mirror still tucked into the spiderskin at her waist.

"Ivy! I was the one who enchanted the mirror back when the tower was first built, and I've got others just like it, better ones, in fact." As if to prove her point, Drusilla withdrew a small gilded hand mirror from the folds of her gown. It was adorned with tiny carved rosebuds and delicately trailing vines.

"I've always had a bit of a fascination with mirrors," she confessed sheepishly, examining her own reflection in the glass. This was entirely unnecessary, as red-rimmed eyes and tear tracks from her recent crying spell did little to diminish her radiant beauty. "People think all you can do is look in them, but mirrors can show you much more than just your reflection. They're quite a useful invention. Take this one, for instance." She gestured toward the dainty golden mirror in her hand. "It's a very powerful instrument. It has a connection to every other mirror in existence. You can see out to the other side. What's even better—you can talk to whoever happens to be there."

"So I could speak to my father?" Ivy was now so worried it was all she could do to keep from snatching the mirror straight out of Drusilla's hands.

"As long as he happens to be near a mirror," said Drusilla, looking supremely pleased with herself. "Clever, don't you think? I once had a sweetheart who was a weather warlock. He chased storm clouds all over the world, making sure they blew in the right direction. This mirror was how we kept in touch while he was away... until he got lost in the foglands along the Memory Coast, that is. There are no mirrors there, so I'm not exactly sure what happened to him. I've never heard from him since... but that's another story." She passed the beautiful mirror to Ivy, who grasped it eagerly by the vine-entwined handle and held it up to her eyes.

"Now, just tell it the location you'd like to see," instructed Drusilla. "It has to be somewhere with a mirror, mind you."

"It's about time for my father's midafternoon nap. I bet he's in his bedchamber," Ivy said. "I'd like to see my father's bedchamber," she told the mirror, taking care to speak clearly so there was no confusion, "in the east wing of the castle in the kingdom of Ardendale."

At once, the surface of the hand mirror began to ripple in the same misty, rolling way the mirror in the tower had. Ivy watched her reflection twist and distort until the ripples cleared, revealing an unobstructed view of a very familiar royal bedchamber. Ivy was seeing the room from above the dressing table, and she realized she was looking through the bedchamber mirror as if it were a window. Her eyes darted about impatiently, taking in every inch of the room in hopes of seeing a familiar gray-bearded figure. Not only was there no sign of the king, but it immediately became clear that something was terribly wrong. Her father's bedchamber was a mess. It was never especially neat, as her father was not inclined to be tidy, but at the moment it looked as if a hurricane had blown through. Clothes had been pulled from the wardrobe and scattered across the floor, the blue draperies that normally hung around the bed lay in a tumbled heap upon the bedsheets, and books and papers had been tossed out of the mahogany chest that sat against the wall beneath the dull-colored tapestry of a hunting scene.

"Something's wrong." Ivy was light-headed with worry. "He's not there—and someone has gone through all of his things."

"Oh dear," Drusilla said. The glow she gave off seemed to soften and diminish with her distress. "Is there someone else you could talk to at the castle? What about Tildy?"

The princess swallowed hard. She didn't think she could bear facing her nursemaid. Tildy probably blamed her for all of this.

"There are my friends Rose and Clarinda," she suggested

instead. "But they could be anywhere—in the kitchen, in the solarium, out in the courtyard, maybe even in the castle garden."

"It probably wouldn't be a good idea for you to pop up in mirrors all over the castle looking for them," said Drusilla. "If something really is wrong, you wouldn't want Prince Romil or one of his goons to catch your reflection in a mirror. They might suspect you were up to something."

"I'll try Rose's bedchamber, but I don't think she'll be there in the middle of the day," Ivy said. Turning her attention back to the mirror, she said, "Show me my friend Rose's bedchamber in the servants' wing of the castle."

This time, when the misty waves cleared, Ivy was surprised to discover that not only was Rose in her bedchamber, but Clarinda was with her. They were sitting on Rose's bed in the tiny, windowless room, deep in whispered conversation. Both girls looked distraught, and Clarinda was crying softly.

"Rose? Clarinda?" Ivy was startled to see her friends so troubled.

"What was that?" Rose looked around, puzzled.

"Over there," Clarinda gasped, pointing at the mirror above the washbasin.

"Ivy? Ivy, is that you?" There was a flash of golden curls as Rose scooted off the bed and positioned herself directly in front of the mirror, Clarinda a few steps behind. Clearly they could see the princess through the glass, just as she could see them.

"Oh, Ivy, where are you?" Clarinda cried, sounding near-hysterical. Words began to gush from her almost as rapidly as tears. "Are you all right? H-how did you get out of the tower? What h-happened to the dragon? H-how did you end up in a m-mirror?"

"Look, I don't have time to explain everything," Ivy said hurriedly. "I found out Romil was planning to murder my father and me once he became king. I had to leave the tower to find Drusilla. She's with me now, and we're coming to stop Romil. But I need to know what's going on at the castle. Is Romil still there? What's happened to my father?"

"Ivy, when Romil got to the tower and you and the dragon weren't there, he was f-f-f-furious," Clarinda said in a tremulous whisper, as if frightened someone would overhear.

"That blubber-brain thought it was some sort of trick to keep him from becoming king," Rose explained, her voice tight with anger and her beautiful blue eyes flashing. "He blamed your father, accused him of working with the dragons, plotting the whole thing."

"Where is my father now?" Ivy wasn't sure she wanted to hear the answer. Dread was seeping into her like bilgewater filling a sinking ship.

"Romil has this ridiculous idea that maybe he can ransom the king for the dragon treasure he didn't get," said Rose. "He's locked your father at the top of the southern tower."

Ivy felt almost giddy, so great was her relief. Her father was alive, for the moment, anyway.

"I th-think it's because the castle doesn't have a d-dungeon," Clarinda stammered. "The King's Guard tried to stop Prince Romil, of course, but Romil's men overpowered them. They've all been l-locked in the cellar."

"Prince Romil and his goons have taken over the entire castle," said Rose hatefully. "They've lowered the gate and posted a guard at the gatehouse and everything. Romil says he's going to send for his army, and that the more the castle staff cooperates now, the better it will be for us when they get here."

"Oh, Ivy, it's horrible," Clarinda sobbed. "They've ransacked the castle, and we have to w-wait on them hand and foot."

"We had to serve them lunch in the Great Hall," said Rose. "The skinny Glacian who looks like a ferret kept trying to kiss me. I nearly dumped an entire bowl of steaming mashed turnips in his lap. He probably would've thrown me into the cellar with the King's Guard, but I think it would have been worth it!"

"Rose, d-don't say that," Clarinda said. "You know we mustn't make them angry."

"They're planning a big celebration for tonight," Rose continued. "They've had Cook ready seven barrels of the king's best elderberry wine."

"They'll g-get so drunk, they'll tear the Great Hall to pieces," wailed Clarinda. "And we're to be there. We're to h-help serve dinner."

"What about everyone else?" Ivy asked worriedly. "What about Tildy? What about Owen?"

"Everyone's all right, just frightened and upset," said Rose. "Owen and some of the others are trying to come up with a plan to free the king, but the Glacians have all the weapons, you see. They disarmed the King's Guard before locking them up. Prince Romil has made it clear that he expects us to fall in line, or else. Ivy, he says that if he can't win the kingdom under the terms of the Dragon Treaty, then he's going to take it by force. Once his army gets here and secures the valley, he's going to declare himself king!"

"Oh, Ivy," Clarinda cried. "What are we to do?"

"Look, try to stay calm. Drusilla and I are on our way." Ivy thought it was pretty feeble of her to tell her friends to stay calm. Her own insides felt as if she had swallowed a handful of moths that were now fluttering around inside her, frantically searching for a way out. "I promise we'll think of something. Just do what the Glacians tell you in the meantime, try not to make them mad, and don't let anyone know that you've talked to me. We're going to need the element of surprise."

As if sensing her desire to end this troubling conversation, the mirror began to fog over once more.

"Ivy, please hurry," pleaded Clarinda before she and Rose both disappeared from view, lost beneath the rippling waves of white.

26

Godmotherly Guidance

"This is all my fault," Ivy said miserably, dipping her head and lowering the golden hand mirror to her lap. "I should have never left the tower. Now Romil has taken over the castle, and once his soldiers arrive from Glacia, he'll have the entire kingdom under his thumb. He'll cut down the Fringed Forest and strip the valley of its crops and force everyone to serve him and his army. I've brought a horrible enemy upon us, and they'll be the ruin of the kingdom—it's Felda's prediction coming true."

"Nonsense," Drusilla declared. "If you had stayed in the tower, you'd probably be preparing for your wedding about now, and the throne would rightfully be Romil's. At least this way we still have a chance against him. He's not king yet."

"And he hasn't made a pincushion out of me with all of his spears," Elridge added gratefully.

Ivy knew that they were trying their best to reassure her, so she mustered a weak smile for their sakes. Inside, however, her heart weighed heavily.

"We must leave for Ardendale at once," Drusilla said. "Elridge, I don't suppose you're up to carrying a couple more passengers? I don't have any method of getting us to Ardendale that's any faster than dragon flight. Flying horses have a surprisingly bad sense of direction...."

"That shouldn't be a problem," said Elridge. "But 'a couple more'? Who else is coming besides you?"

"Why, Toadstool, of course," said Drusilla. "I could never leave her behind." Her gaze drifted lovingly to the tiny goat at her feet, who was just starting to stir from slumber.

"Leave?" mumbled Toadstool, still looking sleepy-eyed. "Whaddaya mean leave? We're not going topside, are we? You know I'm much too delicate for travel, Drusy, especially topside."

"Toadstool, darling, I would never let anything happen to you," Drusilla purred to her pet. Turning her attention back to the dragon, she said wisely, "We can make our way out of the mound now, but we won't be able to fly into Ardendale until after dark. Otherwise, Romil and his men will surely see us coming. It's kind of hard to miss a dragon soaring over the kingdom. It's the sort of thing that gets people's attention."

"It'll probably take us until nightfall to get back to the surface, anyway," Elridge said, a look of dread shadowing his scaly face. "What with the mist and the lake and the giant octopus and all. Dear me, don't know if I can take another run-in with that tentacled terror."

Drusilla brightened at mention of the octopus.

"You've met Snord? What a sweetie," she gushed. "He's our miniature kraken. He didn't give you any trouble, did he? He's got a good temperament for a kraken, but he can be a bit skittish around strangers."

"A bit?" Elridge looked at Drusilla as if she had just said the sun was a bit hot or Glacia was a bit frozen. "And how can anything big enough to nearly drown a dragon be miniature?"

"Well, freshwater kraken are much smaller than the saltwater variety," Drusilla said. "Now *there* are some ill-tempered creatures. On a bad day, they'll take out an entire fleet of sailing ships."

"I may have, sort of . . . poked Snord's eye out with a shard of glass," Ivy confessed reluctantly. She thought Drusilla would be angry, but the beautiful fairy merely waved a hand breezily.

"Oh, it'll grow back," she said. "Snord is resilient that way. He poked his eye out three times this past summer. He keeps forgetting to duck when swimming under low-hanging stalactites. Anyway, if I'm with you on the journey back, he won't give you any trouble. We're old friends."

Drusilla ushered them out of the arbor and led them through the twisting labyrinth of alleyways between buildings, back toward the gated entryway to the fairy kingdom. The once-bustling city was now strangely still and quiet, except for the occasional low rumble of snores. Ivy saw her godmother had been right about the fairies calming down after lunch. They sprawled across marble benches, under trees, or on the quartz-cobbled streets themselves, dozing contentedly, sleepy from their revelries and full bellies.

"Would the other fairies come with us to help save Ardendale?" she asked hopefully.

"No, I'm afraid not," Drusilla sighed. "By and large, the affairs of humans don't concern fairy folk. Many of them have never even been topside. Some of us venture above-ground and spend our time granting mortals' wishes or play-ing tricks on wayward travelers or serving as godparents to the daughters of royal bloodlines, but we're considered a bit odd. The mortal world is one of death and hardship and imperfection. Most fairies don't want anything to do with it—they find it depressing beyond measure. But I discovered that I really enjoyed godmothering. It gave me a sense of purpose for the first time in hundreds of years, and that was nice for a change."

Ivy glanced at the fairies lazing about the beautiful city like useless lumps of white cloth. *What thoroughly frivolous, thoughtless beings,* she thought, a bit amused to find herself sounding so much like Tildy. She was glad Drusilla, at least, had more conscience and heart than most of her kind. Ivy knew she would in all likelihood never return to the fairy kingdom after this day and, for all its splendor, found that she didn't regret this one bit.

The journey back across the underground lake and up to the entrance of the fairy mound was much quicker and easier with Drusilla leading the way. First of all, Snord the miniature kraken didn't make an appearance. Perhaps he was off somewhere nursing his injured eye. Second, a whispered incantation from Drusilla was all it took to blow every last wisp of mist out of their way. Third, when they reached the earthen door that sealed the entrance to the mound, Drusilla simply waved her hand and it lowered at once, admitting them into the sunlit world beyond. The light outside was so bright compared to the soft glow of moss in the mound that Ivy's eyes watered for several minutes before she became accustomed to the glare.

Evening wasn't far off, so they spent an hour or two resting at the base of the Murmurs, awaiting sunset. Each passing minute was maddening for Ivy. She kept picturing her poor father locked in the dusty storeroom that was at the top of the southern tower, huddled among buckets and brooms, confused and befuddled and sick with worry over his missing daughter. Even the ethereal serenade of the stones at the top of the mound couldn't calm her restless mind, nor could the lavish meal Drusilla conjured for dinner—complete with table and chairs, tablecloth, cutlery, and a centerpiece of roses and daylilies blooming out of a polished silver bowl. There was even a large platter of stuffed mushrooms for Toadstool, which the little goat set upon immediately. Elridge was still not hungry, and Ivy's own stomach was too jumbled by nerves to allow her much of an appetite.

Drusilla met the princess's eyes over the steaming dishes on the well-laden table. "We need to talk about what we're going to do once we reach Ardendale. I've been giving it a lot of thought. There are a couple of villages just to the north of the castle. I think our best bet is to rally the villagers. If we can storm the castle before daybreak, we may catch Prince Romil and his men off guard. You said there's fewer than two dozen of them. We should be able to overtake them and free the king."

"But my father—and the entire staff—is practically being held hostage inside the castle," said Ivy. "People could get hurt—the villagers, too. Most of them are farmers and tradesmen. They don't know how to take on trained warriors like the Glacians."

"Rescuing the king is not without its risks." Drusilla looked solemn. "But Ivy, I don't see that we have any other choice. We have to act before Romil's army arrives."

The princess sighed heavily. She had never felt so helpless—she should be protecting the people of her kingdom, not leading them into battle against such savage brutes.

"You have my word I'll use my magic to do whatever I can to help," Drusilla promised.

"I'll...I'll help, too, Ivy," said Elridge from where he rested in the grass at the foot of the fairy mound.

"You, Elridge?" Ivy couldn't help feeling surprised. She hadn't expected the dragon to simply abandon them, of course, but neither had she thought he would be willing to come anywhere near the castle or the bloodthirsty Glacian prince. "What about Romil and his dragon-claw spears?"

"I can't just sit by and twiddle my talons while you plunge headfirst into danger," said Elridge, his voice more steady and certain now. "Good goat fur, Romil can't be much worse than trolls or swamp sprites or a miniature kraken, and we've faced all of those." The dragon gave a loose shrug of his scaly shoulders. "I probably won't be that much help, anyway. You know I'm not a particularly capable dragon...."

"Don't be silly," said Ivy. "You'll be a great help. You're quick and cunning and a fantastic flier. We're lucky to have you along." In a rush of affection for her steadfast friend, she sprang from her seat and wrapped her arms around his long neck, squeezing tight.

"Yes, well, you'd do the same for me," mumbled Elridge, looking embarrassed.

"Having a dragon with us when we take the castle will be a great help indeed," Drusilla said approvingly. "Your friend Rose said the Glacians had posted a guard at the gatehouse. They might be watching for an attack from the ground— but Elridge can help us drop in from the air."

When the sun, at long last, drifted west below the jagged silhouette of the Craggies and made way for the usurping moon, Ivy and Drusilla clambered aboard Elridge's back. Toadstool nestled in Drusilla's lap, a disagreeable expression on her stubby little face. One of the fairy's arms clutched the dragon spine in front of her, the other wrapped protectively around the little goat. Toadstool was in a foul mood. She didn't care for the world aboveground at all. She had done nothing but complain bitterly: the sun was too bright and hurt her eyes, the grass and mud stuck to the bottom of her hooves, and who had ever heard of trees that were green and didn't glisten? She hated being on the ground; there was no doubt she would hate flying over it. Ivy could tell that Elridge, who didn't have a high opinion of goats to begin with, was quickly tiring of her constant complaints.

The princess grasped the last shard of magic mirror in one of her hands, having taken the spiderskin from her waist and knotted it firmly to the tip of Elridge's tail. When the dragon took flight, it streamed behind him like a white banner in the moonlight. Ivy hoped the trolls would spot it as they crossed the sharp peaks of the Craggies and let them pass unhindered as the Guamp had promised.

"I don't like this. I don't like this one bit," Toadstool started up at once, looking rather pale and nervous. "This flying stuff is for the birds. Why do we have to go this high? Delicate creatures like myself are not made for heights, you know."

"We're not going to make it over a mountain range flying a hairbreadth off the ground," grumbled Elridge. "Besides, you live on an island surrounded by cliffs."

"Yes, but it's not like I have to look over the edge, is it, Scaly Legs?" the little goat said peevishly.

"Well, don't look now," snapped Elridge. He shot higher with a sudden and, Ivy suspected, quite purposeful burst of speed. With a little squeal, Toadstool retreated deeper into Drusilla's arms and screwed her eyes shut as tightly as clamshells.

"I c-c-can't believe how c-c-cold it is up here," she whined minutes later, after they had soared over the treetops of Wrathful Swamp and into the snow-strewn heights of the Craggies. "No wonder no one wants to leave the mound. The mortal world is awful."

"Do all pixie goats talk this much?" Elridge asked irritably, turning his head in the direction of his passengers and glaring at the little goat—who, with her eyes still scrunched up tightly, couldn't see the nasty look he gave her.

"Goodness, no!" exclaimed Drusilla. "Pixie goats don't talk at all, usually. They're topside creatures, bred by dwarves in the eastern Moondew Mountains. I got Toadstool when she was just a baby. She was a gift from Brutus, a handsome rogue of a fairy who hoped to entice me into running away with him to the Elfin Isles. I almost went, too, but then I found out he was seeing this bit of wood nymph on the side—fluffy as flitweed, that girl was—and...well, let's just say it all turned out very badly. But at least I got my little Toadstool out of the deal. I loved her so much, I gave her the gift of speech. Fortunately, enchanting small creatures isn't much more difficult than enchanting furniture or mirrors. Now we can all enjoy her delightful conversation."

"Lucky us," muttered Elridge as he turned to face forward again.

The dragon flew onward and in a matter of moments crested the tops of the snowy peaks. The night was clear, the moon was bright, and far below, the valley kingdom of Ardendale came into view. Ivy felt her heart flutter despite herself. She was headed home.

Flight of Fancy

They could see the valley surprisingly well in the light of the nearly full moon. It was a long sweep of silver and shadow, and from this height it looked more like a patchwork quilt than ever. Parcels of land were divided by long dirt roads, dark rows of trees and hedges, and silver strands of river. Nestled here and there among the rise and fall of the landscape were villages and the odd farmhouse or barn, glints of gray with darkened roofs. To the north, far in the distance, the trees of the Fringed Forest were a black mass in the night.

"Oh, the valley looks just as I remember," Drusilla breathed. "Only darker, of course. I've never been much of a night person."

Elridge started his sweeping descent toward the valley floor. The rush of cold air made Ivy's eyes water. She heard a muffled whimpering and realized that Toadstool had now completely buried her face in the folds of Drusilla's gown.

"I think your mother would be very proud of what you're doing, you know," her godmother called over the rumble of wind streaming past their ears. "Trying to save the kingdom, I mean. Traveling all this way, facing so much peril."

"I've always thought if my mother knew what I was like, she'd be disappointed that I wasn't a better princess," said Ivy. It felt good to be able to confess this to someone. She always told herself that she didn't mind not being "proper," and this was mostly true. But there was a tiny, nagging voice in the back of her mind that she could never completely silence. It sounded a little like Tildy, but also a little like her own voice, and it insisted that she was the most selfish and ungrateful of daughters, and that she was letting her royal mother down.

"That's pure rot," Drusilla said firmly. "Your mother's biggest regret was that she never had any of the grand adventures she dreamed of. She just wasn't daring enough. She cared too much about what Tildy and the rest of the kingdom thought, so she played the part of obedient princess and dutiful queen. In a way, she lived her life for other people. You live your life for you, and I think your mother would admire that very much."

This both lifted Ivy's spirits and, oddly enough, made her a little sad at the same time. Who would have guessed that the beautiful, perfect queen had been so discontent?

"The one thing she never regretted was marrying your father," said Drusilla. "She adored him, and he loved her so dearly. He was such a magnificent king, so devoted to his people."

"Father?" Ivy asked, astonished. "I never knew that. These days he's a little...scattered."

"So I've heard. But back when he first took the throne, you couldn't have asked for a better king. He was kind and conscientious and noble, everything Prince Romil will never be."

Ivy was taken aback. It seemed both of her parents were not at all what she had thought.

Elridge had reached the bottom of the massive mountain range. He soared past the white tower where he and Ivy had first met, its stone bright in the moonlight, stark against the night sky.

"At least my treasure is okay," he said, surveying the rocks near the tower with a look of relief. "Your friend Rose said Romil didn't find it."

Ivy suppressed a smile. Even if Romil had found an old book by the tower, it would have never occurred to him that it was dragon treasure. He'd go through the castle roof if he knew there were no gold or gems waiting for him to claim.

"Shall I head for those villages you were talking about?" the dragon asked, swinging his head around to look back at them.

"Yes," said Drusilla. Toadstool's face was still buried in the silky fabric of her gown, and she stroked a soothing hand across the goat's white fur. "They're near the center of the valley, along the bend in the largest river."

With a whoosh of his broad, batlike wings, Elridge veered slightly, setting a course for the heart of the valley.

"There's something I don't quite understand," Ivy said.

"Why did Felda read my tea leaves when I went to see her? Why would she help me at all, knowing that I was going to bring destruction and ruin and all that?"

Drusilla thought carefully before answering. "I think if your mother's death taught Felda one thing, it was that you can't escape what fortune has in store for you," she said. "Your poor mother tried to run from it, and look what happened to her. Perhaps Felda thought it best if you faced your fortune straight on, good or bad."

"Faced my fortune..." mused Ivy. The words pushed into her mind like a key forcing its way into a stubborn lock, groves and ridges scraping and grinding until finally, in a moment of perfect alignment, something clicked.

"There's the largest river," Elridge called out, his voice breaking into her thoughts. "If I turn and follow it south, we should arrive at the first of those villages in no time."

"No," said Ivy, her voice so firm and full of purpose that it took even her by surprise. "That's not the way we're going. We need to keep heading west, to the Smoke Sand Hills."

"The Smoke Sands?" Drusilla looked baffled. "Ivy, why would you want to go there?"

Elridge was less gracious.

"Good goat fur, have you gone mad?" he squawked, his voice cracking slightly on the last word. His large head had swung around again, each of his golden eyes almost as wide as a round of bread.

"I know it sounds crazy, but I think it's what we're supposed to do," Ivy told her friends. "Drusilla, back in the mound, you said I couldn't hide from Felda's predictions, and Elridge, you've been telling me all along that I should trust what Felda sees in the leaves.

"Well, I think you're both right," the princess announced. "Everything Felda foresaw in my teacup has come to pass, just not always in the way I expected. I thought the dragon she saw meant I should play my part in the Dragon Treaty, let myself be locked in the tower where I'd be guarded by a dragon, but now I think the leaves were being more specific. I think that dragon in my teacup was you, Elridge. The tea leaves were trying to guide me to you, trying to tell me I could trust you and that you'd help me.

"And the window in the leaves *was* an answer I needed, just not in the way I first thought. And the mountains, the Craggies—remember how I thought it would be foolish to go there, Elridge?—but we would never have found Drusilla if the tea leaves hadn't pointed us in that direction. Don't you see? Whenever I've followed the guidance of the leaves, everything has worked out in the end."

Even now, Ivy could hear Felda's musical voice echoing in her ears: "The leaves never lie, and I have never known them to be wrong...."

"I still don't see what Felda's predictions have to do with the Smoke Sands," said Elridge.

"What if what Felda sees in the leaves is what's *supposed* to happen—something you can't change and shouldn't try to?" said Ivy. "I'm not going to do what my mother did. I'm not going to try to escape from that awful prediction about me—I'm going to do everything I can to make sure it comes true." Her voice filled with resolution. "I'm going to bring a great enemy to the castle, or at least someone who might be considered an enemy at the moment, but I'm hoping once they hear what I have to say, they'll be willing to join us against Romil."

"You mean the other dragons? You want to bring them into the valley, to help you?" Elridge looked thoroughly shocked by the idea.

"I knew coming topside was a bad idea! I just knew it!" cried Toadstool, lifting her head from Drusilla's gown to roll back her eyes in a long-suffering expression. "Freezing mountains, evil princes, predictions of destruction and ruin—and now more dragons! I don't want to deal with a bunch of oversize desert-dwellers—Scaly Legs here is bad enough." The goat shot Elridge a dirty look.

"Romil's a threat to the dragons, too," Ivy pointed out, ignoring Toadstool's dramatics. "If he becomes king, he'll see to it they're all slain.

"Drusilla, you were the one who told me that Felda's predictions were unpredictable, that they weren't always as bad as you might think," the princess said, casting an imploring look at her godmother.

"How can destruction and ruin *not* be bad?" snapped Toadstool.

"The kingdom's going to be ruined anyway if Romil takes the throne," Ivy retorted. *I must be getting awfully desperate*, she thought, *to be arguing with a goat.*

Toadstool opened her mouth to deliver what was sure to be a scathing reply, but Drusilla cut her short.

"Hush," said the fairy, placing a gentle, calming hand

on the pixie goat's back. She turned her violet gaze upon the princess. "Ivy, I know you want to do what's best for the kingdom, but I don't know if this is such a good idea. We could only secure the assistance of the dragons with the Dragon Queen's consent. Unfortunately, she can be a bit…" Drusilla looked at Elridge cautiously, clearly not wanting to say anything that might offend him.

"Difficult?" Elridge supplied readily. "Set in her ways? Spiteful and narrow-minded and hardheaded?"

"Something like that," said Drusilla, looking amused. "She's very wary of humans—and with good reason. Relations between humans and dragons have hardly been peaceful throughout the centuries. It's a miracle the Dragon Treaty has held up as long as it has." Ivy had a sinking feeling she was arguing a lost cause, but, to her utmost surprise, her godmother's face suddenly took on a hopeful light. "But there are so few dragons left that maybe the Dragon Queen will do whatever it takes to protect her kindred," she said thoughtfully. "If we can convince her that Prince Romil really is a threat, we might be able to garner her support. …"

"We already have one dragon on our side," said Ivy, looking at Elridge brightly. "That should help."

"Don't expect my word to count for much with the Dragon Queen," Elridge sniffed. Bitterness tinged his usually congenial voice. "She's going to be furious with me for leaving the tower. She'll say the dragonly thing would have been to stay and make toast out of Prince Romil—that would've solved all our problems. Never mind that I had absolutely no chance of accomplishing that. . . . Good goat fur, it's so hard to reason with her."

"We have to try," said Drusilla. "I helped the king who negotiated the Dragon Treaty. Hopefully, the Dragon Queen will remember me."

"So we're going, then?" Ivy asked hopefully.

"How could we fail to defeat Prince Romil with an entire host of dragons on our side?" said Drusilla, nodding her head as if it made all the sense in the world. "It's just crazy enough to work—if the dragons don't incinerate us in a ball of flames first."

"I'll take you to the Smoke Sands if you think that's best," said Elridge, looking none too happy. "But Ivy, please be careful. Dear me, you don't know what you're up against. Dragons can be nasty, vicious creatures—believe me, I know."

28

An Audience with the Dragon Queen

Ivy saw the smoke before she saw anything else. It was visible even in the dark of night, eerily writhing columns rising in the moonlight over the black shapes that were the Smoke Sand Hills. The princess had never seen the Smoke Sands up close before, so she was surprised at how blocky they were. These were not the gently rolling hills of the Fringed Forest, but the sharp sandstone rises of a high desert. By the time Elridge left the valley floor and glided over the first of the barren ridges of rock, the air was so thick with smoke that Ivy's eyes burned and her breathing grew labored.

Toadstool erupted into a fit of drawn-out coughs and promptly began to complain. "I was right before—the mortal world *is* awful, and it just keeps getting worse and worse," the little goat whined.

"Now, Toadstool, you must give it a chance," said Drusilla, who didn't seem bothered by the smoke at all. "The topside world has many charms. There are those who would never leave it, not even if they had the chance. Why, I was once in love with a delightfully roguish human sailor. I offered to whisk him away to a life of luxury in the fairy realm, but he preferred to join a band of pirates and raid coastal villages rather than retire peacefully to a fairy kingdom, even one as nice as the Isle of Mist." The beautiful fairy sighed rather dolefully.

"I still say this is the worst place yet," Toadstool wheezed, her voice scratchy and even more shrill than usual. "And meeting a swarm of smoke-spewing dragons isn't going to make it any better, let me tell you," she added with a dark look at Elridge, as if this were somehow all his fault.

"You know goats are dragons' favorite food, right?" said Elridge. His tone was casual, but there was an exceedingly satisfied grin on his face.

Toadstool's eyes widened, and she visibly shrank in Drusilla's arms. She kept quiet after that.

Elridge headed for the source of the smoke, a jagged line on the horizon from which it rose in spiraling columns. Upon approach, the line grew larger and wider, until Ivy could see it was a deep canyon cutting through the desert stone. She made out the red glow of what must be an enormous bonfire burning in its depths.

Elridge banked to one side and started his descent into the canyon. The smoke was all but suffocating now. A thick, charred odor filled the air. Ivy's eyes were tearing so badly she had to squint to see through the smoke.

"Remember, the Dragon Queen has a hot temper and is easily offended," said Drusilla. "Be sure to show her the utmost respect. It might help if you compliment her—extravagantly and as often as possible. Dragons like to hear about how grand they are. Um, sorry, Elridge."

"That's okay." Elridge shrugged. "It's true. Most of my kindred have big heads. It's one of the things I can't stand about them."

He landed on the canyon floor, barely making a sound as his feet sank into the loose red sand. The bonfire Ivy had spotted earlier was not twenty paces in front of them, burning in the center of a ring of stones. It was massive, with giant red and orange flames that leaped toward the sky, casting light and eerie, flickering shadows across the canyon's walls. Ivy barely contained a gasp, for in the firelight she could see that a number of towering structures had been carved into the face of the striated cliffs. They looked like temples, with smooth, timeworn columns in front, and windows and doors where smoke drifted out lazily. Magnificent carvings adorned the ruddy sandstone surfaces, depicting dragons with wings spread in flight or rearing up and billowing flame. They were elaborate and detailed, but also crumbling. This was the ancient work of human hands, the princess realized with astonishment.

The doors of the temples were so enormous a ship could have sailed through them. As Ivy watched, they darkened with gigantic, looming shapes.

"Who isss there?" hissed a voice from the shadows. It was hard to imagine a more foreboding sound; it was like the angry hiss of a snake and the rumble of distant thunder rolled into one. "Who daresss enter our realm?"

"Um, it's me," Elridge answered hesitantly, sounding very small. "It's Elridge."

"Elridge," the voice spat out angrily. "You have a great deal of gall, young one, returning here after all you've done. Word hasss reached usss that the tower goesss unguarded."

Up and down the canyon the shadowy figures emerged into the firelight, and Ivy was stunned by the sight of them. There were only about fifteen dragons altogether, but they made for a terrible and impressive scene. They were absolutely enormous—easily twice the size of Elridge. There was something else different about them, too. There was a heat to them, a fiery quality that Elridge lacked. It was as if great fires smoldered within their bodies. Tendrils of smoke curled from their nostrils, and a strange light burned behind their eyes. Their scaly faces were grim and heavy with displeasure. A tremor of fear ran the length of Ivy's body all the way to her toes. One of these dragons could easily squash her like a bug or crush her like a grape between its dagger-size teeth.

The dragon who had spoken strode to the front of the crowd, the others quickly moving out of her way. Her scales were the same purple-black as Elridge's but had a dullness that spoke of age rather than a bright, shiny sheen. She wasn't the biggest of the lot, yet she had a powerful presence. Her reptilian face was severe, and her eyes shone with fierceness and wisdom. There was a terrifying majesty about her. She could only be the Dragon Queen.

"What isss on your back?" she demanded, casting her fiery eyes upon Elridge.

"Oh, uh, this is Ivy—I mean Princess Ivory of

Ardendale—and her fairy godmother, Drusilla," stammered Elridge, not quite daring to meet the Dragon Queen's penetrating gaze.

Drusilla slid to the ground, still clutching a terrified Toadstool in her arms. The little goat was trembling uncontrollably, her lips quivering like leaves battered about in a breeze.

"Your Majesty," Drusilla greeted the dragon formally and dropped into a low curtsy the best she could with a goat in her arms. She looked amazingly calm given the situation, but perhaps fairies didn't scare easily.

Ivy followed her godmother's cue and dropped to the ground, dipping into a curtsy. It felt awkward and ungraceful, for the princess didn't have much practice curtsying.

"Isss thissss an offering, then?" the Dragon Queen asked, eyeing Toadstool, who squealed and clamped her eyes shut tightly. "A bit sssmall, don't you think? I'd be lucky to get two bitesss out of it."

"Oh no, Your Majesty," said Drusilla. "This is my pixie goat, Toadstool. She accompanied me on my journey here. I would have very much liked to have brought you an offering, something worthy of your great splendor and magnificence, but I'm afraid the circumstances that brought us here left no time to gather a gift."

The Dragon Queen looked disappointed by this.

"Drusssilla, did you sssay?" she hissed. "Weren't you that twig of a fairy who helped the humansss negotiate our treaty?"

"Yes, Your Majesty, that *was* me." Drusilla looked delighted to be remembered. "You obviously have a superb memory. It's no wonder dragons are so famed for their intelligence."

"I am not easssily ssswayed by flattery," the Dragon Queen said warningly, but she looked pleased by Drusilla's praise all the same. Quick as lightening, however, her scaled features hardened once more. "And the fact remainsss that you are tressspasssing in our realm, fairy. I could do little to hurt an immortal like you, I know, but perhapsss I will eat your companionsss for thisss great insssult."

"Please, Mother—if you'd just listen to them, you'd see they have good cause to be here," Elridge said shakily.

Ivy's insides lurched, and she had to struggle not to let her astonishment show. The Dragon Queen, this most frightening and ferocious of creatures, was Elridge's *mother?*

"Do NOT call me that, you firelesss fool!" the Dragon Queen roared. "No ssson of mine would abandon the tower like a coward, then have the insssolence to return home with thisss rabble of sssoft-ssskinsss." The Dragon Queen cast a look at Ivy that made the princess's knees buckle. "Including the puny offssspring of that brute who ssslew Boldrisss, my worthy and true ssson." Her furious gaze returned to Elridge. "You have broken the Dragon Treaty, the only thing that keepsss the sssoft-ssskinsssss from our realm—you may have well doomed usss all. Boldrisss met hisss death proudly. But you—you are nothing more than a craven, pathetic, firelesss little runt."

Rumbles of agreement ran through the gathered dragons. It was obvious they were furious with Elridge, but Ivy was angry, too. Elridge didn't deserve such scorn. He looked thoroughly ashamed of himself, his head hung low and his shoulders slumped. No wonder he hadn't been in any rush to return to the Smoke Sands and face the wrath of his kindred. He was nothing like his proud and ferocious mother and the rest of her clan.

"I ssshould let our kindred take you to the tar pitsss at the edge of the desssert and tosss you in," the Dragon Queen roared at her son. "I ssshould throw all of you in for even daring to ssset foot here."

"Now, wait just a minute," shouted Ivy. "You're being completely unfair. You have no idea what Elridge has been through on your behalf, and this is how you repay him—by yelling and threatening and trying to humiliate him?"

The Dragon Queen turned a fiery, disbelieving stare upon the princess. Two round puffs of smoke issued from her nostrils as they flared. Ivy probably would have been petrified if she hadn't been so mad.

"Ivy, what are you doing?" Drusilla said in an urgent whisper. "You can't shout at the Dragon Queen. Maybe you should let me do the rest of the talking. . . ."

But words were already pouring from Ivy, tumbling out of her in a hot rush of anger. "This prince coming to slay the dragon—Romil—he's dreadful," she said. "Not only is he planning to murder me and my father, but he's going to legalize dragon slaying again. I heard him say so in a magic mirror when he didn't think anyone was listening. He's got a whole army of soldiers just jumping at the chance to face a dragon. He's been planning to break the Dragon Treaty all along—so, you see, it would be a disaster for all of us if he became king.

"Elridge used his brain," Ivy declared. "He knew he had no chance against Romil. You said it yourself, he's...well, runty and fireless. So he had a choice—he could stay at the tower and be slain, or give his kindred a chance by finding some other way to keep Romil from the throne. That's why he agreed to help me. He wasn't thinking of himself when he left the tower, he was thinking of all of you, and I think that's very noble."

The Dragon Queen still looked angry, but now her brow was furrowed as well, as if she was trying to decide whether to listen to Ivy or roast her on the spot.

"You're obviously an exceptionally smart dragon," the princess said, deciding to go the route of compliments as Drusilla had recommended. "Surely you can see that Elridge made a wise decision. Besides, it's not like we've been off on a picnic somewhere. Elridge has been very brave. We flew to the Craggies and had to free ourselves from trolls, and fought off a kraken, and even grappled our way through a haunted swamp in the middle of the night." This last part wasn't exactly a lie. The trolls believed Wrathful Swamp was haunted, and Ivy thought it sounded a lot better than saying they had nearly been done in by cranky swamp sprites.

"We had to find my godmother, Drusilla, so she could help us keep Romil from the throne, and now we need your help to finish the job."

The Dragon Queen's eyes were guarded. "I have been deceived by humansss before," she growled, the sound rising from deep in the back of her throat. "There wassss a time when humansss practically worssshiped dragonsss.

Centuriesss ago, they built thessse great templesss to honor usss, back when the human race wasss ssstill humble enough to revere that which isss greater than itsssself. They would leave usss offeringsss of gold and gemsss and meat. Today, they treat usss no better than animalsss, trophiesss to be hunted and ssslain."

"I'm not deceiving you, Your Majesty," Ivy said in as firm a voice as she could muster. "Your son has saved my life more than once since I've met him. I can assure you I have the greatest respect for dragonkind."

Her features softened slightly, but the Dragon Queen still didn't look convinced.

Ivy felt a surge of desperation. "Look, I'm sure if you help save his kingdom, my father will consider putting a stop to this tower and dragon slaying business once and for all." Drusilla and Elridge both looked at her with startled expressions. Ivy didn't know what had possessed her to say such a thing. She wasn't sure of anything of the sort. In truth, her father would probably set fire to his own beard before he'd agree to put an end to the Dragon Treaty. But it just didn't seem right to let someone who had helped you be slayed. Even her father should be able to see that. "Allies don't slay each other in battle, right? If you help us stop Romil, I promise to talk to my father about it myself."

The Dragon Queen had grown very quiet. She studied Ivy for several long moments, the expression on her face unreadable.

"I need proof of what you claim," she said finally. "You sssay you learned of Romil'ssss plansss in a magic mirror. I want to sssee for myssself. Ssshow thisss Romil to me in your mirror."

"Well, I can't, exactly." Ivy felt herself break into a sweat that had nothing to do with the bonfire or the desert heat. "I, sort of, broke the mirror. I only have one piece left, and it doesn't work properly." She looked down at her waist forlornly, then she pulled out the last useless shard of glass.

"Maybe not," said Drusilla, "but we still should be able to see Romil. Mirrors have memories as surely as people and dragons do. It's just a matter of stirring them up. Here, will you hold Toadstool for a moment?"

Without waiting for an answer, Drusilla dumped the little goat into Ivy's arms and seized the shard from the princess's hand. Toadstool was all legs for a moment as she struggled to settle into a secure position.

"Don't you dare drop me," she shrilled at Ivy, shooting a cowering look at the nearby drove of dragons as if she thought one of them would surely gobble her up as soon as her feet touched the ground.

Ivy barely heard Toadstool's sharp command, for Drusilla had just done something remarkable. She had run one finger along the shard's glassy surface—and then pushed it straight through. Ivy couldn't see her godmother's finger sticking out the other side, but it had to have gone *somewhere*—her finger had disappeared into the glass all the way up to the second knuckle. Leaning closer, Ivy saw the shard had filled with misty white waves yet again. Drusilla's finger was actually *inside* the fragment of mirror—she seemed to be stirring the mist, digging around, searching for something.

"Ah-hah—here it is!" she sang out, apparently finding what she was looking for, although the shard looked no different to Ivy. "Now we just need something to see it with. A piece of broken mirror won't do."

The fairy strode past the giant bonfire to a dim pool of water Ivy hadn't noticed before—a desert spring, undoubtedly where the dragons got their drinking water.

Drusilla whispered something Ivy couldn't hear and tossed the shard into the center of the pool. It struck with a small plop and sank quickly, sending a ring of ripples across the water. The pool grew misty and rolling, just as Drusilla's mirrors did when working their magic. When the last of the waves trailed off, the mist parted, and there, reflected on the surface, were Romil and Gar in a corner of the castle's courtyard. Romil was sharpening a sword.

"It won't be long now before you're sitting on the throne of this filthy little valley. 'Your Majesty' has a nice ring to it, don't you think?" said the Gar in the water.

With a start, Ivy realized this was the exact same conversation she had seen in the mirror, the one that had driven her to escape from the tower and search for Drusilla.

"And the first thing I'm going to do as king of this backwoods kingdom is lift that ridiculous ban on dragon slaying." Romil's tone was hard, his eyes a glacial glare. "When my soldiers arrive from Glacia, they will want some challenging sport. It's not like there's anything else for them to do around here."

The image of Romil began to waver.

"Besides, I can't have those filthy beasts living so close to my new lands, now, can I?"

Then, as quickly as it had come, the snippet of memory faded away, leaving the waters of the pool as smooth and untroubled as before.

The Dragon Queen was not nearly as serene. Ivy could practically feel the rage rising off her scales like steam. Smoke was pouring from each of her nostrils in great gray bursts.

"Treacherousss, dissshonorable human fiend," she seethed.

She turned toward Ivy and Drusilla, her eyes blazing like hot coals.

"Very well," she ground out between gritted teeth, "what would you have me do?"

29

The Southern Tower

"**W**hat we need is a way to get Prince Romil out of the castle," said Drusilla.

Ivy and her godmother were sitting on the sandy floor of the canyon, having a grave discussion with the Dragon Queen in the light of the bonfire. The other dragons lingered nearby. Elridge cast anxious glances at his mother as if he still expected her to turn on him any moment now, and Toadstool lay in Drusilla's lap shaking like a nervous kitten.

"Easssssily done," hissed the Dragon Queen. "My kindred and I will ssset the cassstle ablaze and bring down itsss wallsss. Romil will sssurely flee—if he isss not consssumed by the flamesss."

"But my father and the castle staff are in there!" cried Ivy, horrified.

"I guess what I really should have said was that we need

a way to get Romil out of the castle without any of the residents getting hurt," corrected Drusilla.

"That will be much more difficult." The Dragon Queen sniffed, and two puffs of gray smoke billowed from her nostrils. "You sssaid Romil hasss the king and hisss guard under lock and key. It would be very hard to free them without alerting the Glacianssss. Doing it my way would be far quicker and sssimpler."

"I'm sure the king of Ardendale would consider it a royal courtesy if you left his people and his castle intact," said Drusilla, choosing her words carefully so as not to offend the easily angered dragon.

"Very well," the Dragon Queen sighed. "My kindred and I will sssettle for eating the Glacianssss *after* they leave the cassstle."

"Eating the Glacians?" Ivy's stomach plunged all the way to her toes. Ardendale was a peaceful kingdom; banishment was the harshest punishment any king had handed down in centuries. And as much as she despised Romil and his lackeys, the princess didn't want to see them get eaten by dragons. She certainly didn't want the dragons to develop a taste for human flesh, or think they could solve all their disputes with humans by simply eating the source of the problem.

Her shock must have shown, for the Dragon Queen arched a ridge above one enormous eye. "You don't expect usss to jussst let them leave, do you?"

Drusilla came to her goddaughter's rescue. "That's exactly what we want them to do, Your Majesty." She gave Ivy a sly wink. "We want Romil and his men to spread word of your great prowess far and wide, to dissuade others from plotting against the dragons of the Smoke Sand Hills."

The Dragon Queen looked pleased by this. "Agreed," she said. "But if Romil or hisss men ssshould threaten any of my kindred, I cannot guarantee there will not be lossss of limb."

"Fair enough," said Drusilla.

"We're not doing anything until I know my father is safe," Ivy said stubbornly. "If we stand against him, Romil will threaten to hurt my father—I know he will. I'm not going to let that happen."

"Getting to the king would be hard," said Drusilla, her voice doubtful. "We'd have to either sneak or fight our way through the castle to the southern tower...."

"No, we wouldn't," said Elridge. He strode forward, giving his mother a tentative look. When she didn't voice any objections, he continued quickly. "The southern tower has a window, right? Ivy and I could fly up and retrieve the king. Once he's been whisked to safety, then we can confront Romil."

"A tolerable idea," the Dragon Queen said grudgingly. She looked at her son with wary eyes. "But perhapsss one of the more...capable...of our kindred ssshould be the one to fly up to the tower."

"No, it has to be Elridge." Ivy's tone was resolute, and Elridge shot her a thankful look. "He's a superb flier. Being small makes him quick and quiet—and he's the least likely to be spotted. His scales are a little glossy, but otherwise they blend in with the night fairly well. One of your other

kindred would be much more noticeable in the moonlight."
Ivy looked pointedly at the surrounding dragons, all of
whom were much lighter in color than Elridge—green, gold,
brown, even a couple of reddish-orange ones.

"Fine," snapped the Dragon Queen, who didn't look
happy. "But sssee to it you don't messss up as usssual," she
hissed at Elridge.

Elridge's face fell at her words, and Ivy felt a stab of pity.

"We still have to decide what to do once we have the
king," said Drusilla.

"I've been thinking about that." Ivy met her godmother's eyes in the flickering firelight "Do you think Romil has
posted guards outside the southern tower to watch over my
father?"

"Why?"

"Since I'll already be there, if there was some way I could
get out of the tower, I could sneak down to the cellar and
free the King's Guard," Ivy said. "The dragons are far too big
to fit inside the castle—not without causing a lot of damage,
anyway—but if the King's Guard could drive Romil's men
through the castle gate, the dragons could be waiting on the
other side to . . . um, *persuade* . . . them to leave the kingdom."
Ivy grinned at the thought. "It would all be over after that.
A small troop of Glacians is no match for an entire drove of
dragons."

"But they're more than a match for the King's Guard,"
Drusilla said grimly. "They've already defeated them once."

"Sober," Ivy pointed out. "But remember what Rose
and Clarinda said? The Glacians are planning a big feast

tonight—with seven barrels of wine at the ready. I just bet they get roaring drunk. They're probably at it already. Surely the King's Guard can herd a bunch of drunk hooligans out of the castle gate."

"But those drunk hooligans will have weapons," said Elridge, "and the King's Guard will have none. Rose said they'd all been taken away."

"If I can get word to the serving staff, they could help us," said Ivy, growing more and more excited as the plan came together in her mind. "The Glacians don't like to sit at the table with their swords strapped on. They're not comfortable in those narrow chairs in the Great Hall unless they take them off. I saw them do it at meals all the time—they set their swords on the floor next to their chairs or lay them on the table beside their plates. The serving staff can keep the wine flowing, make sure the Glacians get good and drunk, then slip away their swords when they're not looking." She tapped her lips thoughtfully with one finger. "But I still don't know how I can get out of the southern tower. Oh, I wish I could pick locks...."

"I think I have a way you can get past them," said Drusilla. "But Ivy, I'm not sure I like this idea of you wandering around the castle by yourself. Not all of the Glacians will be feasting in the Great Hall, you know. Romil will have lookouts posted. The cellar and the tower could both be guarded, for all we know."

"I have to take that chance," Ivy said. "Since we can't bring the dragons to the Glacians, we'll have to bring the Glacians to the dragons."

Drusilla didn't look convinced.

"There isss ssstill my idea," the Dragon Queen reminded her eagerly. "Jussst dessstroy the cassstle and everyone inssside."

"All right, then," chirped Drusilla. "Freeing the King's Guard it is!"

The Dragon Queen was reluctant to bring all of her kindred into human territory, so in the end she selected five of the largest and most ferocious of her dragons to accompany her into Ardendale.

"Seven altogether, counting the Dragon Queen and Elridge," Drusilla said cheerfully as they glided into the valley atop Elridge's back. "That should be plenty to quash a handful of Glacian usurpers."

"*If* the dragons keep away from Romil's armor and spears," Ivy added, earnestly hoping the pasty prince had put away his dragon-slaying gear after finding the white tower empty.

"Oh, it's really too bad we didn't have a chance to see the tar pits before we left," mourned Drusilla, watching the Smoke Sands shrink into distant, dark bumps on the horizon. "I was once courted by a charming desert sheikh who had his own tar pit, you know. Unfortunately, one day he accidentally fell in."

The dragons soared low over the kingdom, giving wide berth to villages and farmhouses, lest they be spotted by some hapless resident up after dark. Finally, they set down just to the north of the castle, in the miller's meadow, which was skirted by a thick screen of hornbeam trees that autumn had yet to rob of their leaves. One had only to peer through the tangle of branches to see a stretch of the Inland Road and the castle gate just beyond.

"The dragons will have to stay out of sight for now," Drusilla said, sliding to the ground, "but Toadstool and I will keep a lookout in the trees and alert them once the Glacians have been flushed out of the castle gate."

"Are you sure you don't want to come inside?" asked Ivy, trying very hard to make it sound like a casual question. She couldn't help thinking it would be useful to have Drusilla's fairy magic at hand if something should go wrong—and she could think of plenty of things that could go wrong.

"I think it best that I stay here with the Dragon Queen," Drusilla said regretfully. Leaning in close, she whispered, "To make sure she doesn't change her mind about burning the castle to the ground."

"Besides, *I'm* not going into that pile of rubble, and Drusy would never leave me here at the mercy of these overgrown lizards," Toadstool declared, not even bothering to lower her voice.

"Now, Toadstool, you mustn't talk about our new friends that way," scolded Drusilla, shooting the Dragon Queen an apologetic look. "You must forgive Toadstool, Your Majesty. She's fantastically outspoken. But it's quite refreshing and charming to come across a creature who speaks her mind so freely, don't you think?"

The Dragon Queen muttered something that sounded like, "Charming," under her breath in a way that reminded Ivy so much of Elridge that she nearly smiled.

"Didn't you say you had a way for me to get past locks?" she asked her godmother.

"Oh, yes, I nearly forgot." Drusilla withdrew yet another hand mirror from one of the bell-shaped sleeves of her gown. This mirror was tiny and had a little bronze sun in the top corner of its frame, the rays extending out to artfully encircle the glass. "This is my melting mirror."

"Melting mirror?"

"Yes, it's quite powerful," Drusilla said proudly. "It will take any form of light and concentrate the rays to a single point hot enough to melt...well, just about anything. I use it to melt pieces off the chocolate statues they serve for dessert back in the mound when I'm not that hungry and all I want is a toe....But it will work on harder substances like wood and iron, too, and you only need a smidgen of light. Sunlight, moonlight, firelight—any of it will do. You'll be able to melt locks right off."

"Thanks." Ivy tucked the mirror into the spiderskin. Since there was no longer any need for it to be tied to Elridge's tail, the princess had wrapped it around her own waist again before they had left the Smoke Sands.

"Please be careful, Ivy," Drusilla said, and for the first time something close to worry darkened her beautiful features. "You and I still have a lot of catching up to do when all this is over. If you can't get to the cellar safely, just come back and we'll find some other way to get the Glacians out of the castle."

"All right," said Ivy, although secretly she had made up

her mind to get to the cellar if she had to plow through every single one of Romil's guards to do it.

"I think you and Elridge should approach the castle from the rear," said Drusilla. "Remember Rose said there was a Glacian on watch at the castle gate."

"Yes, they must have locked Boggs in the cellar, too," grumbled Ivy, thinking the fussy little gatekeeper would have never willingly abandoned his post.

"Boggs?" Drusilla's face lit up like a candelabra. "Is that charming rapscallion still at the castle? Goodness me, that man was ever so dashing and handsome. . . ."

Boggs?! Ivy started so violently she nearly fell over. *Boggs must have looked a lot better back when he still had hair and all of his teeth,* she thought.

Drusilla gave her a quick hug, then waved good-bye as the princess clambered aboard Elridge's back and the two of them set off for the castle. Ivy was strangely comforted by the fact that Elridge seemed just as nervous as she. His dark scales looked paler than usual, and his wings trembled on the wind in a way that was not entirely normal.

They circled the castle and approached its stony parapets from behind, hidden from the view of the gatehouse.

"There it is," Ivy said, pointing to a small gray tower that faced the beach and the roiling waves of the Speckled Sea. She was careful to keep her voice low, so no one would hear them coming.

Elridge had been unusually quiet. He spoke for the first time in several minutes. "Do you really think your father would let the dragons out of guarding the tower?" he asked.

Even though his voice was barely above a whisper, Ivy could still hear the trace of hope in it.

"I don't know," she admitted. "I'll do whatever I can to convince him." The thought of Elridge being slain tore at her heart like never before. "I truly hope it's enough."

"Me, too," the dragon said wistfully. There was a long silence before he spoke again. "By the way, thanks for sticking up for me back in the Smoke Sands. If my mother had her way, I'd be at the bottom of a tar pit right now. She's really not glad I'm here."

"Well, for what it's worth, I'm glad you're here," said Ivy, giving his shoulder an affectionate squeeze. Elridge cast a wan smile in her direction. She couldn't help asking, "Why didn't you tell me you were the Dragon Queen's son?"

"Sorry—it's not like I was trying to keep it from you," said Elridge. "I guess I just don't like to talk about it. I mean, everyone expects me to be like her, just because she's my mother."

"Tell me about it," Ivy muttered under her breath.

They had reached the small window at the top of the southern tower. Elridge glided up to it, flapping his wings as gently and soundlessly as possible. The room looked dark, with not even the flicker of a flame cutting through the black. Ivy felt a hot surge of anger. Romil and his louts hadn't even seen fit to give her father so much as a candle.

"Father," she called in a loud whisper, her heart fluttering with a combination of excitement and nerves.

There was no answer, and Ivy wondered if perhaps he was asleep.

"Elridge, can you pull closer to the window?" she asked. "I'm going inside to get him."

Elridge edged as close to the side of the tower as possible and hovered alongside the window ledge.

"I'll help my father out the window and onto your back," Ivy told the dragon. "Then you can fly him to safety while I melt the lock off the door and head for the cellar."

"Dear me, it looks dark in there," said Elridge, looking worriedly at the black square of window. "I thought Drusilla said there had to be light for the mirror to work."

"I think there's enough moonlight coming in," said Ivy, raising her eyes hopefully to the large silver moon overhead. "Drusilla said it didn't take much."

She carefully climbed down Elridge's scales and scrambled over the window ledge. Thankfully, enough watery moonlight did spill inside for her to see, although barely. The circular room she found herself in was as tiny, cramped, and cluttered as she remembered, buckets and broom handles making strange shapes and shadows against the walls. It took a moment for Ivy's eyes to adjust to the dimness, but she finally made out a figure curled near the door, hunched beneath a hooded cloak.

"Father!"

She dashed across the room and fell on her knees beside him.

"It's all right, Father," she said, shaking his shoulder gently, trying to wake him. "You're safe now. I'm going to get you out of here."

"Is that so?" he answered in a voice that was not only

wide awake, but strangely cold and unfeeling. He raised a pale hand and pushed back the hood of his cloak, but beneath it wasn't the warm, gray-bearded face Ivy longed to see. It was, in fact, the last person in the world she wanted to set eyes upon at that moment.

"Well, well," said Prince Romil frostily, seizing her tightly by the arm. "If it isn't my wayward bride-to-be."

Inside the Captive Castle

"**Y**ou!" Ivy tried to wrench her arm free, but Romil's grip was like an iron vice.

"My guards overheard some of the castle's residents plotting to free the king," said Romil, an exceedingly satisfied look on his face. "I had them thrown into the cellar with the rest of the king's riffraff, but I suspected some over-devoted yokel might still try to rescue him. I didn't expect that yokel to be you," he sneered at Ivy, "but no matter. I was wise enough to take the precaution of removing the king and setting up my own little trap in turn."

"WHAT HAVE YOU DONE WITH MY FATHER?"

"Ivy?" came Elridge's anxious voice from the other side of the tower wall. "Dear me, is something wrong? What's going on in there?"

In a rush of wings and scales, the dragon repositioned

himself at the window so he could peer inside, gripping the window ledge with his front claws for purchase.

"Ivy!" he squawked, freezing as he caught sight of her in Romil's grasp, no doubt recognizing the prince from the memory Drusilla had extracted out of the last fragment of magic mirror.

Romil, too, seemed stunned for a moment. He looked back and forth between the princess and the dragon, his eyes slowly darkening with realization and rage.

"I knew it!" he bellowed, turning on Ivy. "You scheming little harpy," he snarled, giving her a look that would have surely melted the ice palace back in Glacia. "There was never going to be a dragon waiting at that tower at the foot of the Craggies, was there? You've been working with the filthy beast all along—you and your father both. I bet the castle staff is in on the plot, too, aren't they? Everyone in this pathetic little kingdom has been conspiring to humiliate me and keep me from the throne, haven't they? *Haven't they?*"

He shook Ivy violently, as if he thought he could shake a confession right out of her.

"Leave her alone, you big bully," screeched Elridge, his voice cracking wildly. His claws clutched the window ledge so tightly, little holes were bored into the stone.

Ivy could see anger in his eyes, but it was overshadowed by fear and uncertainty, and somehow there wasn't a lot of power behind his choked-out command.

With his free hand Romil drew the sword buckled at his side, never once loosening his grip on Ivy.

"So, it would seem I may get my chance to slay the dragon after all," said the prince, his pale face lighting up as if someone had given him a longed-for gift.

He advanced several steps, dragging the squirming princess behind. The small window was just wide enough to frame Elridge's face like a painting, leaving the dragon no room to maneuver his claws or horns inside, and giving Romil the perfect target. Ivy stumbled and felt her knees go weak. She had read of dragons being slain through the head. A sword could pierce the soft roof of a dragon's mouth and cut straight through to its brain.

"Elridge, fly! Get out of here!" she cried, panic-stricken.

Elridge's eyes had been fixed upon the sword, wide and terrified, but Ivy's voice seemed to snap him out of his trance. She saw his muscles tense as if ready to take flight, but still he clung to the window ledge, looking torn.

"Ivy," he faltered. "I can't just leave you here...."

Romil was inching ever closer to the window, despite Ivy's attempts to drag her feet and slow him down. Soon he'd be within striking distance of the skittish dragon.

"Just go!" Ivy pleaded with her friend.

With one last forlorn look at the princess, Elridge released his grip on the window ledge and launched himself into the air. He didn't fly far, however, hovering several arm lengths from the window, just out of reach of Romil's sword. It was an immense stroke of luck that Romil didn't have his dragon-claw spears to throw.

The Glacian prince darted the last few steps to the window, his jaw clenched tightly. He seized a fistful of Ivy's gown at the shoulder and hauled her up next to him.

"I'll tell you what, dragon," he called. "Since you seem so reluctant to leave your precious princess, I'll make you a deal. I came to this forsaken valley to do battle with one of your kind, and I loathe to be robbed of that chance. Meet me in the castle courtyard in twenty minutes, and I promise no harm will come to Princess Ivory. The two of us can face each other in battle as we were meant to do at the foot of the white tower."

"B-b-battle?" Elridge's mouth fell open. "With you?"

"If you defeat me, the princess and her father will go free," Romil said. "But if you fail to appear for my challenge, I can assure you that little Ivy here will meet a most unfortunate end."

Romil laid the edge of his blade against Ivy's neck as if to prove he meant business. She shuddered at the feel of cold, sharp steel against her skin.

Elridge was starting to look angry again.

"Let her go, you piece of goat gut!"

"Ah, but you will have to win her freedom first," Romil taunted. "Unless you're too cowardly to even try. Quite puny for a dragon, aren't you, and spineless, too, running from an unarmored man with a simple sword? To tell the truth, I wouldn't be terribly disappointed if you didn't come. I'd quite enjoy devising some horrible, messy fate for this little monstrosity they call a princess." Ivy gave a sharp gasp as his sword pressed into the side of her neck. She felt warm, wet blood oozing onto the surface of her skin.

In that moment, something about Elridge seemed to change. The anger positively burned behind his eyes.

Romil didn't seem to notice. "Twenty minutes, dragon," he said, and turned away from the window, towing Ivy to the door on the other side of the small room.

"Ivy!" Elridge shouted. The princess managed one quick glance back before Romil flung open the tower door and dragged her roughly down the stairs.

Ivy would have been sorely tempted to try to break free and run, if not for the sword still grasped at the ready in Romil's hand. At the bottom of the stairwell, they were met by two burly Glacian guards.

"Your Highness—" began the taller of the two, but he stopped short when his eyes landed upon Ivy. "The princess? But where did she come from? We've been watching the stairs to the southern tower as you commanded, my prince. No one passed this way. How did she—"

"I don't have time to explain," Romil said sharply. He pushed Ivy toward the guard. "Take her to the cellar and lock her up with the rest of the prisoners. Make sure the cellar door remains guarded at all times. I don't want any distractions. I have armor to don and a dragon to slay."

"Yes, Your Highness." Neither of the guards asked any more questions. They bowed crisply as Romil strode past.

"I confess I don't expect it to be much of a battle," said the prince. "Still, a puny dragon makes a better trophy than no dragon at all. Besides, none of the insufferable peasants around here will be able to contest my claim to the throne after this. Ardendale will be mine once and for all." He turned and, with a determined stride, disappeared down the hallway that led to the guest chambers.

"Move, you." One of the guards drew his sword and gave Ivy a none-too-gentle shove. "And don't even think about trying anything funny."

As they made their way down the hall, the princess could hear raucous laughter and the jostle of cutlery coming from the direction of the Great Hall. Those of Romil's men who were lucky enough not to be on guard duty were feasting the night away.

They reached the bustling kitchen far too soon for Ivy's liking. It was full of castle staff. Kitchen maids stirred bubbling pots of soup and ushered loaves of bread out of the ovens. Cook and her helpers were roasting meats and chopping vegetables and preparing sauces. Servants scurried in and out, entering with empty platters and leaving with heaping full ones.

"Better hurry with the next course," one of them said to Cook on his way out. "You wouldn't believe how much those Glacians can eat. It's no wonder it takes a whale to feed them."

But Cook's attention was elsewhere.

"Ivy," she gasped, nearly dropping her saucepan at the sight of the bedraggled princess. The kitchen was suddenly still; everyone had stopped what they were doing to gape and stare.

"Nothing here that concerns any of you," the second of the guards growled at them. "Get back to work."

At the back of the kitchen, a set of stairs led down to the tiny storeroom where the cellar door was located. Another pair of Glacians was on guard here. A small trestle table and two stools had been set near the door so that the bored watchmen could play dice.

"Prince Romil says to lock her up with the others," said the Glacian with the drawn sword, "and to make sure the door stays guarded at all times. As for us, we're off to join the festivities in the Great Hall."

"At least you get to enjoy yourselves," grumbled one of the guards at the table. He stood, fumbled with a key fastened to his belt, and opened the iron padlock that secured the door. "All right, in you go."

Ivy had spent plenty of time in the cellar before. The dark, cool, windowless room was where Cook stored apples and root vegetables, large wheels of cheese, and extra barrels of elderberry wine. It was the perfect place to sneak a midafternoon snack if you could slip in and out without any of the kitchen staff noticing. The door had never been locked before.

As the door shut and she heard the padlock click back into place behind her, Ivy was surprised to find that the cellar wasn't dark for once, but lit by the dim glow of a tin lantern. There was another surprise as well.

"Father!"

The princess flew forward and threw her arms around the old king, who looked as astonished and happy as she felt.

"Ivy, thank the heavens," he said, his voice strangely thick. He squeezed her so tightly it hurt, but the princess couldn't bring herself to care. "I was so worried—none of us knew what had happened to you, or to the dragon for that matter," he told her. "Prince Romil returned from the tower as angry as a hornet. That blackguard took over the castle and swore he would make himself king. He's had me locked in the southern tower all day, and just this evening moved me down here to the cellar. You were right about him all along, my dear. He is a vile villain of the worst sort. I am so sorry I didn't listen to you."

"I'm just glad you're all right," the princess murmured.

"Ivy, you're hurt," cried her father when they had broken apart. He inspected the side of her neck where Romil's blade had bitten into her skin.

"It's just a scratch," she assured him, taking a good look around the small cellar. It was full of familiar faces. There were Boggs and the King's Guard as she had expected, but Absalom the butcher was there as well; and Mortimer, the king's man-in-waiting; and back in the far corner was . . .

"Owen!" cried Ivy, spotting the red-haired stable boy.

"Hullo, Ivy," Owen said. "I'm glad you're all right. I've—I mean—everyone's been really worried about you." The tips of his ears turned as red as his hair.

"What are you doing in here?" the princess asked.

"The guards overheard Absalom and Mortimer and me planning to break the king out of the southern tower. We were going to try to do it tonight."

"That was brave of you," Ivy said admiringly.

"Very brave," agreed the king.

"I suppose," said Owen, looking embarrassed. "Too bad it didn't work."

"Speaking of towers," the king said, "Ivy, dear, however did you get out of yours?"

So Ivy told all of them her story, as briefly and quickly as she possibly could, starting with her escape from the tower and ending with her plan to flush the Glacians out of the castle so they could be captured by the waiting dragons.

"But now Romil wants to fight Elridge in the courtyard in a matter of minutes," Ivy said. "We have to get out of here, or Romil is certain to slay him."

"But you won't be able to melt the padlock off the door from in here," said the king forlornly.

"Drusilla said the mirror could melt through almost anything," said Ivy. "I bet we could melt the door itself using the light from the lantern."

"Clever girl, that Druthee." Boggs beamed.

Ivy studied the door. It was five planks of sturdy oak, held together by iron battens.

"The guards might notice it starting to melt," she said.

"Melt the hinges," suggested Owen, "just enough to get the door good and loose. We can ram it and break it down all at once, catch the guards by surprise."

He carried the tin lantern to the door. The princess pulled the melting mirror from the spiderskin and held it at an angle to the light, trying to cast a ray toward the door. She worried that the flickering glow from the lantern just wasn't strong enough, but then she noticed a small beam of white light reflected upon the wood. It started to smoke. She quickly directed the beam at the highest of the iron hinges. It melted like snow under the sun, rivulets of liquid metal coursing down the side of the door. Steam rose from the hinge in little curling wisps.

"It's working," she exclaimed happily.

"There, that's enough," Owen said. "The hinge is almost melted away."

The princess melted most of the next two hinges as well, then the three largest of the King's Guard lined up before the door.

"Put your backs into it, men," said the king.

The guards ran at the door, ramming their shoulders into the heavy oaken planks. The loosened door swung away from the wall with a loud crash, sending the trestle table on the other side flying. Romil's men were knocked from their stools. They struggled to rise, but a member of the King's Guard whacked one of them on the side of the head with the lantern. The other was felled with a well-placed punch. Neither of the Glacians even had a chance to react. Their swords were snatched up from the floor.

"I bet Cook has some string we can use to tie them up," Owen said, stepping over the unconscious guards and starting up the stairs to the kitchen.

"My daughter's plan is a good one," the king said to those who remained. "No doubt the Glacians are as drunk as fiddlers at a fair by now. I say we have the serving staff slip away their swords, one by one, and bring them to us. When we're fully armed, we'll attack and drive those ruffians out of the castle gate."

"Perhaps it would be best if you wait here, Your Majesty," one of the King's Guard suggested.

"Piffle," said the king. "I was once a master swordsman. I daresay I can still swing a steel blade with the best of them."

Ivy looked uncertain.

"I know sometimes you think I'm just a silly old man," her father said. "You're not going to try to stop me from joining the fight, are you?"

The princess looked at him thoughtfully. "No," she said. "I know how strong and brave you can be, and I know you can do this. But, Father, I need to go help Elridge. I don't think he would just abandon me. I have a feeling he's going to try to fight Romil in the castle courtyard. Are you going to try to stop me?"

The king met her with a level gaze.

"I think anyone who can make it over the Craggies and back and venture into the very heart of the Dragon Queen's realm can take care of herself," he said, his face shining with pride. "Go and help your friend. I shall see you when all this is over."

31

Battle in the Courtyard

Ivy took the steps to the kitchen two at a time and tore through the room. She didn't know how long it had been since Romil had dragged her down from the southern tower, but she guessed it must be close to twenty minutes, maybe longer. Romil could be preparing to sink a spear into Elridge this very moment. The thought made her throat tighten and her heart drum inside her chest. Elridge could already be wounded, or even... but no, she refused to think of that. She *would* get to him in time—she *must*. Vaguely, she heard Cook calling to her, and Owen, too, but didn't dare stop for even a moment to explain herself.

"Sorry, I have to go," she called over her shoulder as she exited the kitchen, narrowly dodging a serving girl who was walking in with another picked-clean platter.

She was now in the main hallway of the castle's west wing and darted along the gray flagstones in the direction of the entry hall, which opened onto the courtyard. She skidded to a stop, however, just before the enormous arched entrance to the Great Hall. Loud voices and drunken laughter drifted out in waves. In her haste, the princess had forgotten she would have to pass this open entryway to reach her destination. Frustration welled up inside her, and she fought the urge to scream. It was a good seven or eight paces wide. There was no way she could cross that space without at least one person in the Great Hall spotting her. It wouldn't do her any good to double back and take the hallway down the east wing of the castle, either, for an identical entryway flanked the Great Hall on that end as well. She was roundly trapped and rapidly running out of time to reach Elridge.

"Pssst."

Ivy started at the sound and turned to find none other than Tildy rushing up the hallway to meet her, carrying a large platter of steaming raspberry scones. The princess's heart leaped at seeing her nursemaid unharmed—and just as quickly fell back to earth. Tildy looked cross and harried, and Ivy had the sinking feeling she was in for the tongue-lashing of a lifetime. She fully expected her nursemaid to launch into a lecture on the impropriety of leaving the tower and the sorry state of her gown, but to her surprise such offenses seemed to be the last thing on Tildy's mind.

"They've put me to work as if I were some common kitchen maid," the nursemaid whispered instead, her voice brimming with indignation. "I spent the entire afternoon scrubbing pots in hot water. It will take weeks for my poor hands to recover, even with my best rose petal and honey hand cream." Her eyes flared angrily, and when she turned her gaze on Ivy, it was filled with a steely determination. "Well, don't just stand there, we have to get you past that door. Get behind me and be sure to keep up."

Tildy stood at the edge of the entryway, facing forward into the Great Hall with the platter held before her. She took a neat step sideways with her left foot, then deftly slid her right foot over to meet it. Somehow she made the movement look natural and graceful, even pretty. Realizing what she was meant to do, Ivy hunkered down and scuffled along behind Tildy, hidden from the sight of those in the Great Hall by the nursemaid's wide girth and generous skirts. Within moments Tildy had sidestepped half the length of the doorway.

"Whaddaya think you're doing?" Ivy heard one of the Glacians slur. He had obviously caught sight of Tildy doing her peculiar sideways slide.

"I am practicing one of the signature steps of the Arden-dale waltz," Tildy said huffily. "It is one of the most fluid and elegant of the traditional ballroom dances. Not that I would expect a drunken barbarian like you to know that," she added under her breath.

"Well, practice on yer own time," the guard half mumbled, half growled, "and get that plate of cakes in here."

Fortunately, by this time, Tildy had reached the opposite end of the doorway.

"They are called scones, and hasn't anyone ever told you patience is a virtue?" she asked imperiously, pausing a moment to give Ivy time to scoot over and flatten herself against the wall, out of the view of the Glacians. "But very well, I am coming."

Tildy gave Ivy a most unladylike wink before sweeping into the Great Hall with her platter.

Ivy was stunned—and more than a little impressed—but she didn't have time to dwell on such thoughts. She pushed away from the wall and continued her frantic flight down the hallway. She reached the entry hall, hurtled the short distance to the door, and burst into the courtyard. A stone portico sheltered the door and the handful of wooden torches that burned in brackets against the wall, casting flickering firelight into the square. Both Romil and Elridge were already there, facing each other from opposite ends of the courtyard: Romil in front of the stables to Ivy's left, and Elridge with his back to the stone wall on her right. The princess felt her body go limp with relief. Elridge was all right; she wasn't too late.

Neither of the courtyard's occupants noticed her. Romil was eyeing Elridge shrewdly as if sizing up his opponent, while Elridge watched the prince guardedly in turn. He paced back and forth, looking uncomfortable but not nearly as scared as Ivy expected. It took a moment for her to realize what was different about him: a thin tendril of smoke snaked lazily out each of his nostrils.

Elridge found his fire, the princess thought. Surprise and delight flooded her in spite of the dire situation. She remembered the burning light she had seen in his eyes in the southern tower. Romil must have made the dragon very angry indeed.

Romil was clad in his glistening dragon-scale armor,

although the visor of his helmet was raised, revealing a face rigid with resolve. A sword was at his hip, and his large quiver of spears stood upright by his side, within easy reach. The pointed tips of at least twenty dragon-claw spears poked menacingly out of the top.

"This is it, dragon," the Glacian prince shouted across the courtyard, the venom in his voice promising a brutal fight. He slipped one of the spears out of the quiver and grasped it tightly in his armored fist. "Let the battle commence!"

The words were barely out of his mouth when the prince drew back his arm and launched the spear straight at Elridge. Ivy gasped, but the dragon was ready for the attack. He darted to one side, the spear bouncing harmlessly off the stone wall behind the spot he had been standing a mere moment before.

Ivy released a breath, but her relief was short-lived. The Glacian prince launched a second spear before she could draw her next lungful of air. Looking slightly nervous, Elridge dodged this second missile as well.

"Confounded dragon," Ivy heard Romil mutter under his breath.

He obviously hadn't realized that Elridge's small size made him that much quicker than the average dragon and that much smaller a target. Still, Romil didn't look too concerned, and it didn't take a scholar to see why.

The courtyard wasn't all that large, and they were closed in by three walls and the castle gate; Elridge couldn't flee far, and anywhere he positioned himself would still be well within the range of a spear. If he took to the air, he exposed his soft underbelly. Elridge may have been doing a grand job of evading spears so far, but clearly his focus was on avoiding the rapid onslaught of spears rather than attacking his opponent. Ivy, however, wasn't about to let the bloated-brained Glacian prince get off so easily.

"Fire, Elridge!" she cried. "Use your fire!"

Both Elridge and Romil turned at the sound of her voice. She wasn't sure which of them was more surprised to see her. Elridge grinned broadly.

"You? You're supposed to be locked in the cellar." A look of disbelief hung upon Romil's pale face.

"Elridge, blast him with your fire!"

Elridge drew a deep breath and released an orange jet of flame directly at the distracted prince. Ivy was expecting Romil to flee in terror, so she was rather disappointed when the prince merely squared his shoulders and stood his ground. Elridge might not have had much experience breathing fire, but his aim was true. The stream struck Romil full-on, only to rebound harmlessly off his glistening armor, scattering in all directions in a magnificent starburst. Fire rained down upon the roof of the stables, the dry thatch bursting into eager flame.

Ivy's rising hope rapidly deflated. She had forgotten that dragon fire was useless against the scaled armor that shielded Romil.

The prince gave a mirthless laugh. "You'll find I'm not so easily defeated, dragon," he said, a note of triumph in his icy voice.

At once, he was on the move again, hurling another of his deadly spears. Ivy felt a cold stab of fear as she watched Elridge barely get out of the way in time. Poor Elridge just wasn't much of a warrior, and his fire wasn't going to do him any good as long as Romil was protected by that infernal armor.

If only Romil had some sort of weakness, Ivy thought bitterly. *A trick knee, bad eyes, a big boil on his nose...anything....*

Bad eyes. At once, Ivy was flooded with the memory of the Smoke Sand Hills. It had been hard to see in the clouds of smoke that engulfed the desert realm, and even harder to breathe. But the dragons had gone unbothered, even though she, a human, had fought for breath....

"Elridge, make smoke," Ivy cried. "A lot of it!"

"Be quiet! Stay out of this," Romil growled at her. He had taken up another of his claw-tipped spears. For a moment, Ivy was afraid he planned to hurl it at her, but the pale prince had other plans. He turned and took aim at the dragon yet again.

Elridge was already hard at work. Ivy hadn't thought one small dragon could produce so much smoke so quickly. Maybe Elridge was showing off a bit now that he could actually make smoke for the first time in his life. She could hear the dragon snorting loudly as he ducked beneath the arc of Romil's throw. Puffs of thick, black smoke mushroomed from his nostrils. Heavy and rolling, they began filling the courtyard, trapped between the sturdy stone walls. It was even worse than the Smoke Sands; there was so much smoke in such a confined space. In a matter of moments, Elridge was completely hidden from view.

Romil had snatched up another spear, but even he couldn't fight the effects of the suffocating smoke. He began to make choking sounds, then started to cough furiously. Ivy's eyes landed on the large quiver, left unattended several steps behind the hacking prince. She knew she would have to act fast—now—while she could still see the quiver and Romil was still distracted by his coughing fit. Taking a deep breath and holding it tightly, she bolted from the safety of the portico and plunged into the sea of smoke, making a mad dash toward the hazy figure of the Glacian prince. He was nearly bent double now, struggling to expel the acrid smoke from his lungs.

Without warning, a long, scaled tail snaked out of the billows and whipped the prince's ankles out from underneath him. He hit the ground with a curse and a loud thud but was thinking like a hunter even then. Without missing a beat, he hurled his spear in the telltale direction of the dragon's tail with all the strength he could muster.

There was a short, strangled cry, then Elridge's tail jerked backward into the smoke like a fleeing eel and disappeared from sight.

"Elridge?" Ivy breathed, stopping mere footsteps from the quiver of spears—and from where the Glacian prince sat sprawled upon the ground.

The name hung in the air, unanswered.

Romil turned then, his gray eyes falling upon her, icy and hard.

Ivy's heart jumped ferociously in her chest as she remembered why she was there. She didn't know how badly Elridge was hurt, but she wasn't about to let Romil launch any more spears at the dragon. Without further thought, she snatched the quiver and ran for all she was worth.

32

A Castle Reclaimed

"**M**iserable...little...wretch..." Romil hacked between coughs from somewhere behind Ivy, hidden from view in the clouds of smoke.

The princess's speed was frustratingly slow. The spears were heavier than she had expected, and she practically had to drag the quiver along the ground behind her. She could hold her breath no longer. She permitted herself only tiny inhales, trying to take in as little of the smoke as possible, but found herself coughing and wheezing all the same. Though she knew the courtyard like the back of her hand, she didn't see the small stone well near the northwest corner until she almost ran straight into it. She worked quickly, hoisting the quiver and laying it across the lip of the well where it balanced like a plank. With a grunt, she heaved the back end higher and higher, until the quiver and all its contents upended into the well's shaft. She heard several splashes as they hit the water far below.

There, she thought, supremely satisfied with herself. *He'll never get them out.*

"WHAT HAVE YOU DONE?"

Ivy turned to find Romil stumbling toward her out of the smoke. It was starting to thin—Elridge obviously wasn't producing any more, she thought with a sinking heart—and the sound of splashing water had probably led the prince straight to her in any case. He clearly grasped what she had done to his precious spears, for his normally pale face had turned a shocking shade of crimson, as if his blood were about to boil over. There was the sharp ring of steel, and Ivy realized Romil had drawn his sword.

"You have been a thorn in my side from the moment I set foot in this accursed kingdom." His voice was low and deadly, his eyes wild with rage. Ivy had seen him angry plenty of times, but she had never seen him like this. "All that is at an end. I finished off that wretched dragon, and now I'm going to finish you, too."

He advanced several steps. Ivy found herself trapped, her back against the well, the sound of her own heartbeat pounding in her ears. Romil was mere steps from her now, his eyes still wild. He lifted his sword . . . and, with a sudden cry, dropped the weapon and clutched at his chest. A spot of hot, white light had appeared over his heart, steaming and smoking of its own accord.

The melting mirror. Ivy looked down to see the very top

of the mirror poking out of her spiderskin sash. The fire on the stable roof was spreading rapidly, and a section of thatch behind Romil had flared furiously, its light catching the mirror's reflective surface just right. Ivy could barely believe her eyes. The dragon scales across Romil's chest were melting— but then, Drusilla had said the mirror would melt just about anything. Undoubtedly Romil's skin was steaming underneath, like a crab being cooked in its shell.

"What... sorcery... is this?" panted Romil. Had he realized the source of his distress was merely a shaft of light cast by an enchanted mirror, he could have simply stepped out of the way.

Unfortunately, the fire rolled onward, and the flames shifted course. The beam of light dimmed and faded. Romil gasped for breath and gawked at his ruined armor. It gaped open at the chest, a white substance resembling melted candle wax caking the front.

"You little witch." His strength returning, Romil lunged at her with the ferocity of an enraged mountain cat.

Ivy flinched, expecting his hands to close around her throat, when a sudden jet of flame roared past her left ear. It struck Romil full in the chest, the force knocking him on his back. His armor repelled most of it, but the front of his gray undershirt, peeking out from the gap in the chest plate, caught fire as surely as tinder. Romil thrashed about on the ground, yelping and slapping at the flames with his hands.

Elridge strode through the last remaining wisps of smoke, looking alive and well except for a nasty gash on his right flank. He towered over the fallen prince. For a moment, Ivy thought he simply planned to watch as Romil burned, but then the dragon leaned down and looked the writhing prince full in the face.

"Dear me, that looks unpleasant," he said, a wide grin revealing rows of long, pointed dragon teeth. "Here, let me help you with that."

He clamped one of his front claws down tightly over Romil's torso, pinning the prince to the ground and snuffing out the flames at the same time. Romil moaned and sagged in relief. Ivy doubted he had suffered any serious injury, although between the melting mirror and the fire, he probably wouldn't have any chest hair for some time to come.

"Elridge, you're all right!" she cried, giddy with a mixture of joy and relief.

"Right as rain," said the dragon, tipping his head to look down at her affectionately. "With a little help." He flashed a grateful smile, and the princess grinned back, her rush of elation broken only by the sound of a familiar voice.

"Ivy! Ivy, are you all right?" Owen raced up from the direction of the entry hall, his eyes drifting from the princess to the burning stables, where fingers of flame had started to creep down what was left of the thatched roof to the walls and wooden support beams. Fire had already spread to the west wing of the castle, behind the stables, and Ivy could see the tall parapets beginning to blacken. Flames glowed a threatening orange against the night sky.

The whinnies of horses, frantic and high-pitched, carried across the courtyard. Ivy could hear them thrashing in their stalls, trying to paw their way out. Cold panic gripped her.

Frederick's in there, she thought.

"I have to get the horses out," said Owen. "If the fire spreads further, the whole castle could burn down." He darted toward the burning stables.

At that point, a number of things happened in quick succession. It began with a rolling clap of thunder. The sky opened, and rain pelted down. Ivy was astonished, as the night had been perfectly clear only moments before. But a bank of swollen storm clouds had formed in the sky like magic and promptly proceeded to drench the courtyard and everything in it. The raging flames sputtered and died, leaving the charred remains of the stable roof and a blackened wall of castle. The dirt floor of the courtyard darkened into a mire of mud and loose bits of hay.

Elridge stared up into the sky, his golden eyes wide. Romil used that moment of distraction to wriggle free from beneath the dragon's claw. He took off running but quickly lost his footing on the slick, muddy ground.

"Whooooaaaa..."

The prince fell backward into the mud with a splat and proceeded to slide across the courtyard on his backside until he slammed into one of the stone walls. After that, he didn't have the wherewithal to do anything but lie in the mud, once again groaning loudly.

Next, a clamor of angry voices caught Ivy's attention. She looked up in time to see a horde of drunken Glacians stumble out the door of the entry hall and into the mud-filled courtyard. On their heels was a mob of castle residents. Absalom, Boggs, and the King's Guard were waving swords, and many of the others had taken up makeshift weapons of their own. A number of the kitchen staff had meat mallets and carving knives clutched in their hands, and Ivy saw shovels, hoes, and hammers from the storage closet off the east hallway. Cook grasped a frying pan. The king was at the head of the crowd, lavishly brandishing a sword and looking as if he was enjoying every moment of it.

"Out of our castle, you ill-mannered vermin," he shouted as the mob advanced into the courtyard. "Out, out, out!

"And you, too, you travesty of a prince," he added, leaning down to seize a dazed Romil by what remained of his undershirt. "Leave before we decide to cover you in mustard sauce and send you to the trolls as an offering." With a strength Ivy didn't know her father possessed, the king hauled the mud-covered prince to his feet and roughly shoved him in the direction of the castle gate.

The Glacian manning the gatehouse abandoned his post after being confronted with five swords and a meat mallet. Boggs assumed his rightful place next to the gatehouse door and turned the crank to raise the portcullis. The King's Guard drove the Glacians out of the gate at swordpoint while the castle's residents cheered.

Last of all, the princess heard frightened cries erupt on the other side.

"You mussst be the Prince Romil I've heard sssso much about," came the rumble of the Dragon Queen's voice.

Ivy began to laugh.

33

Mud and Other Matters

The strange storm petered out as quickly as it had come, the liquid light of the moon spilling through rapidly dissolving clouds. The torches on the portico had been protected from the wet weather and burned as brightly as they had before the downpour, casting a welcome glow upon the courtyard and those who celebrated within its walls.

"I don't understand," said Elridge, still staring into the sky with a look of bewilderment. "Where did all that rain come from?"

"Elridge," laughed Ivy, "don't you remember Drusilla saying she used to tinker with the weather?"

The furrows on Elridge's face melted into a huge grin. "You know something? I really like that godmother of yours."

"Elridge, you're bleeding," Ivy said, gasping as the firelight caught the red slash in the dragon's side. She examined the cut carefully. It was long but mercifully shallow, barely breaking the surface of Elridge's hard, glossy scales.

"It's just a scrape," he assured her. "Romil caught me off guard with that last spear, but I still managed to get out of the way in time. It just nicked me. The sight of my own blood gave me a bit of a turn, however," he admitted sheepishly. "Good goat fur, it was so bright and red and kind of shocking... but I got over it... after a minute or two."

Ivy laughed and threw her arms around him—or more truthfully just kind of leaned into his uninjured side with her arms spread wide, since her arms weren't actually long enough to fit around a dragon.

"You silly thing," she said, "why did you try to fight Romil all by yourself? Why didn't you get the other dragons to help?"

"The other dragons?" Elridge looked as if such an idea had never occurred to him. "There isn't enough room for them to maneuver inside this puny courtyard. The best they could have done was hover over it and try to strike at Romil from the air—and Romil would have speared them for sure. I couldn't put my kindred in that kind of danger."

"It must have been scary," said Ivy, "the thought of facing Romil on your own."

"Well, finding my fire made it a little easier," said Elridge. "It happened at the southern tower, you know, after Romil threatened you and cut your neck with his sword. The thought of him hurting you made me so angry. I felt all this heat build up inside me, and then it just kind of... sparked." The dragon's eyes softened. "Besides, I couldn't just leave you at Romil's mercy. You're the only reason I didn't get slain at the foot of the white tower in the first place. You're the first true friend I've ever had."

His words filled Ivy with warmth. "You really are the kindest, bravest dragon in all the world, aren't you?" she said.

Elridge was so pleased by this, he couldn't bring himself to answer.

Everyone around them was soaking wet and splattered with mud, yet no one—not even Tildy—seemed to care. The castle residents celebrated with unsuppressed abandon under the night sky. Cook and several of her helpers brought out heated wine and spiced cider to ward off the chill, although most of the crowd seemed far too exuberant to be bothered by the cold. Word must have gotten out that the dragons were on their side this night, for no one seemed the least bit perturbed that a dragon lingered in their midst.

And, suddenly, there were Rose and Clarinda, rushing out of the crowd to greet the princess, their pretty faces flushed and rosy and beaming with delight.

"I got the sword away from the ferrety one," boasted Rose, proudly hoisting a thin blade into the air like a trophy. "I pretended to trip and spilled cranberry sauce all over it. Then I fluttered my eyelashes at him, begged his forgiveness, and asked wouldn't he let me take it and clean it off. And—can you believe it?—the brainless nit actually gave it to me!" She turned to grin at her dark-haired companion. "Clarinda got a sword, too. She gave it to one of the King's Guard."

"Clarinda!" Ivy gasped, looking at their timid friend in astonishment.

"It wasn't anything special," said Clarinda, her cheeks turning a pretty shade of pink. "I just slipped it out from under one of the Glacians' chairs in the Great Hall when he wasn't looking. He was too drunk to notice."

"That's fantastic!" Ivy hugged each of them. "You've both been so brave."

"Not as brave as you, Ivy," Clarinda said, her soft voice filled with admiration.

The king found his daughter, wrapped an arm around her, his blue eyes twinkling merrily, and shook Elridge's claw as cheerfully as if they were old friends bumping into each other on a stroll to the market.

"You have saved this kingdom and everyone in it," he said. "You are true heroes, both of you."

He opened his mouth to say more, but his speech was cut short by a shrill, angry shriek.

"You!" cried Tildy. Ivy turned to see her nursemaid leveling an accusing finger in the direction of the castle gate, where Drusilla had just breezed in, glowing and glistening like the rare gem she was. As she crossed the courtyard, her white gown remained unsoiled by even a single drop of mud, no doubt protected by some form of fairy magic. Toadstool was not so lucky. The little goat plodded along behind her mistress, scrunching up her nose as she tried to shake mud off her hooves after each and every step.

"Druthee?" Boggs gaped at the beautiful fairy as if seeing a vision from a dream.

"How dare you—how dare you show your flighty fairy face here, after all you've done...abandoning poor Ivory when she was no more than a baby? Have you no shame?" Tildy looked ready to explode.

"Tildy, I'm so sorry about what happened." Drusilla hung her head remorsefully. "After Gwenda died, I just couldn't think straight. I...I felt so terribly guilty. I thought it was all my fault, and I thought it would be for the best if I left the kingdom."

"Well, it's easy to say you're sorry now, isn't it?" Tildy's voice was indignant. "But your apology is fourteen years late."

"Tildy, please," Ivy beseeched her nursemaid. "Romil would still have control of the castle if it wasn't for Drusilla. She was the one who convinced the dragons to help us and gave me the melting mirror that got us out of the cellar, and it was her magic that put out the fire. The whole castle might have burned down if it wasn't for her!"

"It was wrong of me to leave," Drusilla said, tears glistening in her violet eyes, "and I can't tell you how sorry I am, all of you. But I'm here now, and I'd really like to be a part of Ivy's life. She's an amazing young lady."

"Yes, she is," agreed Tildy, so fiercely that it took Ivy by surprise. "Ivory might not be the most well-behaved or best mannered of princesses, and goodness knows her skin-care regimen and grooming habits leave a lot to be desired, but she has a good heart, and I'll be the first to admit that her... unconventionality...has served us all well in recent days." The tight lines around her lips softened slightly. "I suppose she deserves a fairy godmother as much as any other princess," she relented, before adding sternly, "as long as you stick with the job this time."

Drusilla gave the nursemaid a grateful smile. "I will—I promise—you have my word," she said, hastily wiping away tears with the back of her hand.

And the next thing Ivy knew, both Tildy and Drusilla had their arms around her, squeezing so tightly one might have thought she was a pair of blacksmith's bellows they were determined to empty of air. It was a surprisingly nice feeling.

When they finally let go, Drusilla gave her a wry smile. "So, it would appear you led a great enemy to the castle, after all," she said, "but they turned out to be an enemy of our enemy in the end."

"You brought destruction and ruin, too." Toadstool observed the aftermath of the fire with distaste. "You're lucky Scaly Legs didn't burn the whole place down."

"The destruction of a stable roof and the ruin of a castle wall aren't too bad, all things considered," said Drusilla.

Boggs, still standing at attention next to the gatehouse, hadn't been able to tear his eyes from the lovely fairy.

"Druthee, I never thought I'd thee you again," he said. "You're even more beautiful than I remember."

"Darling Boggs, just as charming as ever, I see." Drusilla giggled and peered at the gap-toothed gatekeeper closely. "You know, if you'd like, I could fix those teeth for you. . . ."

"Well, now that all our happy reunions are over, I think it only fitting that I venture out front and thank the Dragon Queen properly for her assistance," the king said cheerfully.

Ivy hadn't been able to bring herself to tell him about the Dragon Queen's connection to Boldris. She wasn't sure how the Dragon Queen would react to meeting the man who had slain her favorite son. "Father, no, wait!" But her words were too late. The king had already swept through the castle gate, the rest of the courtyard eagerly filing after him.

"Fairy cakes, we have to get out there!" she told Drusilla and Elridge, dashing after the crowd.

On the other side of the gate, Romil and his men cowered, muddy and weaponless, in the center of a ring of fuming dragons. Some of them were so fuddled with wine, it was all they could do to stay on their feet.

The king had strolled straight up to the enormous Dragon Queen.

"Most noble queen, I cannot thank you and your kindred enough for your help in subduing these ruffians," he declared. "The people of this kingdom are eternally in your debt."

The Dragon Queen looked down on him as if he were an insect she was considering squashing. Her eyes blazed threateningly.

"Sssso, you are the puny sssoft-ssskin who ssslayed my ssson," she hissed.

"Your…son?" The cheer drained from the king's cheeks. "You mean…that dragon at the tower, all those years ago… that was your…oh dear." Any further words died on his lips.

"Would you sssee the remainder of my kindred ssslain, one by one, until none are left?" demanded the Dragon Queen, as if she expected no less from a human. "Now that we have helped sssave your cassstle and your beloved kingdom? Will you ssstill hold usss to the treaty, force usss to guard your white tower ssso your championsss can play dragon ssslayer and rob usss of the lassst of our treasssure?"

The king was too flabbergasted to answer.

"Father." Ivy touched his elbow gently. "There's something I need to talk to you about, something I didn't have the chance to mention earlier. The Dragon Queen was kind enough to help us capture Romil, but we had hoped—I had hoped—that in exchange you'd reconsider making the dragons guard the tower." The king's startled gaze moved from the Dragon Queen to his daughter. "I know how strongly you feel about the Dragon Treaty," she said hurriedly, "and it was a good idea at the time. It saved lives, made things better between us. We've been locking up princesses and slaying dragons for so long, we've come to believe that's the only way there can be peace between humans and dragons. But there has to be something better—a way that doesn't cost princesses their freedom and dragons their lives." The king remained silent, and Ivy felt a stab of desperation. She leaned toward him and lowered her voice, not wanting Elridge or his mother to hear. "*Please*, Father," she whispered urgently. "The Dragon Queen has already lost one son, and now she stands to lose another." Ivy's eyes drifted toward Elridge. The dragon, who had been too large to fit through the castle gate, had leaped over it instead with a flap of his wings. Now he stood before the gatehouse, looking nervous despite the thin streams of smoke that still issued from his nostrils. The king followed her gaze, eyes widening in realization.

"Your Majesty," said Drusilla, stepping forward and taking one of the king's hands in her own, "I think if tonight's events proved anything, it's that the humans of Ardendale and the dragons of the Smoke Sand Hills make much better allies than enemies. Besides," she said wisely, "after all Ivy and Elridge have done, sending them back to the tower would be a rather poor way to repay their brave deeds, wouldn't you agree?"

Ivy's heart gave a hopeful leap when her father merely sighed and lowered his head meekly.

"I cannot bring back the son you lost," he said to the Dragon Queen, his voice thick with emotion. "But I can see to it that none of your other kindred meet the same fate. We have managed to live in peace for some time now under the terms of the Dragon Treaty; I see no reason why we can't live peacefully without it—no tower, no royal suitors, no dragon slaying."

"But Your Majesty," said Tildy, finding the nerve to speak, though she glanced at the Dragon Queen with anxious eyes, "if there is no dragon to slay and no treasure to claim, how are we to lure a prince to the kingdom to marry Princess Ivory?"

"Why do I have to marry a prince? Why can't I marry who I want?" Ivy asked, and her cheeks grew warm as the image of a certain red-haired stable boy drifted into her mind, quite unbidden.

"It would be most improper for you to marry anyone else," Tildy insisted.

The king cleared his throat.

"It was foolish of me to suppose that because Prince Romil was of noble birth, it meant he had a noble heart," he said. "I believe it would be equally foolish to assume that a common man must have a common one. Besides, I was locked in a tower myself for a bit, and I know how dreadfully unpleasant it can be." The king shuddered, obviously recalling his time in the cramped southern tower. "Ivy, my dear, when the time comes, you may marry whomever you choose with my most heartfelt blessing."

Ivy felt much as she had that moment Elridge had first lifted her off the ground. The same, wonderful soaring sensation filled her chest.

"I am willing to abandon this ancient treaty between our peoples—er, kindreds—if you are," the king said to the Dragon Queen. "What do you say?"

"Mossst definitely," she replied, and for the first time since the princess had met her, her mouth crooked into the tiniest hint of a half smile. The effect was actually a little unnerving, what with her enormous daggerlike teeth showing and all.

"I do hope my rather...er, unfortunate history...with your kindred is forgiven," the king said tentatively.

The Dragon Queen regarded him thoughtfully, something close to respect in her fiery eyes. "It wasss a very honorable death for Boldrisss. You mussst be quite the opponent, to defeat sssuch a mighty foe. I approve. I think the ability to quasssh thossse who ssstand againssst you isss an admirable trait in a leader."

"Well, um, thank you," said the king, looking greatly relieved.

"From thisss day forth, we are alliesss againssst thossse who would do usss harm."

For a moment, the king seemed quite pleased, but then his eyes clouded and the lines on his face deepened. "My only regret is that Ardendale will have to forgo having a young new king," he said.

"Other monarchs rule their entire lives," said Ivy. "I don't see any reason why you couldn't do the same."

The king brightened, and he stood straighter. "Why, neither do I," he said. "Especially when I'll have such capable assistance, from good friends, old and new." The king gazed at those gathered around him. With a smile and a gracious nod, he acknowledged Tildy, Drusilla, and each of his counselors, and then the Dragon Queen and her kindred in turn. He looked happier and more in his right mind than Ivy had ever seen him.

"And when it does come time for me to leave this world, I daresay I will leave a most worthy heir in my stead," the king declared, and this time when he smiled, it was at Ivy.

34

Departures and Dwellings

Dawn was rapidly approaching by the time the Glacians were loaded aboard their bone ship and cast unceremoniously from the kingdom.

"You are lucky we are not a vengeful people," the king told Romil and his men. "The Dragon Queen kindly offered to dispose of the lot of you. She thought you'd make very tasty snacks for her kindred." There were cries of dismay from the Glacians, and several of them shrank back in fear. "But I have opted for banishment. I plan to send word of your treachery to the king of Glacia," he informed Romil. "Perhaps your brother is a forgiving man and will receive you back into his court, but considering your plot included overthrowing his reign... I'd rather doubt it. I also doubt that army of yours will follow you now that you have no kingdom to rule. I don't know where you and your men will go, and, frankly, I don't care. Perhaps you can find a deserted island or remote iceberg to call home. But one thing is for certain: if you dare set foot in Ardendale again, the good Dragon Queen here has my leave to do with you what she will. We will not be so generous as to let you leave a second time."

Romil shot a nervous glance at the Dragon Queen, who ran the tip of her long tongue over her lips hungrily. Ivy had the great satisfaction of watching his face go whiter than his bone ship.

"My Guard and I will escort you to the beach, and I'm sure the Dragon Queen and her kindred would be happy to accompany us as well," said the king.

"Oh yesss," hissed the Dragon Queen. "We wouldn't missss it."

"I suggest you board your ship and leave our shores immediately, before we change our minds about letting you go."

The King's Guard retrieved the two Glacians that Owen had tied up in the kitchen, and Gar was dragged from the castle as well, wearing nothing but a fur-trimmed nightshirt, for he had been sound asleep the whole time.

"How dare you treat me in this manner," he raged as he was led roughly through the courtyard, his bare legs becoming coated with thick, cold mud.

A well-mannered young lady would have turned away at the sight of a half-dressed man being handled so, but Ivy watched to her heart's content and giggled most ungraciously.

"We owe you many thanks," the king said to the Dragon Queen as they stood upon the shore and watched the Glacian ship drift out of sight on the horizon.

"It wasss your daughter who warned usss of the threat of thessse dragon-ssslaying invadersss," said the Dragon Queen, as if it was she who owed thanks.

"And it was your son who defeated Prince Romil in battle," the king replied congenially. "You must be very proud."

The Dragon Queen looked surprised but vaguely pleased by this news. Elridge was standing with Ivy on the stretch of pebbled sand. The Dragon Queen inclined her head toward him in acknowledgment. It was a tiny, almost imperceptible gesture, but Ivy had never seen Elridge look so happy.

"I believe our cook and kitchen staff are preparing a large breakfast even as we speak," said the king, "seeing as the whole castle has been up all night long and could use some nourishment before heading off to bed...and a much-needed bath," he added, looking down at his own mud-splattered robes. "Would you care to join us?"

"Perhapsss another time," said the Dragon Queen. "At the moment, we'd bessst return to our own home and the ressst of our kindred." That was just as well, Ivy thought, as she doubted Cook had anywhere close to enough food to feed seven dragons.

"You'll come and visit me, won't you, Elridge?" she asked, filled with a sudden terrible fear that she would never see her friend again.

"Swamp sprites couldn't keep me away," said Elridge, giving her a playful wink.

Despite his pledge to return, Ivy still found it hard to watch the dragon fly away from the castle with his kindred, growing smaller and smaller until he was just a tiny speck in the distance, then gone altogether. It felt strange and empty without him nearby. But as the others left the beach to head back to the castle, Drusilla came forward and laid a comforting hand on her goddaughter's shoulder, and the princess felt her gloom dispelling.

"You said you wanted to be a part of my life. Does that mean you're staying?" she asked.

"Yes," declared Drusilla. "Our time together has made me realize that my place is with you, Ivy, here at the castle. I *am* your godmother, after all. The king even said I could have my old bedchamber back, the one overlooking the castle garden. What's more—Boggs has asked me to marry him!"

As if on cue, the old gatekeeper was suddenly at Drusilla's side, his arm around her waist and his eyes all soft and misty as he gazed at his beautiful bride.

"What?" Ivy looked from one to the other, stunned. "The two of you are getting married?"

"I've missed Drusy so much these past fourteen years," Boggs said, pronouncing each word perfectly. "As soon as I saw her, I knew I couldn't let her get away from me a second time." His face broke into a huge, happy grin, and Ivy could see that, for the first time in many years, he had a full set of pearly white teeth.

"I think that's wonderful," she told them.

"I know we'll be very happy here," said Drusilla, who was glowing brighter than ever, "but I'm afraid Toadstool is going to need some time to adjust to the idea that we're not returning to the Isle of Mist. She's a teensy-weensy bit upset." She glanced down worriedly at her beloved pet.

"I can't believe you want us to live topside in this smoldering heap of stones, when we could be leading a life of luxury back in the mound," whined the querulous little goat.

"Well, Ardendale might not be as beautiful or luxurious as the Isle of Mist," Ivy said, "but we're famous for our curly cap mushrooms. There's a huge harvest every year, enough to last the whole winter through, so you'll never be without mushrooms. Cook makes all sorts of wonderful dishes with them, too—mushroom casserole, cream of mushroom soup, mushrooms on toast, mushroom and gravy pie...."

Toadstool still didn't look happy, but she grumbled a little less.

"It's going to be ever so nice to officially resume my role as fairy godmother to the royal princesses of Ardendale," Drusilla said happily.

"I always thought it was strange that only princesses were born to the royal family," said Ivy.

"Well...I'm afraid that's my doing," Drusilla admitted awkwardly. "One of the earliest kings of Ardendale was a bit of a man's man, if you know what I mean. He liked to spend his days riding and hunting and jousting. He had the nerve to tell me that his daughters would have no need for a fairy godmother because he wasn't planning on having any daughters, thank you very much, only sons. Said he had no use for girls and even less use for a flighty fairy around the castle. Well, I wasn't about to take that lying down." Drusilla giggled, her laughter like a chorus of ringing bells. "One spell was all it took to ensure that only girls would ever be born to him or any of his line, and that I'd always have a place at the castle. He had eight daughters—*eight!* He was positively furious—at first. He did come to love them with time, of course—and got very good at braiding hair." Drusilla looked quite pleased with herself as she remembered her feat. "I'm surprised I even managed to pull it off—hereditary spells are extremely advanced magic, and I *am* only a humble fairy godmother, after all. Don't tell anyone about it, though. They might want me to try to reverse the spell, and, quite frankly, I'm not sure I'd get it right. The royal family might not give birth to anything but footstools after that.

"Well," she went on in a chipper voice, "I think breakfast is almost ready. Shall we head back to the castle?"

Feeling more content than she had in a good while, Ivy fell in step behind her godmother as Drusilla strolled up the hill toward the castle, hand in hand with her husband-to-be.

Epilogue

"**M**other has been . . . well, I wouldn't exactly call it nice—dragons are almost never nice—but a lot less vicious toward me since we returned to the Smoke Sands," Elridge told Ivy happily. "She'd never admit it, but I think she really *is* proud of the way I dealt with Romil that night, and she's thrilled she doesn't have to send any more of our kindred to guard the tower. The other dragons are nicer, too. Oh, and you know those crab apples growing at the edge of Old Man Osbert's oat field? I discovered that if you toast them with a burst of flame, it tastes so much better than eating them raw. I don't know how I ever got by without breathing fire—it's the best thing ever!"

In the days since Prince Romil and the Glacians had been expelled from Ardendale, Elridge had taken to flying down to the castle almost every afternoon, and Ivy was determined to show the dragon every nook and cranny of the beautiful valley kingdom.

"That's great, Elridge," she said, peering into a shadowy crevice at the foot of a small boulder. A frown tugged at her lips. "Fairy cakes, it's not here, either. Are you sure this is where you left it?"

"Positive," said Elridge. "I hid it in the group of rocks that looks like a sand tortoise without a tail. This has to be it." His forehead furrowed in dismay. "You don't think somebody took it, do you? Oh, good goat fur, I knew I should have come back for it sooner. Why did I put it off for so long?"

"It hasn't been that long," Ivy said reassuringly. It was less than a week since she and Elridge had last been at the white tower at the foot of the Craggies. "No one ever comes here, anyway. I'm sure your treasure is fine. We just haven't found the right spot yet."

Suddenly, the dragon's scaly face brightened. "The front leg! Now I remember—I left my treasure under the rock shaped like the tortoise's front leg."

Ivy knelt and groped around the base of a short, pillar-like rock. Her hand found a small hollow.

"There's something in here," she said, feeling inside. She withdrew a tidy bundle wrapped in a piece of frayed cloth.

"That's it," cried Elridge. "Dear me, I'm so happy it's safe!"

Ivy carefully unwrapped the graying cloth, examining the contents within.

"Oh, Elridge," she breathed.

"I know," said Elridge, his face beaming. "It's lovely, isn't it?"

Lying in Ivy's lap was the most beautiful book she had ever seen. The calfskin pages were soft and supple with age, and they were lined with rows of words in script so beautiful and perfect she doubted that there was a single stroke out of place in the entire book. Flowering vines, twisting tree roots, knots, stars, and scrollwork framed each page in lavish reds, blues, greens, and even burnished gold. Tiny animals—birds, harts, and hares—peeked out from in between the designs. The illustrations were even more stunning. Knights, minstrels, and maidens played out their stories on the pages, complete with windswept mountains, white-sailed ships, cities of turrets and towers, and, of course, dragons. No wonder the book had stirred Elridge so. It truly was a treasure.

"I only wish I knew what the words said." Elridge gazed longingly at the pages over Ivy's shoulder. "It must be an incredible story."

"I can read it to you, if you'd like," offered Ivy, grateful to have an excuse to take a closer look at the exquisite book. "Or even better—I can teach you to read, so you can read it yourself, anytime you want."

Elridge's eyes widened and even, Ivy thought, went a little misty. "I'd like that very much," he said. Then he grinned. "But let's not start today. Let's get away from the castle this afternoon. Don't get me wrong—the castle's a nice place and all, but I'm getting tired of watching people haul around stones." The damage done by the fire was not nearly as bad as Ivy had feared, for though the castle wall had blackened and burned, the fire had been quenched before it could break through the thick stones to the interior. The past few afternoons, Ivy and Elridge had watched as workmen went about replacing the worst of the charred stone.

"Maybe we can visit Felda," Elridge suggested brightly. "You promised to introduce me. Owen can come if he likes, and Rose and Clarinda, too. We could even invite Drusilla and Boggs—although I know Drusy will insist on bringing that goat-thing of hers. I'll fly us all to the Fringed Forest in a couple of wing flaps. I know you don't want your fortune told, but maybe Felda can make us some tea, just to plain old drink. I've never had tea before—I'd love to give it a try." The dragon glanced down at his claws with concern. "I hope she has a bucket, though. Dear me, I don't think I could manage a teacup."

"That sounds like a nice idea." Ivy absently ran her finger along a page of the book, tracing the gold-tipped wings of a dragon residing there.

"Something on your mind, Ivy?" Elridge asked, his voice warm with friendly curiosity.

"Sorry," she said, moving her eyes from the dragon on the page to the dragon waiting patiently before her. "I was just thinking...I'm afraid it's going to take a long time for humans and dragons to learn to truly trust one another, maybe generations and generations. Do you think this peace can really last? I'm worried what will happen once we're no longer around to make sure everyone gives it a chance."

The autumn sun caught Elridge's scales, and they sparkled in the light. "You have nothing to worry about, Ivy," he said. "You forget—I'm going to be around for hundreds and hundreds of years yet, so I'll be here to help your daughters, and your daughters' daughters, and even their daughters keep the peace."

At this, Ivy couldn't help but smile. Imagining Elridge spending lazy days like this with her daughters, granddaughters, and great-granddaughters was a very comfortable thought indeed.

Who knows? Maybe there'll even be a proper princess or two in the bunch, she thought, her smile widening. But for now, she hoped Elridge was content to spend some time with the most decidedly improper Princess Ivy, his first true friend.

"What are we waiting for?" she said, rising to her feet. "Let's fly."